"According to Kandida,
can't start until they've appointed an
arbiter," Buffy said.

"Which is what again?" Xander asked.

"Like a referee," Willow explained. "Someone to settle conflicts peacefully."

Faith snickered. "Yep. And they want Summers to do the job. She'd have been my first choice too. Settling conflicts without resorting to violence. That's B, all right."

Buffy rolled her eyes. "Pot, kettle, yadda yadda. But Faith's right. They want me to do the job."

"For God's sake, why?" Giles asked.

"Thanks for the vote of confidence."

"No, Rupert, think about it," Micaela said. "The choice makes perfect sense. Inevitably, there are going to be arguments that could turn the Congress into anarchy. If they all agree to abide by an arbitrator's decisions, they'd have to have someone of a supernatural nature, who understands but is not afraid—someone who could impose order but whom all of the members of the Congress could agree is not beholden to any of them. The Slayer is the only logical choice."

Buffy sat up straight. "Time out. I didn't say I wanted the job. And anyway, I'm not the only Slayer around these days, remember. There are plenty of us to choose from, but they're keeping everyone else out. So why me?"

Oz didn't even look up when he spoke. "Because you're special."

Buffy the Vampire Slayer™

Available from POCKET BOOKS

DARK CONGRESS

Christopher Golden

**An original novel based on the hit television series
created by Joss Whedon**

**POCKET
BOOKS**

LONDON • SYDNEY • NEW YORK • TORONTO

POCKET
BOOKS

An imprint of Simon & Schuster
Africa House, 64–78 Kingsway, London WC2B 6AH
™ & © 2007 Twentieth Century Fox Film Corporation. All Rights Reserved.
All rights reserved, including the right of reproduction in whole or in part in any form.
POCKET BOOKS and related logo are trademarks of
Simon & Schuster, Ltd.
Printed and bound in Great Britain
First Edition 10 9 8 7 6 5 4 3 2 1
ISBN-13: 978-1-84739-119-3
ISBN-10: 1-84739-119-2
A CIP catalogue record for this book is available from the British Library.

For Wendy & Ari

The author would like to thank Emily Westlake and Patrick Price at Simon and Schuster for making this homecoming such a pleasure, and Debbie Olshan at Fox for the opportunity to set right a cosmic injustice. Thanks to Lisa C. for the encouragement and support, all the way back to day one. Special thanks, as always, to Connie and the kids, who won't stop singing "I've Got a Theory." And, of course, thanks to Amber for the inspiration.

DARK CONGRESS

PROLOGUE

On the bank of the River Sebu, the hot wind carrying the strangely spiced aroma of the fertile soil, Micaela Tomasi gazed out across the rushing water and the primeval north African landscape, and wondered how such a serene and beautiful location could ever have been home to warring demons. Yet it had. All of the research that the Watchers Council had discovered had guided them to this very place, an hour's Jeep ride from the walls of Marrakesh.

Dyannah Neville, the sensitive, had drawn a blank while they were in the city. But once they had arrived at the banks of the Sebu, she had closed her eyes, held her fingers out like dowsing rods, and guided them right to the spot.

That had been six days ago. Working as swiftly as possible, the expedition had managed to unearth most of the bizarre tomb that had been buried in the wall of the riverbank. With its large earthen bricks, the tomb seemed quite unlike anything that local peoples would have constructed, instead reminding Micaela of tombs she'd seen in the ruins of some desert civilizations.

As she stood and watched, several of the Watchers Council archaeologists worked carefully trying to open the sealed chamber without damaging the tomb. Watching them work always took her breath away. They were artists, truly. She admired their gracefulness and steady hands, their almost worshipful delicacy.

With a sigh, Micaela strode along the riverbank and picked up a sledgehammer. Gently, she pushed past Dyannah. The nominal leader of this expedition was Trevor Hopkins, who also headed up the Council's archaeological department. Micaela had once betrayed the Council, so no matter how many times she proved herself in the years since, they would never allow her to actually be in charge of an operation of this scale—which, she had been surprised to discover, was all right with her. It made her the maverick, the one everyone watched carefully, and the first one they turned to when trouble began.

"Trevor?" she said.

He had been brushing carefully at the mortar around the door to the chamber. Now his brow furrowed with a bit of pique at her intrusion. Slowly he and his assistant, Roberto Corelli, glanced back.

By then Micaela had already begun to swing the sledgehammer. Both men swore and dove out of the way. The hammer struck the door and an echo that they could hear outside boomed through the tomb. The door cracked in two. Micaela lifted the sledge again, but Marcus Green—an American Watcher she'd once been involved with—grabbed the handle and held her back.

"What the hell are you doing, Mickey?" Marcus demanded.

She hated when he called her that. Slender as she was, Micaela was tall and fit. She twisted the sledgehammer out of Marcus's grip and shoved him away, preparing to swing it again.

"No, Micaela, please!" Trevor said. "You mustn't!"

The white-haired, bespectacled man stepped between her and

the tomb just as she began to bring the hammer around. Micaela faltered, stopped herself, and sighed, dropping the sledge to the ground. The relief on Trevor's face was almost comical. At least a dozen members of the team crowded around now, staring in fascination and horror at both Micaela and the damage she'd done.

"What is wrong with you people?" Micaela demanded. She stared at Trevor a moment, then glanced around at Corelli, Dyannah, Marcus, and the entire crew. "Am I the only one who heard the word 'apocalypse' in the briefing we had on this excursion?"

Trevor's face creased with the air of a scolding parent. "This tomb has lain undisturbed for more than three thousand years. We have an obligation to history, and to the culture of Morocco, to—"

Micaela rolled her eyes. "Spare me."

"Miss Tomasi!" the older man snapped, and this time she realized his expression was not that of a parent, but an irritated teacher, full of self-important condescension.

"My dear Professor Hopkins," she said, "I understand and admire the care you take in your work. Truly I do. But we're not here as archaeologists. We're here as representatives of the Watchers Council, attempting to avert a supernatural cataclysm. There isn't time for the niceties and protocols. You can preserve the sanctity of your dig, or you can save the lives of your children and grand-children."

A murmuring arose among the members of the expedition team, the tone of which seemed to concur with her.

Reluctantly Trevor stepped aside. When he did, Micaela saw that there was no need for another strike with the sledgehammer. The face of the tomb had been broken in half, and one side had already collapsed. She went and knelt in front of the opening, pulling the earthen bricks out and tossing them behind her in the dirt. She heard one bump down the slope and splash in the river. When that happened, Corelli cursed her in Italian, unaware that she knew the language quite well. Micaela ignored him.

In less than three minutes, she'd done what Trevor would have preferred they take that many days to do. On her knees, she dragged a number of the bricks farther away from the entrance.

"Light," she said.

Trevor and Corelli both ignored her, almost as if she hadn't spoken. Unwilling to be a part of what they no doubt thought of as her barbaric assault on the ancient tomb, they watched birds wheeling across the sky. Micaela had a distaste for dramatics, especially from anyone over the age of sixteen, and she didn't bother trying to hide her disapproval.

Marcus stepped forward and handed her a flashlight.

"Thanks," she said, and clicked it on.

She shone the light inside the tomb, which seemed remarkably dry considering its proximity to the river. No groundwater had entered. The sepulchre had been built like a brick oven, but over the course of three millennia, she would have expected deterioration. The bricks showed no streaks from seepage, nothing.

Dry as a bone, she thought.

The flashlight picked out the shape of a casket or coffin of some kind. The burial customs of the local populace, circa 1000 BC, involved nothing of the sort, but that did not trouble Micaela. If all of their research was accurate, they had just opened the tomb of Kandida, alternately called the river demon or water djinni. According to legend, the gods had chosen a young girl of Marrakesh to be their instrument. The girl had defeated Kandida and—unable to destroy her corporeal form—instructed the river people how to bury the demon so that she would not rise again.

Micaela had no doubt that this young girl had been a Slayer. Some of the members of the Council disagreed, but she believed they only did so because they would rather be wrong than agree with her.

The sarcophagus inside the tomb looked almost like a tiny ship, its hull made from strips of polished wood that shone as though the last coat had just been applied to the honeyed planks, another element of the tomb that had been impossibly preserved.

She backed away from the entrance, stood, and brushed dirt off of her pants. "Get it out of there."

Trevor shook his head in disdain. After a moment he came to realize that the entire team was watching him, waiting for a response. He was the leader of the expedition.

"Get on with it," he said, gesturing toward the tomb. Then he turned his back on the rest of them and went down to the edge of the river, gazing out over the water.

Marcus gestured to a couple of diggers, who came down to join him on the bank of the river. Micaela gave them room, backing away but watching carefully. Her golden hair had begun to come undone from her braid and she reached up to loosen it, letting it spill around her shoulders.

"Micaela," Dyannah said. Her voice was quiet but carried a power that belied its softness. The mixture of Indian and British ancestry had given her an exotic, ethereal beauty that seemed appropriate for a psychic sensitive.

"What is it?" Micaela asked.

Dyannah shook her head. "I have a bad feeling about this."

"So do I. In fact, I would rather be almost anywhere else right now. Preferably somewhere with margaritas. But we're out of options, Dyannah."

Micaela turned to look at Corelli, who stood by watching the proceedings with his arms crossed in gruff disapproval.

"Besides, Mr. Corelli has assured me that we've nothing to be worried about."

The Italian turned his dark eyes upon her, his right eye twitching with annoyance. Corelli had the effete demeanor of many of his peers, perhaps learned from Trevor Hopkins, but Micaela found him troubling because he was startlingly handsome, like some thirties movie star. It pissed her off that a man that attractive could be so thoroughly unlikable. Looks weren't everything, of course, but they'd been wasted on him.

"We have been through this many times, Micaela," Corelli said. "Yes, the research seems to indicate that a Slayer was involved in Kandida's defeat. Certainly the construction of the tomb has some significance. But I suspect when we have a closer look, we'll discover sigils and wards etched on the interior that will hold her there. As long as we don't remove the remains completely from the tomb, and seal it up again quickly thereafter, we're in no danger."

Micaela slid her hands into her pockets. "So why is the Maghrebi Ivory buried with her?"

Corelli's upper lip actually curled in a momentary sneer. "I have never met a woman as arrogant as you. Maybe that pleases you. I suspect it does. But you have only guesses, Micaela. They are not logical. You have seen all of the research. In the lore surrounding the Maghrebi Ivory, there is no reference to the amulet having the sort of magic required to restrain or negate the mystic power of a goddess."

"But we think we can use it to avert an apocalypse?"

Now she was just trying to aggravate him. The more pissed off Corelli became, the more she wanted to kiss him. Not that she would. She'd punch him in the nose first.

"The last time a rip appeared in the membrane between our dimension and the Nargoth Fashi Netherrealm, the amulet both repelled the evil influence leaking through and healed the rift."

"Four-thousand-year-old hearsay. The truth is, you don't know what the Maghrebi Ivory was created for, or why it was buried here."

Corelli scowled. "Based on the fact that the situation with the Nargoth Fashi is precisely the same as described in the legends, I am entirely confident that the amulet's purpose is to reknit the fabric of the curtain between dimensions, not simply to be some sort of magical sponge. If the Slayer buried it here, she did so to keep it out of the hands of those who might have wished to destroy it. We've come here to avert an apocalypse, not create one."

He spun on one foot and marched away from her.

At the tomb Marcus and the diggers had begun the process of gently sliding the wooden sarcophagus—that odd ship's hull—to the entrance so that they could open it without actually removing it from its brick enclosure.

Micaela glanced at Dyannah. "Do you believe Corelli?"

"I wish that I could," the psychic said. "The dread I feel may simply be resonance in this location. It's not impossible."

"But you don't think so."

"No." Dyannah reached inside the light cotton shirt she wore and produced a leather thong, at the end of which dangled a small pouch of herbs, dried apples, and a withered sliver of a raven's heart.

Micaela knew exactly what the pouch contained because she had one exactly like it in the right front pocket of her pants. Dyannah had made it up for her upon request. No matter what Corelli insisted, both of them had decided it was best to take precautions.

"It's open!" Marcus called.

Trevor turned from the river and marched back toward the tomb without so much as a glance at Micaela.

From their vantage point slightly higher on the riverbank, Micaela and Dyannah could see down over the shoulders of the crouched archaeologists and into the mouth of the tomb. They had set aside the wooden lid of the sarcophagus. Inside the vessel lay a small, withered body, a dried-out husk of a thing. It looked like the remains of a tiny child, burned down to ash in the doomed city of Pompeii.

Trevor pulled on a latex glove and reached down into the gleaming ship. Still its sides gleamed, and the inside of the tomb remained completely dry, the demon of the river deprived of all moisture.

A terrible dread seized Micaela's heart. But they had a job to do. For all of her doubts, and all of her taunting of Corelli, they were out of options.

With a smile of something like triumph, Trevor lifted the Maghrebi Ivory from the sarcophagus. He held it up for all of them to see. The amulet must have been four or five inches in diameter, a beautiful piece of glittering gold with a disk of pure ivory at its center.

Dyannah screamed.

Micaela glanced at her, followed her terrified gaze, and saw a gigantic, three-taloned hand thrusting up from the river. The water had taken on the shape of the hand, and it reached up the riverbank and into the tomb, knocking Trevor away from the sarcophagus.

The talons thrust down into the wooden ship and raised up the withered husk of the demon, forming a fist around it. The nearly fetal cadaver seemed to absorb the water, and began to grow. The water rushed around it in a maelstrom, and then the demon stood naked on the bank of the River Sebu. Nine feet tall, beautiful, and terrifying to behold, her flesh the color of copper and her hair the flowing blue of the river, Kandida opened her arms, flashing three long talons on each hand, and smiled.

In that moment, Micaela loved her, wanted to go to her, but that was the djinni's magic.

"Look away," Dyannah said.

Micaela reached out and took the psychic's hand, and the two of them embraced, closing their eyes tightly and praying that the wards Dyannah had prepared would protect them.

Then the screaming began.

CHAPTER ONE

Standing on the corner of Benefit Street, sweltering in the heat of August, Buffy Summers felt as though she were peering into a tunnel that led back through time. The eighteenth-century houses that lined the street fronted right on the road, with only the brick sidewalk separating them from the pavement. The street lanterns were electrical now instead of gas, but during the day the illusion was complete. Trees cast long blocks in shadow that seemed to blur her view of the clapboard houses with their heavy shutters and sturdy doors.

Once upon a time Edgar Allan Poe had walked this street, over and over, while courting a young woman who'd lived here. The local legends of Providence, Rhode Island, claimed the ghost of Poe could often be seen standing beneath the boughs of the old trees, looking up at the face of 88 Benefit Street, or walking back and forth along the block.

But in broad daylight, nobody would be out looking for ghosts.

Nobody except Buffy Summers. It came with the job, after all.

Slayer. Chosen One. Meant to stand in the face of evil, combat the darkness, blah, blah, blah. But these days, Buffy was more House Mother than Chosen One. The Slayer gig wasn't a solo act anymore. Thanks to some serious desperation and Willow's witchery, all the girls in the world with the potential to become a Slayer had been transformed all at once.

Now, along with friends and allies, Buffy spent just as much time traveling the world in search of those new Slayers, helping to gather them and explain their destiny, as she did fighting the forces of darkness. The Slayers were being trained, as well, and some of them were much further along in the process than others. It had taken an enormous amount of pressure off of Buffy to have so many other Slayers in the world. There were always evils to be confronted and crises to be averted, but she wasn't alone anymore. Sometimes she could even take a little time for herself.

On the other hand, she'd sort of lost the knack for vacations during her years as *the* Slayer.

And sometimes it was nice to get off on her own, find a little bee's nest of evil, and start poking it with a sharp stick.

"Is this hell?" a voice called.

Buffy glanced down the side street she had just ascended, a steep hill that led up to the plateau that was Benefit Street. Xander Harris might have been in the best physical shape of his life—with the possible exception of that stint working construction—but he looked like he was climbing Mount Everest. Bent toward the incline, he trudged up the last hundred feet or so to the top of the hill, reaching the corner of Benefit Street. His T-shirt clung to his sweaty body in a few places. The plastic bottle of water in his hand had only a few ounces left in it.

"Not hell. Rhode Island in August."

Xander grunted and flopped down to sit on the curb. "Funny. Kinda seems like hell. Or San Francisco. Steep. Hell is steep. And sweaty."

"The sweat just makes you look manly," Buffy assured him. "Look, and smell."

Xander glanced up at her. "Smell?"

"Nah. That was me mocking you. Has it been so long that you've forgotten what that's like?"

"Twelve minutes. Maybe thirteen, tops. I haven't forgotten."

Xander lay back on the brick sidewalk. He squinted against the sunlight, though Buffy could only tell judging by his right eye. The left was covered with a black patch. Technically, of course, it was the eye socket that the patch covered, because there wasn't an eye in it anymore. An evil bastard named Caleb had torn it out. The patch served as a constant reminder to Buffy of who Xander really was, beneath the kidding around and the self-deprecation. Of course, she'd learned his true nature long before he'd lost the eye.

"Y'know, it's actually hotter down here on the ground," he said. "Do you smell that? I think I'm frying. Or broiling. And now I'm debating whether I should get up or have you baste me with my own juices."

"Thanks for that image. I have enough trouble sleeping."

Buffy reached down. Xander took her hand and she pulled him to his feet. He uncapped his water bottle and drained the last few swigs, then looked at her guiltily.

"Sorry. Guess I should have offered you a sip."

She put a hand over her belly. "Mmm, yummy, but I already had my backwash cocktail for the day."

"That's repulsive."

Buffy smiled. "My point."

Xander gestured toward the long, shady blocks of Benefit Street off to the left. "So, what've we got?"

Frying a little herself, Buffy lifted her ponytail off her neck to let what little breeze there was caress her skin. This close to the ocean, she would have expected at least some relief from a sea breeze, but no such luck. Not today, at least. It had to be nearly a hundred degrees, maybe more up here on the bricks.

"Not much. I was just waiting for you. You ready to go on?"

He nodded. "There's shade. Let's dive in."

They crossed the intersection toward the tree-lined block ahead. Buffy again felt that sense of passing backward through time. If the street had been cobblestoned, she was sure she would've heard the clip-clop of horses' hooves as they drew carriages through Providence.

"Y'know, it doesn't really seem like the Hellmouthy kind of neighborhood," Xander said.

Buffy narrowed her eyes, studying the street ahead. "What does? Hellmouths don't tend to open up in the places you'd expect them, like Calcutta or Las Vegas."

"I guess . . ."

"Besides, the Hellmouth that was here has been closed since the mid-nineteenth century," she reminded him.

"We hope."

Xander fished a hand into the pocket of his light cotton pants and pulled out his cell phone, checking the time and seeing if he had any messages. Buffy didn't understand why he wasn't wearing shorts on such a steamy day. She had on a dark, floral-patterned skirt and sandals. If evil reared its ugly head, it wasn't the best outfit for a brawl, but in weather like this, a girl had to sacrifice practicality for comfort.

They'd come to Providence because of a recent spate of apparently supernatural occurrences. The sightings of supposed ghosts in the area had increased twenty times over in the past week. Several people had vanished in the vicinity of Benefit Street. Local authorities had captured a huge reptilian creature that zoo officials and university professors had been unable to identify as any existing species. Two Providence police officers had been badly wounded in an altercation with a bar patron who'd resisted arrest and escaped after biting one of the officers in the throat. Then, less than forty-eight hours ago, hundreds of people across the city had apparently witnessed some kind of bizarre manifestation. For two full minutes, they had seen a cyclops—a one-eyed giant with a single horn on its head—towering above the trees in the woods at the far side of town. Then, in a blink, it had disappeared.

Ordinarily Buffy might have sent a team of Slayers-in-training, probably with Xander as an escort. With Giles in London, and Willow and Kennedy in Greece, that would have been the sensible move.

But with a Hellmouth involved, dormant or not, she'd decided to come to Rhode Island herself. It felt good to be away from all of the Slayers-in-training for a while. Xander knew her so well and they had been friends for so long that she could just be herself with him. No need to perform for the trainees, try to be a good role model, or teach anyone anything.

Here, she could just be Buffy.

"It could all be normal supernatural activity," she said as they reached the other side of the intersection and stepped up onto the sidewalk. "Providence is one of the most haunted cities in America. Or, hey, it could just be pranksters."

"Wacky kids?" Xander said.

"Exactly."

They stepped at last into the shade of the massive oak trees that lined Benefit Street. Immediately the coolness of the shadows enveloped them and it felt delicious. Even the breeze seemed cooler here. Buffy actually shivered with the temperature change.

"Okay," Xander said, "this is me officially achieving Nirvana."

Buffy smiled as they walked past the first of the houses on the block. She admired the construction, which seemed both rough and formidable.

She shivered again, gooseflesh rising on her skin. She hugged herself against the sudden chill and faltered. Buffy and Xander looked at each other.

"I know I asked for this, but—," Xander started.

"Definitely not normal," Buffy said.

"What number was the Hellmouth house again?"

"Eighty-eight."

They kept walking. As they went on, the effect began to diminish, and by the time they came to 88 Benefit Street, the heat of the day had returned. Yet somehow the climate still was not quite the same. Xander had been sweating before, and Buffy had also built up a light sheen of sweat, but now the air felt so dry it was almost arid.

"This is weird," Xander said.

Buffy only shot him a glance. If it wasn't weird, they wouldn't have been there. He knew that.

"So what now?" he asked.

"What do you think? We knock on the door?" Buffy replied.

"So simple, right?" Xander said. "Why does it feel like a really stupid idea?"

For a long moment, the two of them gazed up at the silent house, its windows staring back like dark, empty eyes. They shared a glance, exchanged a pair of shrugs, and then started up to the door.

The wind kicked up. A sudden gust whipped at Buffy's skirt and she had to hold it down. Sand skittered along the brick sidewalk, blowing hard enough that the grains stung as they peppered Buffy's legs.

Xander said her name.

Buffy followed his gaze and saw that farther down the street a storm had begun brewing. Her eyes widened and a trickle of fear slid down her spine. Whatever this was, fists weren't going to stop it. A cloud of churning air spun in the middle of the street, blooming larger, growing and spreading, and it began to move toward them.

Impossibly, a sandstorm had blown up along Benefit Street,

where neither sand nor storm could have been found moments before. In the midst of the sandstorm, Buffy could make out the silhouette of a man—or what appeared to be a man.

The wind howled and gusted harder, and Buffy squinted against the flying grit.

"Ever see anything like this before?" Xander asked.

"No!" she called, having to raise her voice over the howling of the wind. "I'm guessing magick."

"Ya think?"

Buffy took a step toward the storm and the dark figure in its midst. Xander grabbed her arm to hold her back, shouting something at her, but she couldn't make out the words.

Then the sandstorm began to roar. It tore down the street toward them. Street lanterns bent over with a shriek of metal. Shutters tore off of houses. The sand stripped paint from clapboard siding and shattered windows. A car parked halfway up the block rocked and trembled, and then its windows simply imploded from the force of the wind.

A three-legged German shepherd charged into the middle of the street and started barking like a lunatic at the oncoming storm. Buffy shouted to the dog, but it couldn't hear her over the screaming of the wind, and then it was too late. The raging, churning storm sucked the dog into its twisting heart, and the animal vanished in the swirl of sand.

Buffy took a step back.

"The house!" she shouted to Xander.

He cupped a hand to his hear, squinting his one eye.

"Get inside!" Buffy yelled.

But she knew words would do no good. She grabbed Xander by the hand and pulled him back to the door of 88 Benefit Street. The sandstorm surged toward them. Buffy shot a kick at the door, just beside the lock, and wood splintered as it burst inward. The wind did the rest of the work, practically tearing the door off its hinges.

They ran inside and took cover behind furniture in the living room as the storm reached the house. Glass shattered. The wind pushed inside, tore knickknacks off of shelves and paintings off of walls. The sand scoured every surface in the rooms on the first floor. Thankfully, it didn't seem like anybody was home. Whatever was going on, it hadn't originated in the former Hellmouth.

"Stay here!" Buffy shouted at Xander.

Another guy might have tried to stop her, or exhibited foolish heroics. But Xander had learned the hard way what the limits of an ordinary guy were, and what the Slayer could do when she set her mind to it. He wasn't going to get macho about it.

He gave her a thumbs-up from his fetal position behind the couch.

Buffy vaulted over the sofa and headed for the door. The wind thrashed her but she struggled through it, bent over. Whoever the man at the center of the sandstorm was, he had to be responsible for it. She had a theory that beating him unconscious might put an end to the storm.

As she reached the door, the wind died.

Sand cascaded to the pavement and the brick sidewalk, covering every visible surface as though a beach had just fallen from the sky.

Buffy stepped out onto the sidewalk, her sandals sliding into the sifting sand.

"Well, that's new," she said.

Xander came out the door behind her, looking around. "I'm gonna go out on a limb and guess the weatherman didn't see that coming."

As the sun rose over the Mediterranean, Willow Rosenberg rode her rented bicycle along the narrow streets of Thira, the largest of the islands that made up the group that the Greeks called Santorini. In a way, it was all one island, since the entire land mass—the large island and her smaller sisters—had once been whole, and the people who lived on Santorini spent their days and nights on the rim of an active volcano, as if it were the most ordinary thing in the world.

Willow thought Santorini looked more the way she imagined heaven ought to than any other place she'd ever been. The sky seemed an endless blue, and the ocean had a deep azure hue like nowhere else in the world. The whole island of Thira had a rare beauty, dotted with whitewashed buildings, shops, and churches, many of which had blue tile roofs and blue shutters that blended with that particular shade of the ocean. And the people . . .

As she rode her bike up long hills, passing wineries, and then through the rows of boutiques and restaurants that catered mostly to tourists, the island came alive. Many of the locals were up and about their business before dawn, when it was coolest. Willow waved to them as they passed, and received kind smiles in return. She and her girlfriend, Kennedy, had made several stops on other Greek islands before coming to Santorini. Several friends had raved about Mykonos, and everything had been much less expensive there than elsewhere, but Willow and Kennedy had not felt very welcome. On Santorini, everyone seemed happy to meet them.

Of course, with the prices they charged for everything, they ought to be very happy indeed. Still, Willow had fallen in love with Santorini. She had found a serenity here that she had never achieved anywhere else in the world. The heat baked the streets, so she kept her fair skin covered by light cotton as much as possible, but otherwise it all seemed so pure, and everyone so alive.

Tara would have loved it here.

The thought took her so much by surprise that her foot slipped off the pedal. She scrambled to get control of the bike again as it wobbled, and squeezed the brakes so that the tires slid on the dusty street. When she looked up, a white-haired old man was watching her with concern. Willow smiled at him and he smiled back, nodding, happy she was all right.

Yet another example of the very thing she'd just been thinking of. Tara truly would have loved it on Santorini. There seemed a general benevolence, a respect for one another that had become rarer and rarer in most of the world. That had been all Tara had ever really wanted from the moment Willow had first met her—and fallen in love with her. Peace. Kindness. She had grown up in difficult circumstances, never accepted, never fully embraced for who she was. Willow knew that most people would be hard-pressed not to become spiteful after having endured that kind of childhood.

Tara wasn't like most people.

She had been the light of Willow's life, but more than that, her presence had always made it much easier for those around her to feel hopeful, to be optimistic about the future, and to search for peace within themselves and with others, as well.

Right up until a stray bullet took her life.

The heat baked into Willow's back as she bent over the bike, pedaling harder as she began to ride up a hill. Cars swept by her on streets barely narrow enough for two of them to pass each other, never mind with a bicycle on the shoulder. At least the buses hadn't started running yet. The drivers were lunatics who would pay little attention to the redheaded tourist girl on the bike.

If they knew she could put a hex on them, they might be more careful—the Greeks had a lot more belief in witches than Americans, that was for sure—but Willow didn't use her magick that way.

Not anymore.

A chill went through her as she remembered the terrible things she had done, the savage magick she had performed in the madness that had overtaken her after Tara's death. Darkness had seized her for a while—revenge, as well.

She pedaled harder. Tiny rivulets of sweat ran down her face and chest.

The darkness was behind her now. Tara's murder had left a hole in her heart that no amount of time would ever heal. Her life would always be split between the person she had been before and the person she had become after, forever in the shadow of that loss. But people endured the loss of love and the tragedy of murder every day. They went on. They lived their lives.

Willow had done the same. It was what Tara would have wanted.

With a sigh, she reached the top of the hill and coasted on the bike, catching her breath. In the distance she could see the small, whitewashed villa that she and Kennedy had rented for their stay here. Beyond it the land fell away in a precipitous cliff, overlooking the ocean below and the other islands of Santorini.

The peace of the place seeped back into her, easing her heart.

Kennedy would be sleeping still, no doubt. Even on her best day, she would have to be dragged out of bed this early in the morning. A mischievous little smile touched the corners of Willow's mouth. She could think of a few fun ways to wake Kennedy up.

Willow felt so grateful for her. After all she'd been through—meeting Tara, falling in love with a woman, losing her to violence, and then turning to dark magick—Kennedy had helped her to put the pieces of her life back together. Willow had spent a long time working to find her center again, to be at ease with even the gentlest magick, to remember who she'd been, once upon a time.

Sometimes she had felt like she might stumble, but then Kennedy had entered her life and helped to steady her. She would never replace Tara—no one ever could—but Willow had fallen hard for Kennedy. It didn't hurt that she could not have been more the opposite of Tara. Kennedy was brash where Tara had been so shy. Kennedy had ebony hair and olive skin, while Tara had been blond and fair. Kennedy was volatile, and Tara had only ever sought to soothe.

"Morning, babe," Willow said to the breeze that rose off the ocean as she let the bike cruise downhill toward the villa.

She and Kennedy had made a life together. Willow still had her witchcraft and Kennedy had been trained to become a Slayer before the spell had given all Potentials that power. They made a hell of a team. A community had begun to spring up around the world as Buffy, Xander, Giles, Willow, and Kennedy sought out Slayers and brought them together for training. And Faith loved teaching the new girls combat.

Somehow the world had shifted on its axis, but they had all survived. She supposed everyone felt that way when they reached a certain age.

When she reached the front walk, she climbed off the bike and set it down on its side. There was no kickstand. Willow stretched, feeling the muscles in her legs throbbing from the ride. She had spent the entire night halfway across the island studying ancient Greek witchcraft rituals at a supernatural locus on the limestone rocks at Mesa Vouno.

It had been a wonderful night, but she hadn't gotten much sleep. All she wanted to do now was climb into bed beside Kennedy.

Willow used her key to unlock the front door and slipped it back into her pocket. The windows were all wide open and the sheer white curtains billowed in the breeze, keeping much of the morning heat at bay.

As she entered, she heard the refrigerator in the tiny kitchen shut and blinked in surprise. Smiling, she moved through the living room and came around the corner.

The girl in the kitchen wasn't Kennedy.

She had a glass of juice tipped back, but froze when she saw Willow, staring over the rim of the glass before she lowered it. Her smile was lopsided and awkward as she reached up to push her unruly black hair away from her face.

Willow's studies had been only a happy by-product of this trip. Their real purpose for coming here had been to seek out a nineteen-year-old island girl named Stefania Kamari, whom they believed had become a Slayer. Willow recognized the girl from her photograph. But in the picture Stefania had been wearing more than a black lacy thong.

Her smudged makeup, wild hair, and almost total nakedness told Willow all she needed to know. If any confirmation had been necessary, there was no sign that anyone had slept in the living room, and the villa had only one bedroom.

Only one bed.

A strange calm fell over her, a kind of icy silence that gripped her heart. Brittle.

The Greek Slayer tried to talk to her in halting English, but Willow barely heard her, and was grateful that Stefania did not try to follow her as she strode back through the living room and into the bedroom.

Kennedy lay sprawled upon the bed, gloriously nude, the single light cotton sheet wrapped around one leg as she snored softly. An almost empty bottle of ouzo sat on the nightstand and another lay on the floor at the foot of the bed. The place reeked of licorice.

As quickly as she could, Willow packed her suitcase, grateful that it had little wheels on it so that she could carry it swiftly away from here. She knelt on the floor and removed her things from drawers and from the closet, folding them neatly, and then, as her hands began to shake, throwing them into the suitcase.

She sniffled, and realized she had started to cry.

She heard a tiny sound, full of sorrow, and it surprised her to realize it hadn't come from her. Willow looked up to see that Kennedy had woken. The Slayer sat up in bed, watching her pack, tears in her eyes. She raised a hand to cover her mouth as though she might scream.

"Baby, I'm sorry."

Willow shook as she zipped the suitcase closed and stood, sliding out its handle.

"Please," Kennedy said, "just let me explain."

With a laugh full of grief, Willow paused and looked at her. "You have an explanation you think will make me understand *this*?"

Kennedy's eyes hardened. "We both knew it wasn't going to be forever, Willow. I've never been one to be tied down. I wanted to give it a shot with you. I love you. But you? You loved me with everything you had, but it'd never be enough. When it comes down to it, Tara's always going to be first in your heart. I can't compete with a dead girl."

Willow stared at her in horror and revulsion. "I never asked you to compete. But you know what? You're right. You could never have competed with her. Tara . . . she'd never have done this to me."

Kennedy could only look away.

"Stay away from me," Willow told her, and then she rolled her suitcase out of the bedroom and across the living room.

Stefania hadn't moved. She stood in the kitchen with half a glass of juice in her hand, watching her leave. Willow left the door open, and left her rented bike lying in front of the villa, then started up the hill toward the busier sections of the island, where she could find a taxi to take her down to the harbor. The sooner she left Santorini, the better.

She thought of John Milton, and wondered if Kennedy would even get the reference.

Paradise Lost.

The bar had the atmosphere of a London pub, all brass and dark wood, and the earthy odor of hops and barley seemed ingrained in every surface. Like thousands of other such establishments in North America, it had at some point in the nineties become a microbrewery, and that beer aroma would never go away.

Oz called it home.

Well, maybe home was stretching it a little, but he and his buddy Eric Katz had picked up a regular gig here, and for the past three weeks had played almost every night in a little corner for decent pay, plus beer and chow. The setup was pretty sweet. Oz had played with various bands and assorted other guitarists and singers up and down the West Coast over the past few years, but Portland, Oregon, had become a kind of second home to him of late.

Even with all of that, he might never have agreed to stick around at one gig for so long if it hadn't been for the name of the place. How could a guy not want to spend time in a bar called Hootenanny's? Oz loved words, the more antique the better. Hootenanny's seemed like heaven to him.

On a rainy Wednesday night, he and Eric ran through a couple of old Grateful Dead tunes, a recent Jack Johnson, and a drawling Bob Dylan, which was the only tune Oz sang vocals on. He didn't have the voice, really, but that had never stopped Dylan.

As he sang, fat-bellied acoustic resting on his hip, his gaze kept tracking back to Victoria, the barmaid he'd become intrigued by ever since first setting foot in Hootenanny's. Word had it that Victoria—never Vicky—had just broken things off with her boyfriend. Oz knew better than to get involved with a girl on the rebound, especially when he himself was just passing through. The life of a troubadour wasn't nearly as romantic as people imagined. Papa was a rolling stone, and all that.

But he couldn't keep his eyes off Victoria, the way she laughed as she talked to the customers, and the way the multicolored lights of the bar played off of her ebony skin.

Oz didn't have a lot of "wow" moments when it came to women. The first had been with Willow Rosenberg, back in high school, and he still felt wowed when he thought about her. There'd been one, maybe two others since Willow.

Victoria, though—she took his breath away.

He finished the song, strummed the last chord, and inclined his head in thanks at the polite smattering of applause from the Wednesday night crowd. According to Victoria, Hootenanny's had been much busier on weeknights since Oz and Eric had started playing there.

It felt a little like a place he could stay—at least for a while.

Eric picked out the first few notes of "Come on in My Kitchen," a bit of old blues from Robert Johnson, and Oz jumped right in. Halfway through the song, though, his brow furrowed and he began to sniff the air.

Beneath the beer odor was another scent.

The little hairs on the back of his neck rose and Oz had to fight to keep from baring his teeth. He knew that animal stink all too well. His eyes scanned the bar. At the tables, people were drinking and eating pub food, mostly couples and groups of friends. Even at the counter, the patrons were in groups of two or three. But over by the door, a man had just come in from the rain, and though no one else in Hootenanny's could have smelled it, Oz wrinkled his nose at the wet-dog stink that came off of him.

A werewolf.

The guy moved to the bar and sat on a stool, not ordering anything, not even bothering to remove his jacket. He just watched Oz, not breaking the gaze no matter how long Oz stared back.

To anyone else, he would have seemed like an ordinary guy who'd come into the wrong bar if he was looking to meet single women. But Oz knew the scent immediately and recognized the feral nature in his eyes.

It took one to know one.

When the Robert Johnson tune finished, Eric turned his back to the crowd. Under the pretense of tuning his guitar, he leaned over to Oz.

"You feeling all right?"

Oz nodded. "Yeah. Let's take a break, though, okay?"

Eric raised an eyebrow but said nothing. That was one of the reasons Oz liked gigging with him. He didn't talk too much, and didn't expect any more from Oz.

"Folks, thanks for coming out tonight. Hope you're enjoying the music. We'll be back with a lot more in just a few minutes," Eric said.

Oz slid off his guitar strap and propped the instrument on its stand. He made his way across the bar. When Victoria passed by, he caught the scent of her vanilla body wash, but didn't blink. Right now his only focus was making sure nobody in the bar ended the night with their throat torn out.

The other wolf had been watching him closely, so Oz didn't bother trying to be inconspicuous. He walked straight up to the guy, a tall, broad-shouldered man with shaggy blond hair and a week's worth of beard.

Oz and the visitor sized each other up, cocking their heads. In a boxing ring, they'd have been dancing around, looking for an opening. When the guy didn't speak up, Oz took a step closer. His hackles rose and he could feel his teeth get a bit sharper. When he'd first become a werewolf, he'd been unable to control the change. Now he and the wolf inside of him had come to an understanding. He'd found unity.

Which meant he could transform anytime he wanted. *Anytime I need to, not want.* He never wanted to be the wolf.

"Hunting season's over. Just so you know," he said.

The other wolf smiled. His teeth were sharp. Oz wondered if he could control the change as well. Most couldn't. This guy looked like he had the beast pretty much on a leash.

"I'm not hunting anything except you," the wolf said.

Oz didn't flinch, but his breathing evened out. If the guy wanted to go, they'd go. It'd be ugly and bloody and a lot of things would get broken—not to mention that having a hundred people witness him wolfing out would kill any chance he had of gigging in Portland ever again—but no way would he let some wolf track prey right in front of him and not make himself a nuisance.

"Settle down, Mr. Osbourne. That's not what I meant."

Oz blinked. The guy knew who he was. It was peculiar as hell. "What do you want?"

Glasses clinked and voices droned on around them in one huge conversation. Rain spattered the plate glass windows of the bar. Oz stared at the wolf and waited.

"The packs are gathering. We've scented it on the wind," the man said. "Events are conspiring to draw us together. The wolves need to speak with one voice."

Oz arched an eyebrow. "I've never been good with unions. Can never seem to pay the dues."

"We've done our research on you. It's important that we speak with you."

Hands sliding into his pockets, Oz nodded. "Yeah. You'd think I'd be flattered, but seriously not. Whoever you've been talking to, they're pretty much morons."

"Mr. Osbourne—"

"No killing. Kind of a rule."

"The packs—"

"I'm not part of a pack."

The wolf growled in frustration. "Shut your mouth, pup, and listen a moment. This is not about killing. Not yet. It's about listening and deciding where we stand, what our place is in the world. All the wolves."

It was a question he had been asking himself for a long time. Oz hesitated.

"I'm not much for the big philosophical questions."

"That's not what I've heard."

Oz narrowed his eyes. "You should go. I've got to play another set. The crowd gets restless without the soothing tonic we provide."

The man's mask of arrogance faltered and Oz saw confusion in his eyes. The wolf reached up to scratch idly at the side of his head with claws too long to belong on human fingers. He was dressed stylishly enough not to be totally out of place in Hootenanny's, but something about him spoke of another age. Oz wondered how old he was.

From his back pocket, the man produced an envelope. He handed it to Oz, who hesitated before taking it from him. What harm could there be? It was just an envelope.

Inside was a plane ticket.

"What's in Providence, Rhode Island?" Oz asked.

The wolf stood a little straighter.

"Answers."

CHAPTER TWO

On a gray London morning, Rupert Giles drove his car slowly along Great Russell Street in search of a place to park. The windows were cranked down and the heat had become quite irritating. Perhaps it was only nostalgia, but he didn't recall it ever getting quite this hot in England during his youth. August it might be, but still, it felt more like the American southwest than London.

Days like this, he missed the States, with America's ubiquitous air-conditioning. They knew how to deal with heat like this. Londoners had a tendency to abandon all courtesy when the mercury rose this high.

A horn blared and a car darted out, roaring past him, the driver glaring impatiently at Giles as he went by.

"Sod off," Giles muttered.

His mood had been foul this morning as well, but not because of the weather. Anything that drew him away from home these days was unwelcome, unless it involved the gathering and training of new Slayers that Buffy and her associates were engaged in. Ostensibly, Giles still had a role with the Watchers Council, but he felt far more loyalty toward the Slayer he himself had trained. Buffy had made it clear that the Slayers no longer had any relationship with the Council, but that didn't include Giles. They were in frequent contact, but it took a real crisis to drag him away from the quiet country home he had made his own.

A real crisis. Now, for instance.

"At last," he said to himself, and he pulled into a parking space where the pavement had cracked inward a few centimeters and partially sunk. He didn't care. If the street opened up and swallowed his car, he'd be rid of the damn thing. It spent far too much time in for repairs anyway.

He stepped out, nearly twisted his ankle in a pothole, and slammed the door without bothering to lock it. Nothing in the car would be worth stealing. His shirtsleeves were rolled up, but the heat was merciless. The gray sky seemed to be promising rain, but for now it only brought humidity.

Giles pulled his collar away from his neck and started down the block. At the corner, he found the old building where the Watchers Council had made its headquarters during World War II. His own grandmother had been a member in those days, and had visited these premises often. In later years it had been abandoned, and only recently reclaimed by the Council and reinhabited. Their last headquarters had been destroyed, taking dozens of lives along with it, nearly destroying the organization forever.

Now the Council had several different offices throughout London, and others elsewhere in Europe. The survivors of the massacre had been forced to begin with far smaller numbers, to find copies of ancient texts that were often among only a few copies available in the world, and to learn to redefine their purpose now that they were no longer affiliated with the Slayers. They were still quite involved in trying to avert supernatural disasters and to combat lesser evils where they appeared, but research and observation made up an equal portion of their endeavors.

His own relationship with the Council remained uneasy. They considered him a Watcher still, but always at arm's length. Giles preferred it this way. Their methods were often questionable.

He knocked on the door of the building on Great Russell Street and was shown in immediately by a young woman of exotic beauty and severe demeanor. She seated him in the front parlor, but within moments returned to tell him that he could proceed upstairs to the office of Rory Kinnear, the branch director. Without a word, she left him outside the open door.

Giles rapped on the door frame as he entered. Kinnear sat behind a heavy desk in a tall leather chair to which Giles imagined he must be sticking, given the weather. The windows in his office were open, as were most of the windows in the building, but the air had been still for hours. Only when at last the sky opened up and it rained would they get a cool breeze in there.

Two others were in Kinnear's office. A dignified old man in his mid-seventies with a thick gray mustache and a cane stood by the window, peering out at the city, perhaps trying to see if he could get a view of the British Museum. Seated before the desk was a black woman of perhaps forty with purple eyes that must have been attributable to contacts.

"Ah, Rupert," Kinnear said as he spotted Giles. He rose from his desk and came over, hand extended. They shook, and the man led him further into the office, gesturing toward the others. "Thank you for coming in. You know Sir Thomas Fox, of course. And this is Malaika Kehinde, a recent arrival to our branch after years of service in Kenya."

Greetings were exchanged. Giles had met Tom Fox many times over the years, but felt sure this was the first time the old man had ever really noticed him. The weight of expectation hung behind Fox's eyes when they shook hands.

Malaika Kehinde began to stand.

"Please, don't get up on my account," Giles said, taking her proffered hand.

With that preamble concluded, an awkward moment passed, as it seemed both Giles and Kinnear expected the other to begin the conversation. When neither ventured to do so, Malaika intervened.

"Mr. Giles," she said, her accent lilting and lovely, "Director Kinnear tells us that you've filed several reports recently about unusual and sudden movements of several demonic tribes."

Giles nodded. "I have. It's of growing concern to me, actually, as the timing seems to coincide with other events."

"Such as?" Rory Kinnear asked.

With a smile for Malaika, Giles turned to him and let the smile fade. "You asked me here, Kinnear. Presumably you had some purpose in doing so. Why not share it, and we'll see where we are?"

For a moment it seemed the man might invoke his authority, but then he obviously thought better of it. Giles would only have told him—as he had a dozen times before—that what he held was merely the illusion of authority. When one wouldn't hesitate to walk away, and nothing stood a chance of stopping one from doing so, authority held no sway.

Kinnear nodded. "All right. Sir Thomas?"

Fox had returned to the window as though being near it might provide some additional relief from the heat. The old man turned toward his colleagues and steadied himself on his cane.

"We have begun a series of inquiries prompted by your reports," Fox said. "The tribes you've mentioned are not merely migrating. They are diminishing. As they move, some of their members seem to have vanished, or perhaps infiltrated the human populations of the environments they have entered. They haven't attacked or harmed anyone as yet. What's more, it seems the last of the Miquot clan have come back to this plane of existence, and—"

"I'm aware of the Miquot's return. I've had at least half a dozen contacts remarking upon their arrival," Giles interrupted. "In every case I've asked my contacts to keep me apprised of their activities, and in every case that has proven impossible. The Miquot arrived in different locations around the world, but now seem to have vanished, as well."

Giles crossed his arms, contemplating unpleasant things. "What's even more troubling is that there have been a number of other dimensional breaches recently that can't be attributed to the Miquot. I know several sensitives who have felt these intrusions into our dimension—"

"But we haven't heard a thing," Malaika interrupted, a deep frown creasing her forehead. "If demons have breached the dimensional walls on the magnitude necessary to be noticed by your sensitives, they would be powerful enough to do vast amounts of damage."

"Indeed," Giles said, unfolding his arms and gesturing toward his colleagues. "And so there is our question. If they haven't come to wreak havoc and spread chaos, why are they here? Better yet, where are they?"

Malaika lowered her head, shaking it slowly with worry. "There is more. Watchers in both the Alps and the Sudan have reported that old gods in those regions—weak and ancient beings only worshipped by handfuls of people, but kept alive and cared for as part of tradition—have also vanished. These things must be related."

Sir Thomas Fox rapped his cane on the floor. "And if they are, something enormous is brewing on the horizon, a storm so large we can only see the edges of it now."

"So there it is, Rupert," Kinnear said, leaning forward in his chair. "You've always said that you'd be with us in a crisis. I believe the time has come."

"So it seems," Giles agreed.

Kinnear stood. He wore a grim expression, nothing like the

self-satisfied smirk Giles would have expected. He studied the man closely.

"There's something you're not telling me, Rory."

The branch director hesitated, but only a moment. He glanced at the Watchers gathered in his office. "Something I haven't told any of you, I'm afraid, because I've only just learned of it myself. As you may know, we have an archaeological team on site near Marrakesh, searching for the Maghreb's Ivory."

"They've found it?" Fox asked hopefully.

Kinnear's expression darkened. "I'm afraid I have no idea. We lost contact with the expedition three days ago."

"And you're just learning of this now?" Malaika asked.

"We're only one branch," Kinnear replied. "the Council has many at the moment, and you know how paranoid the directors have become about security since the breach that nearly destroyed the entire organization. I suspect that the only reason the directors bothered to inform me at all was because they knew I would bring you into it."

Giles stared at him. The implication that the directors of the Council preferred not to have direct contact with him did not trouble him at all—the feeling was mutual—but something else had set alarm bells off in his head.

"This team? This is the expedition you sent Micaela on?"

Kinnear nodded reluctantly. "But you can't go to Africa, Rupert. This mystery is far too ominous to be ignored. A recovery team has been sent after them. We'll know in the next twenty-four to forty-eight hours what happened to our expedition. There's nothing to be done about it until then."

Once upon a time Rupert Giles had not been the rational intellectual he had later become. A streak of rebelliousness had always been in him, along with more than a bit of violence. During the darkest period of his youth, his friends had given him the nickname Ripper, and he'd gone out of his way to find trouble instead of waiting for it to find him.

He worked hard at keeping Ripper nothing more than a part of his past. Sometimes the past came back to haunt him. The desire to beat Kinnear bloody was almost irresistible.

Everyone had demons on the inside. People spent a lot of time trying to exorcise them, to drive them out. That was a mistake. The only way to beat them was to keep them under control.

Especially because, from time to time, you wanted to let them out.

"Tell me the moment you've heard," he said.

Then Giles turned on his heel and left the office. They could compare notes about the growing crisis later, after his fists unclenched.

Willow could not find the beauty in Athens. She knew it existed, somewhere beneath the layers of grime that the centuries had spread across the city. Beneath the modernity of Athens there still lingered the power of the belief of the ancient Greeks, the worship of the old gods. She could sense it, but could not quite reach it.

She had made her pilgrimage to the Acropolis, had stood upon the steps of the Parthenon and felt the searing heat of its nearness to the sun, slitted her eyes against the dust and grit that blew up from the path that the buzzing crowd followed to the cliff edge at the top. There she had felt as though she might cry out and have her voice heard even atop Mount Olympus. Despite the milling people in their wide-brimmed hats and layers of sunscreen, brandishing their cameras, there remained a purity of spirit to the place.

The gods had never completely abandoned Athens.

But once she descended from the Acropolis, putting the trees and the sandstone and the Theater of Dionysus behind her, the corruption of civilization swallowed that spirituality completely. Athens consisted of groaning, laboring buses that belched black exhaust, and tourist traps where trinkets and chalky statuary sold for ten times their value. Only the strip joints outnumbered the gift shops.

What she needed was a flight out of there, to almost anywhere. The problem was, Willow couldn't decide where she wanted to go. Buffy and Xander, last she checked, had been headed to Rhode Island, and Giles was in London. The idea of calling any of them at the moment and admitting what had happened with Kennedy held very little appeal. There would be no avoiding it, not for long, but she wasn't quite ready yet.

Tonight she would spend one more night in the hotel, a marble sanctuary that kept out the filthy ruin of a once glorious city, and tomorrow morning she would make those calls. Tomorrow she would get the hell out of Greece.

With a sigh, she glanced out the window and watched the traffic roaring past—buses and taxis and tourists.

She sat by herself at a small table with a perfect white tablecloth. After her trip to the Acropolis, she'd returned to her room and showered and dressed in clean clothes. The effort would hardly have been worth it if she had gone back out into the grimy city, so she had traveled no farther from her room than the hotel restaurant.

The waiter had brought dolmades—grape leaves—and a couple of other things she could not pronounce but that were suitably vegetarian. The feta cheese on her salad seemed incredibly fresh. The thin, elegant waiter with his dark eyes came and smiled at her as he refilled her wineglass. Willow thought he might be flirting, and it amused her. Fortunately, he said nothing, because she didn't know how to say "You're not my type" in Greek.

Sipping the wine, she thought that if she could just stay in the hotel, eating and sleeping there indefinitely, that would be all right. At least for a while. But no. Tomorrow she would leave Athens for somewhere she didn't have to climb to the tallest peak to escape the stink of exhaust fumes.

Willow set her glass down and picked up her fork. As she bent to take a bite of eggplant, she felt her face flush and the skin prickle at the back of her neck. Troubled, she glanced around the restaurant.

There were several couples and one large group of women, obviously some kind of tour group.

Her gaze came to rest on a silver-haired woman who sat by herself at the table nearest the door. The slender woman had narrow, beautiful features, and did not seem nearly old enough to have gone gray. Her eyes were alight with a kind of gleam that could not be accounted for by the last of the sunshine outside the windows.

Upon her lap there sat a sleek cat with cinnamon fur. The woman stroked the cat, which arched its back in hedonistic surrender.

The woman stood, holding the cat in the crook of her arm, and crossed the restaurant to stand beside Willow's table.

"Miss Rosenberg," she said, "may I sit?"

Willow stiffened. Silently, she began to summon a defensive spell, its magic beginning to spark at the tips of her fingers like static electricity.

The woman smiled as though in appreciation. "I mean you no harm."

Warily, Willow nodded. "A girl can't be too careful. If that's true, with the no harm and all, then have a seat."

She'd worded her invitation carefully. Magick had its rules. The woman had to be a witch—Willow could feel the power in her—and if she sat down, she was accepting the invitation with the condition that she would not attempt to do any harm.

The cat purred as the woman scratched behind its ears. Cradling the animal, she sat down.

"I'm surprised they let you in here with a cat," Willow said, unable to stop herself from admiring the animal. She loved cats. The temptation to take the cinnamon into her lap and stroke its fur was great. But she needed to remain on guard.

"They would not allow this sweet girl to join us, if they could see her," the woman replied, her accent some indefinable European lilt.

The cat purred and looked up at Willow with exquisite eyes.

"Can they see you?" she asked.

The silver-haired woman smiled. "A perceptive question. But yes, they can. I would not wish you to be embarrassed by being seen talking to an empty chair."

Willow nodded. "Thanks for that. Though, really, wouldn't be the first time. Kinda immune to embarrassment by now."

A silent moment passed between them. Willow glanced down at her plate, but found she had lost her appetite. Instead, she picked up her wineglass and took a sip. Once she would have babbled in the presence of this woman, trying to unravel the mystery. Now she only waited.

The woman smiled. She reached up to brush a lock of her silver hair away from her face. The cat stretched, as though anxious for her stroking hand to return, and the woman rubbed its neck, eliciting a deep purr.

"I wondered," she finally said. "But I am satisfied that you are ready."

"Which is, y'know, nice," Willow assured her. "But, okay. A, ready for what? And B, who are you, exactly? I mean, I know you're a witch, but that's not a who, it's a what."

The witch reached out as though to pick up a glass of wine with her fingers; an odd gesture, considering there was only one glass on the table. Yet when she raised her hand, she held a crystal goblet of red wine. She took a sip, licking the last drop from her upper lip, and set the glass down again. Willow had to glance at the table to make sure it had not vanished, but the glass was still there.

"Your frankness is lovely. All right, my dear. A direct approach, then. My name is Catherine Cadiere. I have been practicing the craft for a very long time. Consider a moment how old you imagine I could possibly be. Now multiply that age tenfold and you will be closer to the truth."

She stroked the cat's cinnamon fur. Its eyes were slitted and it seemed to have fallen asleep, but the low purr continued.

"I have been aware of you for some time, Willow. In truth, I first sensed your power nearly two years ago, from across the world. You shone like a beacon. Yet you have barely begun to explore the limits of the magick within you, and the witchery you can accomplish with appropriate guidance and study of spell-craft."

A tremor of fear passed through Willow. Yet she was not afraid of Catherine Cadiere. The only witch Willow feared was herself.

"So, what? You tracked me down to offer me your guidance?"

Catherine smiled. "You could consider me a mentor, or a teacher."

Willow lost any trace of a smile, any semblance of courtesy. "I've had my fill of teachers. And I don't have any interest in exploring anything, thanks. Magick is like anything else. It's best in small doses."

"Ah," Catherine said, scrutinizing her. "You've ventured into darkness."

Willow glanced away. This was too personal. Too intimate. She wasn't going to talk to a stranger about any of it.

Catherine reached out and touched her hand. A surge of warmth spread through Willow upon contact with the witch.

"You came back, Willow," she said. "You have even more power than I could have wished for in a student. You have seen the darkness in yourself and returned from that place, learned disci-pline. You are ready to fulfill your true potential. You have spent your formative years with Slayers, and because of that you are mis-guided. It is the duty of witches, not of Slayers, to subjugate the world's monstrosities. I can teach you how to wield magick with utter confidence."

Willow raised a hand to signal the flirty waiter. He walked by, ignoring her, which seemed strange until Willow realized that he wasn't being rude at all. He simply no longer noticed her presence, thanks to Catherine Cadiere.

Willow put her napkin on the table beside her plate and started to rise.

"I'm going to turn in. It was a pleasure meeting you," she said.

The cat opened its eyes. They bore a sadness that seemed extraordinary for an animal. Or perhaps, Willow thought, she was just projecting.

"Magick is about intent, Willow," Catherine went on. "It influences us, but if magick is well intended, its influence is benevolent."

Willow began to walk away, her back to the witch, wondering if Catherine would try to stop her with a hex.

"Tara's death, for instance."

Breath hitching in her chest, Willow froze. Fury began to roil in her and she felt her face grow hot. How dare this woman bring Tara into this conversation. She spun on one heel, prepared to tell off the silver-haired witch.

But Catherine had not finished.

"If only you'd been willing to be creative with your magick, you need not have lost her at all."

Willow felt her legs going weak. She couldn't breathe. How cruel the witch was to hurt her like this.

"What?" she said, the only word she could muster.

"Sit," said Catherine.

Barely aware of it, Willow went back to her chair, moving like a sleepwalker. She sat staring at the woman, but Catherine did not even meet her gaze now. The ageless, beautiful witch rose, kissed the cinnamon cat on its head, and then set the feline down on her chair.

At last she smiled at Willow. "A powerful witch needs a familiar."

Catherine passed her hand across the air like a common stage magician and produced a small, yellowed parchment scroll, perhaps four inches wide.

"This spell comes down to us from ancient Chaldea. Only a handful of witches in history have ever learned it. I give it to you as a gesture of good faith and friendship. I swear upon my mother's soul that it will do you no harm. They are only words on paper, Willow, but for a witch with the sort of innate magick that exists within you, the words become something wondrous."

Silver hair spilling down like a veil across her face, Catherine bent to stroke the cat a final time, then glanced at Willow.

"I'll leave you to yourselves now. You'll want some privacy, I expect."

Catherine Cadiere turned and strolled from the restaurant into the lobby of the hotel as though she were a princess on a promenade.

Willow shifted her gaze, staring at the cat, eyebrows raised in confusion and doubt. After a moment's hesitation she unfurled the small scroll. The parchment whispered under her fingers. The words printed on it meant absolutely nothing to her, but as she had grown more powerful as a witch, she had learned that one of the gifts of the craft was a sort of sense about such things. She could not translate the spell, but she could pronounce the inscrutable words.

What are you thinking, Will? she thought. *Only a total idiot would fall for something like this. It's a setup, somehow.*

But her instincts told her otherwise. And Catherine had vowed she would not be harmed by the spell. A thousand other things could go wrong, and she certainly was not ready to trust the ancient witch. The darkness was always alluring. How simple it would be to fall into the cruel joy that came with dark magick, to turn wicked.

She held the scroll in front of her and stared at it. The parchment shook in her hand. A light, self-deprecating laugh escaped her lips. She was like an alcoholic sitting in a bar, staring at a glass of whiskey and trying to rationalize. Just one drink. She could handle just one drink.

It's just like that, a voice in her head insisted.

But Willow wasn't listening. She might not trust Catherine Cadiere, but she trusted her own instincts. The woman had been telling the truth about her age, and her mastery of witchcraft. Just being in her presence had made that much clear. And if Catherine could achieve that kind of power and discipline, why not Willow?

Why can't I?

The cat purred and stared at her with bright eyes. When she looked at it, the little cinnamon girl twitched her tail.

What Catherine had hinted at . . . if it was at all possible, wasn't that worth any sacrifice? Any risk?

Willow held her breath as she gazed at the cat, listening to her purr. She squeezed her eyes closed a moment and then opened them. Looking down at the scroll, she read the ancient spell aloud before she changed her mind. As she spoke the words, her body seemed to rise, to unfurl almost like the stretching feline, while the power in these words combined with the power that was always there inside of her.

She finished the spell, the words tingling her lips, but she kept her head down, afraid to look up. Afraid even to breathe.

The voice was half purr, half question, small and tentative. "Willow?"

She looked up, eyes widening as she drew a sharp breath. Both hands flew to cover her mouth, shaking, and tears sprang to her eyes, sliding quickly down her cheeks. Tears of repressed anguish, of unimaginable gratitude, and impossible joy.

Tara had never looked more beautiful.

She stood, blond hair framing her face, cinnamon dress clinging to her curves, and walked over to kneel beside Willow's chair. Tara reached up to wipe away Willow's tears even as her own began to fall.

"Sssh, baby. Sshhh. It's okay."

Willow grabbed her and pulled her into an embrace, pressing

her face into Tara's hair and inhaling the scent of her—that scent that was only hers, that could not belong to anyone else—and then she knew this was no dream, no illusion.

She shook, crying, and Tara cried with her. Tara cupped the back of her head in her hands and then their lips met in a succession of quick, sensuous kisses. They breathed each other's breath, tasted the salt of each other's tears, and Willow knew that some universal error had been corrected. She had been only a fragment of herself, and now she was whole again.

They were interrupted by the waiter, who stood a few feet away pretending not to look at them even as he cleared his throat.

Startled, Willow looked up and realized that everyone in the restaurant was staring at them. Whatever magick Catherine had used to deflect attention, it had faded.

Tara laughed softly, covering her mouth to hide her smile, one of a thousand habits she had taken with her when she died. Just seeing that single gesture broke Willow's heart all over again.

Blushing, Tara slid into the chair opposite Willow's.

Willow took her hand and glanced up at the waiter. "Check, please?"

CHAPTER THREE

Malik crouched beside the corpse of the little girl, blood rushing through him, flushed with fury and hating himself for having arrived too late. The girl's face had pulled into a rictus of terror, a silent scream that had frozen upon her features as the Veshtitza had eaten her heart.

He kissed the tips of his fingers and used them to close her eyes, then sprang toward the open window and glanced out. Only a handful of people walked the street below, locals coming home from a late dinner or from visiting friends. The tourists didn't stray far from the main street that ran down the gullet of Valletta from the village square to the abandoned fortress on the rocky cliff at the end of the island.

Eyes narrowed, he glanced in both directions, ignoring the street now and scanning the second- and third-story windows of the buildings across the street and the space that separated them. Precious little illumination was available, but he could see quite well in the dark. Even so, his prey was elusive.

Then he saw it, a flicker of deeper black against the indigo nighttime sky visible above the eaves of one of the row houses just down the block. An enormous black moth fluttered through the air, rising on an errant breeze, darting aimlessly. Harmlessly.

Yet Malik knew the moth was anything but aimless. Anything but harmless.

He leaped up onto the windowsill, not sparing the dead girl another glance. The weight of his sword in its scabbard across his back provided familiar reassurance. They were inseparable, Malik and the blade. He had received it as a gift on this very island—the island of Malta—so very long ago, when the Ottoman Turks had lain siege and been turned away by the island's defenders.

Malik did not pause. He bent and pistoned his legs, leaping out over the street. For a moment he felt as though he were flying, but of course he could not fly. He struck the opposing house, boots braced against the wall even as his fingers latched on to the ledge beneath the second-story window. His body bent with the momentum and he moved with it, leaping upward to land with his boots upon the ledge. He grabbed hold of the upper frame of the window with one hand and the top of the thick shutter with the other, and scrambled upward, finding fingerholds in the crevices between stones and toeholds atop the window and shutters, and then he pulled himself onto the roof.

All in the space of a few seconds.

If anyone had heard him down in the street and looked up, at best they would have caught a glance.

Malik set off across the rooftops. His gaze found the black moth against the indigo night again and he gave chase. The row houses had roofs that were uneven. He ran along, dropped down five feet to the next, then leaped and sailed onto the next, which was higher. At the first alley he barely had to spring to cross the dark abyss below. The next was not quite so narrow. At the third, the gulf was simply too far. Sword banging against his back, he leaped across to the open frame of a window ten feet below, then reversed direction to land on the top of a set of stone stairs that led down from the door of an old dress shop.

He launched himself from the steps and onto the street. This part of Valletta was deserted. With a glance upward he located the moth as it flitted, but now it began to descend. Malik slowed his pursuit, taking care on the broken, cracked street.

The moth fluttered across the street and into a side alley. The stink of fish lingered in the air from some fishmonger not careful about where he disposed of his unsold wares. Dark figures rustled in a recessed doorway, a man and woman whose tryst he had just interrupted. Some kind of motor scooter leaned against a wall. A chain had been run through a sewer grating to keep the thing from being stolen.

Malik crouched silently behind the scooter, adept at hiding in shadows and keeping silent. The trysting couple muttered something obscene and left the alley. That was for the best.

The moth danced upon the air. In the dark of the alley Malik could make out the lines of gold on its wings. It fluttered toward the window of a dingy flat and entered through the single broken pane.

Malik's nostrils flared and his upper lip curled with revulsion. He had waited for this moment. The Veshtitza sent its soul out after dark in the form of that black moth to drink the blood and eat the hearts of young girls. Five had already died in Malta, two of them after his arrival, including the one tonight. The demon-witch would not take another.

He drew the Ottoman sword, marched across the street, and kicked the door open wide. It banged off the wall inside, cracking plaster and shaking the already broken window.

Once the Veshtitza did not travel alone, but their numbers had dwindled over the past century so that there were simply not enough of them to form covens anymore. Malik had hunted them before. At the beginning of the eighteenth century they had set upon the Maltese Islands like a plague, and he had dispatched the entire coven.

One little moth presented no challenge. It was merely a pest to be exterminated.

The woman lay upon a rough, soiled mattress on the floor of the main room in the tiny flat. She seemed perfectly ordinary-looking. Middle-aged and slightly overweight, her hair an indefinable brownish, color, and her clothes matronly. The pallor of her flesh gave her away. Anyone else coming upon her might have thought her to be sleeping, but Malik knew the signs.

Her soul had gone abroad. The black moth had drained the blood of that little girl, Tania, and opened her up to feast upon her heart. Now it alighted upon the woman's lips, wings twitching as it tried to crawl inside the Veshtitza's mouth. The noise of the door crashing open would not stir her, since the demon-witch's soul had not yet returned to her.

Malik did not hesitate.

He brought the sword down in a whistling arc. It struck flesh and severed bone like a woodcutter's ax, decapitating the Veshtitza.

The black moth rose up, flitting about madly with disorientation, and then darted for the open door. Malik snatched it from the air with his left hand. He pushed the Veshtitza's soul into his mouth, feeling the struggle of its wings as he swallowed it down.

The soul of the monster would wither and die inside of him. The body would decompose, here in this dingy flat. No more little children would be taken by this beast, but all the prayers in the world would not resurrect those who lives had already been snuffed out.

Malik sheathed his sword. He took no pleasure in this night's work—not when parents were grieving, when innocence had been defiled. Malik had never been a hero, nor imagined himself to be. He simply did what needed doing.

Always and forever.

He stepped from the flat, feeling the soul of the Veshtitza still wriggling in his gut, and cloaked himself in darkness. Anyone who saw him on the streets of Valletta tonight would not notice the sword. They would remember only a dark-haired, dark-eyed man dressed in black, if they remembered him at all.

Malik wound his way through the maze of streets that would take him, in time, to the harbor. Word had come from an old friend that a group of Keres had been hunting policemen and soldiers in northern Greece. He would find and destroy them, and then, perhaps, he might rest, at least for a time.

On a steep, curving road that led down toward the harbor, he gazed out over the ocean and wished that there were still lands across the waves that he had yet to see. His wanderings had taken him on journeys all across the planet. The world had few surprises left for him now.

The darkness rippled on the road just ahead. A silver light glowed and pulsed and coalesced into the phantasm of a little bearded man with eyes like tiny stars. The ghost fidgeted worriedly as Malik approached.

"What is it, Anatoly?" Malik asked.

The Russian ghost tugged on his beard, a habit he had carried over into the afterlife. "The Keres are no longer in Greece."

Malik frowned. "What do you mean? Where have they gone?"

"I am not certain," the specter told him, the twin stars of his eyes flickering as he blinked. "One might hazard a guess, however."

A flash of anger went through Malik. "One had better do so quickly."

"I have heard whispers that the Congress is beginning to gather."

Malik sneered. "Impossible."

"Those same whispers claim that in North Africa, the river goddess Kandida has risen."

Malik felt the anger draining out of him. He sighed and nodded slowly, wondering if he would ever rest again. "We'd best locate the others."

Buffy missed her sister. At the moment, Dawn was back at the castle in Scotland where they were setting up Slayer HQ. But that was probably for the best, since she wasn't really speaking to Buffy anyway. The sisters had had a disagreement over Buffy's intention to send Dawn to boarding school. The matter had not yet been resolved, but it would have to wait until Buffy returned to Scotland.

As much as she missed Dawn, though, Buffy never minded eating alone. Once upon a time it would have driven her crazy the way people looked at a young woman sitting by herself in a restaurant. These days, she hardly noticed. The pleasure of quiet, of a moment's respite from the war that was her life, was always welcome.

The restaurant was a little place called DePasquale Brothers in downtown Providence, just a few blocks from the train station. It apparently had not been there very long, and was the sort of place that would likely be replaced by some other establishment within a year or two. The location saw such turnover that in a decade no one would be able to remember all of the different restaurants that had been there. But the eggplant-and-olive pizza she'd ordered tasted delicious, hot enough to burn the roof of her mouth, and with just a bit of kick from the crushed peppers she'd sprinkled on top.

She'd started with a small Caesar salad. The waiter had warned her the pizza would be too much for one, but Buffy didn't mind. Xander would be along eventually, or she'd bring it back to the hotel for him to eat cold later on. There were very few things in the world Xander Harris liked more than pizza in the middle of the night. And if he pulled off the eggplant and olives, well, that was a fault in his pizza-eating wiring.

Just for something different, she'd ordered a glass of chardonnay to go with the salad, but once the pizza arrived she switched to water with a twist of lemon.

Buffy managed to eat a little more than half of the pizza before she caught sight of Xander coming into the restaurant. He craned his neck, peering around in search of her, looking lost. Buffy waved, and when he spotted her, Xander grinned. Without the eye patch he might have been the slightly gawky high school kid he'd been back when they'd first met. But then the expression faded and he came toward her with purpose etched on his face, and the illusion passed.

Xander tried his best to hold on to the lighthearted guy he'd once been, but all too often the harsh reality of the present fell upon him like a shroud. His missing eye was a constant reminder.

When he slid into the booth with her and saw the pizza, though, his face lit up again. Buffy was glad. Any time she could make Xander forget to be serious, it made her smile. They had that effect on each other.

"Everything okay?" she asked.

"With pizza, all is well," Xander said, even as he began picking the toppings off a slice. "I'll try to overlook the way you've tainted this pie with my archnemesis, the vegetable."

Buffy waited patiently while he demolished his first slice. By then the waiter had brought him a glass of water.

"Xand," she said as he took a sip, "what've you got?"

He held up a finger as he took a deeper drink from his cup, and then he set it down, took a breath, and said, "Absolutely nothing."

"Whoa. Don't hold back on the scintillating details of your day."

Xander shrugged. "What can I say? I got nothing. Obviously, the police don't have a clue what caused that sandstorm. They're not even using the word 'sand.' 'High winds,' I keep hearing. Most of them seem to be busy elsewhere anyway, what with all the sightings of weird crap."

Buffy pointed at him. "Y'know, gotta say, you just never cease to amaze me. All the research you've had to do over the years while I'm out trying not to die—or die again—it's freaky all the snooty academic terminology you've just sucked into your brain by osmosis."

He sighed. "Osmosis. You say stuff like that, and I start missing Willow. And besides, pretty much sure you haven't come up with better terminology for what's going on around here than 'weird crap.'"

"I'm still developing a theory," Buffy said.

"It could be demons? Yeah. Heard that one before. Not much more specific than 'weird crap,' is it?"

Xander redecorated another slice of pizza. Buffy took a sip of her water.

"What about you?" Xander asked, mouth full. "Anything?"

Buffy had spent the past few hours making phone calls, touching base with other Slayers they had brought into their network, many of whom she had helped train.

"No hard evidence yet," she said, "but all of the Slayers I've spoken to are saying it's a little too quiet out there."

"Out where?"

"Everywhere," Buffy said. "Aside from right here in lovely Providence, Rhode Island, there's been a pretty steep drop-off in supernatural activity worldwide. I talked to Faith. She's got some vampire stuff she's investigating in San Francisco. Other than that, she's pretty much on the same page with everyone else."

"Quiet. Too quiet," Xander said, trying to sound all film-noirish around a mouthful of pizza.

"Yep. Meanwhile, we've got oodles of weird crap, including the guy in the middle of that sandstorm, who gave me the serious willies."

Xander swallowed, took a sip, and looked at her oddly. "Oodles?"

Buffy nodded. "Oodles."

"And 'willies'? Really? You never say 'wiggins' anymore. Have you noticed that? I miss it, kinda."

"Everything has its day. Can we go back to the weird crap?"

"Okay. All quiet. So did you call in some reinforcements?" Xander asked.

"I've got Dori, Adrianna, and maybe half a dozen others making their travel arrangements. Not sure about Faith, but she's Faith, right? She'll go where the wind takes her."

Xander nodded, taking another bite of pizza.

Buffy put thirty dollars on the table and slid out of the booth. "Looks like there's only one way tonight's not going to be a waste of time."

"We going on patrol?"

"More like hunting, but yes. I'm gonna go up and put on some comfy, butt-kicking shoes. Meet you in the lobby in twenty minutes?"

Xander gave her a thumbs-up as he chewed.

Buffy made her way to the elevator and rode up to the seventh floor, her mind awhirl. There were so many factors to consider—the drop-off of worldwide supernatural activity, the rash of weird sightings in Providence, and the bizarre lack of accompanying deaths. With this many demons and monsters running around Rhode Island, it ought to have been a bloodbath, but so far it had been strangely quiet. Then there was the sandstorm, and the figure at its center, who really had creeped her out big-time. Was he the cause, or just another symptom?

She needed more than one brain working on the problem. And she needed help from more than just Slayers. She needed scholars. In the morning, she'd call Giles and try to reach Willow as well.

The elevator doors slid open. She pulled out her key card as she walked the long hallway with its endless sameness. Any time she found herself in a long hotel corridor she found herself remembering the boy on his Big Wheel in *The Shining* and she'd get a little shiver thinking about the ghosts of the murdered twins awaiting him around the corner.

Fortunately, that had only been a movie. Unfortunately, Buffy Summers had seen worse.

As she opened the door to her room, her cell phone began to trill. Buffy let the door close as she pulled out the cell and flipped it open, not recognizing the overseas number.

"Hello?"

"Hey, it's me."

Buffy blinked in surprise as she clicked on the light in her room. Willow was in Greece. It had to be two in the morning there, which was why she'd planned to wait until tomorrow to call.

"What's going on, Will? Is everything all right?"

"More than all right," Willow replied, and Buffy could hear breathless excitement in her voice.

"Wait, aren't you and Kennedy still in Santorini?"

"Well, not exactly. Kennedy's still there. I'm in Athens—with Tara."

Buffy caught her breath and sat heavily on the edge of the bed. She felt all the blood rushing from her face and horror blooming in her chest. Something had happened to Willow's mind.

"Will, tell me exactly where you are. I'm going to call Giles and have him fly out there first thing in the morning. I want you to just stay—"

"Quiet. Listen," Willow said, and there came the sound of whispers and a soft giggle as she handed the phone over to someone else.

Cold fingers of dread traced Buffy's spine.

Then there came the voice on the other end of the line.

"B-Buffy?" she asked, tentatively. "Hey. You okay?"

For several seconds, Buffy couldn't reply. At last, she forced herself to speak.

"Tara? Is it—"

"Really me? Yep. I know it's hard to believe. I know . . . Willow explained everything that's happened. But it really is me, Buffy. I'm back. I've missed everyone so much. I can't wait to see you."

Buffy put a hand on her forehead as though taking her own temperature. She let herself fall back onto the bed. As the Slayer, magick wasn't really her area, but there were things that she knew all too well. When Willow had used magick to bring Buffy back to life it had been at a terrible cost, using one-of-a-kind magick. When Buffy's mother had died, nothing in the world could bring her back.

"How?"

Tara giggled—that little "hee-hee-hee" that was so much a part of her. "Witchcraft, silly. It's kind of complicated, but it's mostly because I'm a witch. The body I'm in . . . here, wait, Willow wants the phone."

When Willow came back on, she began by talking about witches' familiars and soul-jumping and Tara being a cat, sort of, and then she backtracked to tell the story of how she came to leave Kennedy and how she met an ancient witch called Catherine Cadiere in Athens.

"I was just so confused after what Kennedy did," she went on, "but now I get it. The Fates, this is what they intended, Buffy. How it was always supposed to be, y'know?"

"I do. But are you sure you can trust this Catherine? Ancient witch shows up, plops your heart's desire in your lap. Usually not the recipe for a happy ending, right? Resurrection is dark magick, no matter how you pretty it up. You told me that yourself. After what you've been through, is it safe to get that close to the dark stuff?"

Willow hesitated. "That's not . . . you're being unfair. Isn't that the pot calling the kettle tainted by darkness? There's more to magick than any of us knows. I did a spell. That's it. No child sacrifice or pledging my soul to lost gods. And, hey, who's cozier with the forces of darkness than the Slayer? That's where the power comes from, right? Sometimes you've gotta fight fire with fire."

Buffy rose and went to the windows, threw open the curtains, and looked out at the night.

"You're right, Will. I'm sorry. I just . . . I'm afraid for you. If this is real and there are no strings attached, I can't think of anything that would make me happier. I wish this for you. And I can't wait to see Tara. But you know how it must sound from half a world away."

"I know. I do."

"Okay," Buffy said. "So what now? I wanted to talk to you about what's going on here, but maybe you should get some sleep and I'll call you in the morning? I could use your research-girl skills, not to mention your witchy mojo."

"We're staying put for a little while. Catherine has offered to mentor me, and I want to see how that goes. I'm thinking I could learn a lot from her. And if she seems like creepy-world-destruction-schemer-type witch, you'll be the first to know.

"But, yeah," Willow continued, "call me when you wake up and we can brainstorm about whatever you've got going on there. You and Xander are safe, though?"

"Safer than we should be, which is the weird part. But we can talk about it tomorrow."

Willow laughed softly and muttered to Tara to stop whatever it was she was doing. "Watch the hands," she whispered.

Buffy's heart ached. For Willow's sake, she hoped it was all real.

"All right. Talk to you then," Willow said. "Night."

"Night," Buffy replied.

She closed her phone and dropped it onto the bed. As she changed into clothes more appropriate for a night hunting monsters, her mind was elsewhere. Willow had proven that she controlled her magick now instead of its controlling her the way it once had. But recovering alcoholics fell off the wagon all the time. If Willow stumbled, the consequences would be dire.

An ocean separated her from her best friend, but Buffy knew she couldn't just let it go. At the very least, she had to see if Giles could find out anything about this Catherine Cadiere.

It was difficult to let herself believe that Tara could be alive again. But if it proved true, if she really was back, what a gift that would be. Willow had never had a chance to say good-bye to her. Now it seemed she hadn't needed to.

CHAPTER FOUR

San Francisco's Haight Street was haunted by the ghost of the 1960s. Much of it had been gentrified, with high-end boutiques and restaurants, and for the most part the street was clean. But junkies still slept in doorways and teenagers and twentysomethings staggered in clusters across intersections with their shirts hanging open and their shoeless feet filthy from the road.

Yet the locals and visitors still loved Haight Street. Mostly because they went home before the lights went out and only the luckless and aimless remained.

Faith Lehane crouched on the roof of Wilkerson's Chop House, scanning the street for dark figures she knew that she would eventually see. They moved without the stagger-step of drunks or the jittery desperation of junkies or the swagger of troubled punks who dared the night to challenge them. The figures she searched the street for would move with a velvet step, sliding in furtive silence toward their destination.

Vampires. But not the typical leeches she and other Slayers

dealt with all the time. She hunted some old ones tonight. And if the rumors were true—the rumors she'd beaten out of some of the street vamps—there were even older bloodsuckers in San Francisco tonight.

She had Robin Wood to thank for the lead that had brought her here in the first place. Out of the blue he had sent her an e-mail. The message had included no information on his current whereabouts and no comment about their brief dalliance, or the calluses on her heart that had prevented it from being more than a dalliance. All Robin had done was send her the information. Faith had flirted with the idea of asking where he was, but in the end she had not bothered to reply to his message. They both knew their limits; why pretend otherwise?

Car doors slammed.

Faith tensed, eyes narrowing. Once again she scanned the street, but her attention came back to the building diagonally across from Wilkerson's. It sat on a corner and behind it was a darkened parking lot. Cars moved up and down Haight Street, but it was after two o'clock in the morning and the traffic was light. An engine roared to life, followed by two others, and moments later a dark sedan with its headlights off rolled out of the parking lot behind the restored office building. The other two streamed after it.

As if responding to some signal, all three drivers clicked their headlights on at the same time, and then the first car turned onto Haight Street.

Faith stood, took two steps back, and then ran to the edge and leaped off the restaurant's roof. Her coat flapped around her as she plummeted, but it was weighted down with the sharpened stakes she kept in the sheaths she'd had specially sewn into the lining.

She hit the pavement, her momentum carrying her forward, and she rolled once before springing to her feet.

Headlights pinned her to the spot and the first car slowed, brake lights shining red on the grill of the car behind it. The engine revved as though the automobile itself were considering what to do next. Faith held her hands by her sides, palms out, empty, hoping they would be stupid enough to get out of the car and try to talk to her, or even try to kill her. Either way would make her job a lot simpler.

The driver hit the brights. Faith squinted and raised a hand to shield her eyes. The engine revved and the car lurched forward. But she was ready. Her reflexes were so acute that her body was in motion almost before she knew it. As the car shot toward her, Faith ran straight at it. Behind the wheel, she imagined the driver must be smiling, anticipating the crunch of metal and the shattering of her bones.

Faith leaped into the air, pulled her jacket around her, and shot out her right foot. Her boot shattered the windshield. Emergency glass exploded in a shower of fragments like rock candy. Faith shot into the car as a human bullet and found herself in a tangle amid a quartet of stunned vampires. She shot one boot into the side of the driver's head as her lower body continued forward between the seats and she lay exposed, on her back, staring up at them as they bared their fangs. But the impact and surprise made the driver swerve. The car hit a fire hydrant and water erupted from it, a fountain that sprayed them all.

The second car clipped the rear bumper, and then all three vehicles were stopped.

Faith sat up and grabbed hold of the two leeches in the back by their shirts and yanked them toward each other with all of her strength. The one on her left had the weaker skull, and it caved in with a terrible crack. Faith used the leverage of her grip on them to pull herself fully into the backseat as the two in the front tried and failed to hold on to her. Still clutching his shirt, she drove the vampire on her left into the window and his head broke the glass.

In that dazed moment, she reached into her coat and produced a pair of stakes. She struck both vampires in the backseat at once, plunging sharpened wood into monstrous hearts, cracking bone and splitting muscle, and the two vampires exploded in twin clouds of dust. The breeze from the broken window sucked some of the dust out, but for a moment it made it impossible to see inside the car.

Dropping a stake, Faith snatched up the shoulder harness of the driver's seat belt and pulled it tight, pinning the vampire to his seat. Then she rammed the other stake through the back of the seat, through leather and padding, through skin and bone. It took all of the strength a Slayer possessed, but the seat belt suddenly gave plenty of slack, and the driver was dust.

That left only one.

Already police sirens wailed in the distance.

The vampire in the front—a blond man whose ears had begun to look pointed and whose fingers were too long to be human, indicating incredible age for one of his kind—tried to run. He opened his door and leaped out. Faith scrambled over the front seat after him. The leech tried to slam the door on her but she stiff-armed it, knocking him away from the car, staggering.

Then they were out in the street. A thin, half-naked man stood in a nearby doorway, gaping at them. Faith ignored him. There would be other witnesses. It didn't matter. Nobody would believe a word, and there weren't any bodies. Vampires made that part easy, at least.

Trickles of blood wept from tiny wounds where glass had punctured or remained stuck in her flesh. Faith ignored them, shook the rock candy shards from her hair, and started toward the vamp, who walked backward toward the other two cars.

All four doors opened on the second car and another quartet of bloodsuckers climbed out, three males and a female.

But then the third car began to back up. Its tires spun, squealing for traction. The driver cranked the wheel around, and the car slewed to one side and then started off in the other direction.

"Damn it!" Faith snapped.

That car had to be the one she'd been looking for, but there were five leeches between her and her goal, and no way to dust them fast enough to give chase.

Only one option.

Police sirens grew louder as she fought, a blur of fists and kicks, of elbows and sharpened stakes. The vampires did what they always did—they threatened and they gnashed their teeth and they promised to eat her eyeballs and her heart, and then she killed them.

Well, four of them.

She left the old blondie with the pointed ears alive. Faith beat him until he stopped trying to fight her. The cops were close enough that she could see lights flashing off of buildings far down the street. She dragged the vampire over to the second car, which had only a little front bumper damage, popped the trunk, and tossed him in.

The keys were still in the ignition. The leech who'd driven it would never be coming back. Faith considered it a loan. She took a page from the vampires and killed the headlights, cranked the wheel around, and disappeared up a side street as the first of the police cars appeared at the scene of the fight.

She drove around for a few minutes to make sure nobody was following and then headed up Twin Peaks Boulevard, following the winding road as it climbed up high above the city. At Christmas Tree Point, where a handful of people were still out and about, checking out the view of the city and the bay and the lights of the bridge far below, Faith pulled into the lot. Nobody paid any attention to her. Their eyes were all on the view.

When she popped the trunk, the vampire tried to attack her. She clamped one hand over his mouth, and with the other she drove the stake through his upper thigh. Her hand muffled his scream.

"You done?" she asked, bending over him. "'Cause you're not getting out of this. Basically, you've got two choices. I can make it quick, or we can get up front, sit in the car together, and wait for the sun to come up. You want to burn to death, on fire from the inside out, screaming, that's all right with me. I've seen it a hundred times, and it's wicked cool, if you wanna know the truth. Takes me to my happy place. Or you can go with a flick of the wrist. It'll hurt for a second, and then you're dust in the wind."

The dull gleam in his eyes told her he was ready to talk. Faith pulled her hand away, ready to slam the trunk if he got out of line or started screaming.

"What do you want?"

Faith smiled. "See? Ain't cooperation much easier?"

The vampire's thin lips pulled back in a sneer of hatred. The feeling was mutual.

"I'm gonna assume Haarmann was in that last car. I know he's here. First time he's ever been in the States, from what I hear. Master vampires don't tend to travel all that much. I want to know who's with him, what they're doing here, and where they're going."

He considered lying. She saw it in his eyes. But the leech must have seen something in hers, because he glanced away in defeat.

"Haarmann is a legend, even in the human world. But even the butcher's not as revered among vampires as Christabel," the bloodsucker said. "She sired me. I am her creature."

Faith smirked. "You were. Now you're mine."

Then the name tweaked something in her mind and suddenly it wasn't funny anymore. "Wait. Christabel? You're saying Christabel de Tournefort is here, in America? That she's alive?"

It was the vampire's turn to smile. "It's your good fortune that they left before you could meet them."

"No one's heard of her since World War One. The Watchers Council thought she was dead."

"We are all dead," the vampire said.

Faith had lost interest in talk. This wasn't a game anymore. "Why are they here, and where are they going?"

"There is a gathering unlike anything humanity has ever imagined. That is their destination."

Faith pressed the point of the stake against his left eyeball, the tip puncturing it so that a little drip of fluid slid out. The vampire hissed in pain.

"Where?"

"In Rhode Island," the vampire said, voice wretched with pain and the understanding that his time had come to an end. "Providence, Rhode Island."

Faith was as good as her word.

She dusted him right there in the trunk just as a couple of half-drunk college boys came along the side of the car, trying to figure out what was going on back there. Faith shut the trunk and smiled at them as she climbed back behind the wheel.

As she drove back down Twin Peaks Boulevard, a grim certainty weighed upon her. Whatever this was, it had to be related to Buffy's phone call. Which meant Faith was headed east. If Christabel de Tournefort and Haarmann were going to New England, Faith Lehane would follow. She hadn't been back east in a long time. Providence wasn't Boston, but it would be sort of like going home.

The thought brought her no pleasure.

Giles had spent most of the night in the library at the building on Great Russell Street. Kinnear had instructed most of his branch operatives and Watchers to focus on the strange migrations of demon tribes and old gods and myths, and Giles understood why. Something terrible must be brewing for such a phenomenon to be so widespread.

He could not bring himself to care. Instead, he stayed in the library and studied the file Kinnear had given him on Micaela Tomasi's Council expedition to unearth the Maghreb's Ivory. The amulet was vital to the Watchers' effort to avert a potential apocalypse, but Kinnear insisted they could not panic about having lost the thing until they had a full report from Morocco and could determine the status of the expedition.

Giles had fallen asleep several times on the table in the library before finally dragging himself upstairs to sleep in one of the branch office's many guest rooms. But he'd woken shortly after seven o'clock and returned to the library to continue. After having reviewed the file on the expedition multiple times the night before, he had focused upon the legend of the river demon Kandida and her destruction and burial in a tomb along the river.

A recipe for disaster if he'd ever seen one. Great care would have had to be taken. In fact, from what he'd read, it would be foolhardy to attempt to remove the Maghreb's Ivory without preparing some other method of containing or destroying Kandida should she be freed by the Ivory's removal. Nothing in the research indicated that was a certainty, but caution demanded it be considered.

Apparently, caution had not prevailed.

Sunlight streamed in, warming him and illuminating half of the table. The other half still lay in shadow. Dust motes danced in the air. Still exhausted, Giles had begun to drift, gazing out the window. In the sunshine, he could easily imagine how beautiful Micaela had been upon their first meeting, long ago. Her golden hair had been quite long then, and bound in a braid. Her dress had been elegant and alluring, and he'd been smitten. That part of their relationship was long behind them now, but after difficulties and misunderstandings and betrayals they had found themselves intimate friends in the way only former lovers and colleagues could become.

He wished he'd been with her in North Africa.

Mind wandering, he barely heard Malaika Kehinde enter the room.

"Mr. Giles," she said, her accent like music.

He glanced up, and from her grim expression he knew that she had brought word. Giles sat up straight, suddenly cold.

"What've you heard?"

Her gaze softened. "Our operatives reached the dig site this morning. You will be happy to know that Micaela survived."

Giles raised his hands, steepled his fingers as though in prayer, and rested his face against them. His chest ached with gratitude, but he could express it only to Miss Kehinde.

"Thank you," he said, lowering his hands. "Thank you so much."

He removed his glasses and rubbed at his tired eyes. As he cleaned the lenses on his shirt, he studied the woman and saw that Micaela's survival was not the only news, and the rest was grave.

"Were there other survivors?"

Malaika shook her head. "None. And it appears the river demon has been released."

"What a disaster," Giles said.

"The Maghreb's Ivory has been recovered, at least."

"One less apocalypse to worry about," Giles noted.

"True," Malaika said. "And now that we know Miss Tomasi is safe, I hope that we can rely on you, Mr. Giles. the Council are frantic about all of this migration. They are unused to puzzles they cannot solve."

Giles nodded. "Right. You've got me, whatever you need. Let's get to work."

The man in the cage screamed. His throat had become raw and his voice ragged from days of screaming, but he had at last stopped shaking the bars of the cage, surrendering to the knowledge that he would not be able to free himself.

Perhaps he thought that when the moon became full, the wolf would be able to free itself.

Tai often wondered what they thought when wearing the guise of humanity. Certainly this man, Kurt Traeger, knew what he was, knew the beast inside of him. But he seemed ordinary enough otherwise. Tai thought this was the most despicable type of werewolf— the one who knew what he was and pretended for the rest of the month to lead an innocent life, pretended that he did not know the beast lived inside of him and needed to be destroyed.

The woman in the cage with Traeger had given her name only as Odessa. She had struggled at first, tried to rip Tai with her fingernails. When she understood that he meant to cage her, only then did she reveal the beast. Traeger could not change himself at will like some of the older and more powerful wolves. Odessa knew how. She had begun to do so, jaws lengthening, fur sprouting from her tender flesh, but Tai had rammed her skull into the bars of the cage and then thrown her through the door and locked it behind her.

Odessa never screamed. When Tai brought the meat to the cage, she tracked him with her eyes, never hiding her predatory nature. He admired her. Such a shame he would have to kill her.

By all rights, he should kill her now, cut her throat like he had done with all of the others. She had revealed herself, after all. Tai knew with utter certainty that she was a wolf. But with Traeger, he had to wait until the full moon arrived and proved his suspicion beyond a doubt—he would never kill an innocent. He had to be sure. Letting Odessa live until the full moon was simply easier. She would be nothing but beast then—just an animal.

Traeger had been in the cage for over a week, ever since Tai had stalked him across the cobblestone streets of Prague. Too many damned werewolves in Prague. He had caught Odessa three nights ago. She was a beautiful specimen with alabaster skin and hair like black silk. He liked to watch her walk the cage. Whenever Traeger tried to speak with her, Odessa would strike him.

Tai did not want to kill her until he could see no trace of her beauty.

The full moon was more than two weeks away. It would be an eternity.

He put two buckets of water through the bars of the cage. Then he slid another, this one full of rare meat and barely cooked potatoes, in to them. Enough to keep them alive until the time came to kill them.

Traeger rushed the bars.

Tai stepped back as the wolf-man reached for him. Odessa only laughed at the vulgar display from the pitiful creature.

"Why do you leave me in here with him?" she asked. "Is there no other cage, nowhere else you can lock me up?"

This was not the first time Odessa had asked the question. Tai only gazed at her a moment, then turned his back and left the basement. Traeger began to scream again, to shriek like a madman, and Tai closed the door quickly behind him, sealing in the asylum sounds.

Tai had not replied to Odessa, nor had he ever replied to any question that the wolves asked of him. In truth, he never spoke. Though he had been born with the ability, he had no memory of speaking, not even as a child in Beijing, when he had still had the capacity. He was not mute, only silent.

The massive hulk of a man locked the cellar door and climbed the stone stairs up to the main floor of the old jail he had taken over three years earlier. The neighborhood was one of Prague's worst, a slum where homeless wandered by night and hid away by day, where buildings were torn down or burned down with regularity. It was a forgotten corner of the Czech capital.

But prosperity had begun to catch up. The city planners had begun to renovate at the edges of the neighborhood, and if they had their way, soon entire blocks would begin to be reimagined as hotels and shops for the tourist trade. Similar transformations had occurred throughout much of Europe over the past century. When gentrification finally reached his location, if Tai had not exterminated the wolves of Prague, he would have to move to another place where his activities would go undiscovered.

He did not relish the thought.

With a sigh, he glanced out the window at the broken street and crumbling edifices of this place, which had remained forgotten for nearly sixty years. Over the rooftops he saw the towers of the

Prague that the government seemed so proud of, and cursed them for their pretense that the city was in no danger.

A figure appeared, coming down the street from the north.

Tai knew him instantly. The wraith in his long, black coat could be mistaken for no one else. The silent hunter arched an eyebrow in curiosity and went to the door, opening it wide.

He waited on the stoop for Malik to arrive.

"Hello, my friend," Malik said as he approached. "You look well."

Tai bowed his head in greeting and thanks, then gave his friend a questioning look.

"The darkness gathers. We are needed," Malik said.

Troubled, Tai glanced back into the house and toward the door that led down to the cellar.

"I know," Malik said. "It is regrettable, but we must go."

Tai sighed. He did not like the idea of executing the wolves before the moon was full. It would be difficult enough to kill the lovely Odessa, but Traeger had not yet proven himself a wolf. Oh, Tai felt certain, and he had never made an error before—never taken an ordinary human accidentally. But still it was not the way he worked.

Saddened, he shrugged his shoulders and went back inside. Malik was both friend and commander, and Tai would follow him, no matter the cost.

He took an ax from its place hanging on the wall and opened the cellar door. For once, Traeger was not screaming.

But he would be.

CHAPTER FIVE

Late Thursday afternoon, Tara wandered beneath the towering trees of Athens's National Gardens and found herself at peace. All morning she had followed a trail of marvels, bits of ancient history and modern pride scattered around the Greek capital. A small guidebook she'd bought in the hotel gift shop had provided all the information she needed. Away from the bustle of the office buildings and hotels she had found Athens a wonder. The city was dotted with places of ancient power that took her breath away, and vast reservoirs of magick that lent her a serenity she doubted she could have found anywhere else.

How had Willow overlooked all of this?

Tara bought a bottle of water from a vendor by the street and then strolled back into the garden. In a shaded spot she sat down cross-legged and hummed softly to herself, gazing out across the green lawn.

Resurrection felt so wonderfully strange. It felt as though she hadn't eaten in a year and then wandered into a marketplace filled with the smells of spice and roasting meat and fresh fruit and baking cookies. Not that she would eat the meat. That wasn't the point.

A smile flickered at the edges of her lips. No, the point was coming back like this made everything so wonderful to her. She wanted to devour the world. Well, not in some world-devouring vengeful goddess sort of way. Tara wanted to take it all in, to breathe in every breath of air in the garden, rich with the earth and growing things, and never exhale. She wanted to embrace it all.

Tara never wanted to let go, or to overlook anything.

A tumble of her blond hair had fallen across her face and she tucked it behind her ear, looking around again. Willow had told her how much she had despised Athens. Tara could only assume it was because Willow had sort of been abandoned here. Not that anyone had left her behind—it was Willow who'd left Kennedy behind, technically. But Willow had come here to escape, to run away, and had been trapped in Athens while waiting for a plane home. It was a way station, not her destination. She hadn't really bothered to go out and try exploring anywhere other than the Acropolis.

Tara hadn't even been up to the Acropolis yet. She loved ancient temples and all of that, and planned to go in the morning. For today she'd just wanted to wander. She would have plenty of time to get to the Acropolis if Catherine Cadiere fulfilled her promises to teach and mentor Willow in the furthering of her magick. For her part, Tara had no real interest in magick anymore. It still existed inside of her, and she still knew witchcraft well enough, but Willow had always been more powerful and more gifted than she was. Tara only wanted to touch the world. To stay in contact.

She reached out and traced her fingers through the grass, then lay back and gazed up at the blue sky and the branches way at the top of the tree. They didn't have trees like this back home, completely bare for 90 percent of their height, then full at the top.

The Mediterranean sun felt wonderful.

Tara closed her eyes, then hissed in a lungful of air as she opened them again. A line of pain seared her left arm, as though a blade had just sliced her skin. In the same moment, she could feel Willow's presence with her, and Tara's senses were filled with her. She could smell Willow's scent and feel her pain in some new, empathic connection greater than anything they had ever had before.

Teeth gritted against the pain—which now dulled to a throb—she scrambled to her feet and began to run. She could feel Willow close by, but the magickal empathy they now shared was not necessary to find her. Catherine Cadiere had taken her to the Temple of Zeus to begin to explore the extent of Willow's knowledge of witchcraft. The ruins were not far away, just across the gardens and then just a block over.

Panic seized Tara. Catherine had been responsible for reuniting them, but she did not trust the witch. She was lovely and silver and ancient and as tempting as the serpent in the garden. Willow had power unlike any other witch Tara had known, but Catherine had knowledge far greater than either of them could imagine.

No. Don't jump to conclusions. Just . . . just run.

Tara bolted past the exhibition halls of the National Gardens, and at the end of the long walkways leading up to them she could see the cars going by on Vas Olgas. Someone shouted, perhaps wondering what she was doing. But were they trying to stop her? Maybe some cop who thought she had done something wrong . . .

She couldn't take that chance, refused to stop.

With the swiftness of thought, she was a cat again, a black, sleek feline who darted along the path toward the road. Her senses flooded with the choking exhaust of cars on the street, and for a moment she saw Athens the way Willow had seen it before they had been reunited. But as a cat—and as a woman—she was Willow's familiar now, and her thoughts and senses remained focused.

The black cat hesitated at the curb. An opening appeared in traffic and she raced across. Horns blared. She paused on the median, then darted again. Tires screeched and she heard a crump of metal. One large wheel nearly crushed her, but she lunged forward, and then she was on the sidewalk on the other side of the street while curses in Greek were bellowed in her wake.

The Temple of Zeus was nothing but rough, barren ground with a handful of standing columns amid the ruin of the magnificence that had once stood there. As the cat paused and blinked, Tara thought for a moment she could see the ghost of what the temple had once been, feel the presence of a being of incredible power—Zeus. Then the moment passed.

In the midst of that barren land, beside a column that had tumbled to broken pieces on the ground, she saw Willow on her knees in the dirt. Catherine Cadiere, radiant and gleaming in the sun, stood above her with both arms raised as though in supplication to the gods.

The black cat could smell Willow's blood, even from that distance. She was the witch's familiar.

As the cat ran, Tara changed again, and then she was running with long strides, her loose peasant blouse rippling in the wind and her hair flying behind her.

Dirt whipped up in a small whirlwind around Catherine, turning her into a strange silhouette. The ancient witch lowered her arms, the dirt spinning around her, and then she turned and simply stepped out of the world.

The dirt settled.

Catherine Cadiere had vanished.

Tara raced to Willow and fell to her knees by her girlfriend's side.

"Sweetie, what did she do? Oh, goddess, what'd she do to you?" she asked, reaching for Willow's hands.

Willow blinked in confusion and lifted her hands. She wore a thin green top with spaghetti straps, her red hair hanging to her shoulders. Tara was struck in that moment by how much older and more sophisticated Willow looked.

Then she saw the blood. Willow's left forearm had been slit open and blood wept from the wound in long streaks that ran down her arm and fell onto her lap. The cut wasn't deep, Tara saw. In her right hand, Willow held a small blade—a box cutter.

"Willow?" Tara asked, staring in horror at the blade, and the blood.

"It's not . . . Catherine didn't do anything," Willow said. At last her eyes locked on Tara's. "I did it myself. All morning we went through spells I've done before and others that were similar. It was like . . . like she was testing me. Then she started in on blood rites."

Tara's heart went cold. She shook her head. "No."

Willow's gaze wavered. She glanced down. "I know." She looked up again. "Catherine said it was about power and devotion, and didn't have to be dark magick. I . . . she started talking about all the good I could do with the kind of power she could teach me. It was a simple spell. Some kind of making. I could make a dagger out of my own blood that would kill any enemy, no matter how much magick they could wield."

Tara held Willow's hands, lifted them up to kiss them, and then looked at her over their clasped fingers. "Tell me you didn't."

"No. No, I didn't do the spell. I started to, but I couldn't do it."

A tiny smile touched Willow's lips and she lifted her hands. "That's why so much blood."

Tara kissed her fingers again. "We'll get you cleaned up. The cut's not deep. It'll be all right."

Together, they stood. Tara glanced around. Catherine had used magick to shield herself and Willow from detection, otherwise they would never have been able to stay out there in the open—in the ruins of the Temple of Zeus—practicing magick all day without being noticed. But now that Catherine was gone, she had to assume the glamour had gone with her.

"Where did she go?" Tara asked.

Willow had her eyes closed. She whispered something in Latin, casting a simple spell that would disguise her wound and bloody clothes from notice. Even Tara had to narrow her eyes and focus on the cut to see it, and she was a witch herself.

"I don't know," Willow replied. "She started to get frustrated because I didn't want to do a blood rite. And, here's me, 'Hello? Black magick woman. Not a good idea.' She tried to convince me, but I told her it would take me a while to be comfortable with it. That I'd have to be confident.

"Then she said something about having other business to attend to, that we'd have to pick things up when all the dust had settled, but that I needed to really think about what I wanted. That I could be one of the most powerful witches in history if I would only accept her guidance. She started chanting a spell, the dirt started to fly, and Catherine said she'd see me again very soon and I could tell her my decision then. And just before she disappeared, she said something kinda odd. Pretty much have no idea what she was talking about."

Tara reached out to brush some dirt from Willow's cheek. "What, sweetie? What'd she say?"

Willow frowned and her gaze shifted, as though she could see Catherine Cadiere's crisp beauty right there between them. Remembering.

"She said, 'It may be possible to control the darkest corners of this world simply by controlling two hearts.'"

Tara stared at her. "And you don't know what that means?"

"Not a clue. But whatever she's up to, I'm pretty sure I don't trust her," Willow replied.

Tara agreed and they held hands as they walked back to the road. They had to get back to the hotel and get Willow's cut cleaned up. Magick might keep them from having to go to the hospital, which would be a very good thing. But even as she worried about Willow, Tara had other concerns.

Neither of them trusted Catherine, but if not for the icily beautiful old witch, Tara could never have been brought back to life. If

Catherine could not be trusted, then could they put their belief in anything that stemmed from her? If Catherine were an evil witch, what did that mean for Tara?

Love and regret flooded through her. Tara clutched Willow's hand more tightly, but neither of them put voice to the question that Tara knew haunted them both.

St. Mark's Square breathed with music. It slid across the stone plaza, echoing back from the facades of buildings, somehow seeming to reach everyone in the vast square. Dozens of little alleys led away from St. Mark's Square, but it seemed closed in upon itself nearly all around its perimeter, save for the opening to the Grand Canal. That view—of boats, of the gondolas, of the water lapping up onto the stones, of the beautiful mosaic of buildings across the canal—that was Venice.

The music came from a miniature orchestra playing in front of a restaurant whose glass and metal face peeked out from the first floor of one of the centuries-old buildings that lined the square. Violins danced sweetly, then sadly. A piano provided the melody. A cello and an array of horns joined in.

Tables and chairs had been arranged on the square. The restaurant had no real patio, but one had been created with velvet ropes that marked out the extent of its influence. There were umbrellas, but as afternoon became evening, the shadows of St. Mark's Square grew long and the umbrellas were no longer needed.

At the end of the bar sat a woman of singular beauty. Her lush red hair had been pulled back off of her shoulders with a bow. Anyone near enough to see her bright green eyes would have presumed them to be contact lenses, but would have been incorrect. In a silk dress that accentuated her curves, she perched on a stool with one leg demurely crossed over the other, drawing attention to her shapely legs and her shoes, which were all black straps and daring heels.

Simone had received many supernatural gifts in her life—all of them dedicated to her mission—but none of them influenced her appearance. Every man who passed within sight of her turned to look, and to linger, and many of the women admired her as well, though some with much spite. No magick was involved.

She could command attention with a movement, a glance. Men had compared her to Aphrodite, to Venus. And some had learned she was more Venus flytrap than goddess.

If she could have been a goddess, Simone would instead have chosen Diana or Artemis—the huntress. And what better huntress than one who could use herself for bait?

The incubus could not stay away.

The demon had been seducing and destroying women throughout Italy for many weeks. Simone had been hunting him for a handful of days. She had tracked his movements and played the odds, but tonight fortune had smiled upon her. The moment she sat down at the end of the bar and saw him, deeper within the shadows of the restaurant—nearer the singles who lingered over their drinks instead of the couples at the tables—she had recognized him for what he was. Perhaps it was the red glint they so often had in their eyes. But Simone had first noticed him because of his arrogance. He seemed ordinary at first glance, but sometimes the way he cocked his head and the calculating ice of his eyes gave him away.

Flirting with him had been simplicity itself. Eye contact, and then studied aloofness. A shifting of her legs, skin caressing skin. Touching her neck, adjusting the thin garland of gold around her throat. Sipping her martini.

And now he made his way toward her, along the bar. He behaved as though shy, but that was part of his game. The incubus always let his prey think that she had drawn him into bed. It made that moment of revelation, when he let his disguise fall away and she saw the face of the demon she was about to have sex with—that was the moment an incubus thrived on.

Tonight's revelation would be slightly different.

Simone kept her gaze averted right up until the moment the incubus came to stand beside her.

"Excuse me," he began, oh so tentatively.

Idly, she ran her tongue over her upper lip and turned to him, eyes searching, gaze curious and open, luring him in.

But then she saw the massive Chinese man standing just behind the incubus, dark-eyed and well dressed, expressionless.

"Tai, no!" Simone said.

Too late. The silent warrior reached out and grabbed the incubus by the head with both hands, and twisted. With a crack of bone and a moist tearing noise, he ripped the demon's head from its body.

The screaming started.

Even as the demon's corpse fell to the ground, Tai took her by the elbow. Simone shouted at him in protest and tried to pull away, but then she felt another hand take her other arm and she turned to see Malik there. Flanking her, they hustled her away from the bar and into one of the busy alleyways off of St. Mark's Square. It was summer in Venice, and they were soon lost in the crush of humanity.

"I am sorry to deprive you, Simone," Malik said. "But we have no time for games."

Just a handful of months ago, Ngaio could not have imagined the way her life would change. For the first seventeen years of her life she had never left New Zealand—barely traveled beyond the village where she and her Maori family had lived. Now she had seen a dozen cities in Australia, Europe, Asia, and America, and she found herself sitting in the back of a Toyota SUV—headed south on Route 95 from Boston, Massachusetts, to Providence, Rhode Island—and chatted happily with girls who had become like sisters to her.

Petite Adrianna, a tiny twenty-year-old girl from Rome, sat in the backseat with Ngaio and Zamira, who was only fifteen and from

Albania. In the front, Mai sat in the passenger seat while Dori drove. Mai was from Vietnam and her name, Ngaio had learned, meant "cherry blossom." The name seemed almost as beautiful as Mai, whom Ngaio looked up to a great deal. Dori was another story completely. She claimed to come from Canada, but had none of the courtesy that seemed always associated with Canadians.

In the field, in the absence of Buffy or Faith, Dori often took charge. Ngaio did not mind—mostly because she did not want the job—but she bristled at Dori's harsh instruction.

A year ago none of these girls—from homes scattered across the globe—had ever imagined meeting one another. But yes, they'd become like sisters, for better or worse.

They had rendezvoused in Paris and flown from there to Boston on the first available flight. Ngaio had slept on the plane and knew she ought to have felt refreshed, but instead she only felt more tired. A storm had moved in and the gray clouds hung low and smothering. The windshield wipers swept back and forth in a hypnotic rhythm and rain spattered the window beside her. The voices of the other Slayers became a drone, and Ngaio started to close her eyes, head lolling toward the window.

With a sharp intake of breath, she forced her eyes open. Ngaio reached up and removed the rubber band with which she'd tied back her black hair, letting it fall in curls around her shoulders. She ought to try to take in her surroundings, but in the rain the scenery from the highway all looked the same. The chatter continued, and once again she began to nod off.

The SUV bumped through a pothole. Dori swore. Mai said something about her driving and they started to bicker.

Jarred awake, Ngaio looked out the window. A drainage ditch ran along the highway and beyond it was a hill. At the top of the hill was a line of evergreen trees.

Demons burst from the trees and raced down the hill, running at infernal speed. They were hideous things with long, streaming hair, but she could not identify them from her studies.

"Dori," Ngaio said.

At the wheel, Dori heaved a sigh. "It's raining, all right? I can't see a damn thing. Cut me some slack!"

Ngaio pressed her face to the window and looked up ahead of them. On the shoulder of the road there were other demons that had already come down from the trees. Her momentary glance told her there were at least three species, one of which was Vahrall. Dread clutched at her heart and she felt ice flowing through her. Few demons were as vicious or efficient as Vahralls. The savage things were marked with tribal tattoos and wore their hair in thick tangled dreadlocks, and their talons and long teeth made them extremely deadly.

She was about to scream.

Zamira beat her to it. "Dori!" the Albanian girl shouted. "Look!"

They all looked. The swift demons with their trailing hair were catching up, running beside the SUV. The Vahralls and others— Were there Miquot? How could there be Miquot?—seemed only to be waiting.

Mai pointed straight ahead, the first of them to put her eyes back on the road.

"Watch out!" she cried.

On the rainswept highway stood a thing thirty or forty feet tall, a hunched and ugly giant with twisted horns on either side of its snout and arms that dangled at its sides like some terrible ape. Its mouth hung agape and a torrent spilled from its lower jaw, either of collected rainwater or viscous drool.

Dori swore and cut the wheel hard to the right.

The highway was slick with rain.

At that speed, they had no chance. The SUV flipped. Screams echoed in Ngaio's ears. She tried to hold on to something, anything, but could not. The SUV rolled. Her head struck the window, which shattered. Safety glass flew everywhere, but Ngaio had her eyes shut tight. Adrianna slammed into her and they battered against each other.

Time slid. Darkness fell.

When her eyes fluttered open she could hear the wheels spinning and the hiss of rain falling on the hot undercarriage of the car. She hung upside down from her seat belt. As she blinked her vision clear, she saw Mai hanging in the passenger seat. Her head hung to one side and her left cheek had been torn and now seeped blood.

Someone groaned.

In the driver's seat, Dori's breathing was ragged and she choked, but did not speak.

Beside her, hanging like a marionette, Adrianna was unconscious.

"Zamira," Ngaio said. "We've . . . we have to get them out."

"I think . . . I think my arm is broken," Zamira said.

Ngaio took a deep breath. She wondered if Dori would die. Carefully, making sure that she had no severe injuries herself, she unbuckled her seat belt and let herself down onto the underside of the SUV's roof. The whole world had turned upside down.

Carefully, aware of the still spinning tires and the smell of gasoline, she crawled from the wreckage, emerging through her broken window on her hands and knees.

She looked up.

The demons stood in the rain. She could barely make out their silhouettes in the gray of the storm, but she could hear the low grunt of their breathing. There were Vahralls and Fyarl and at least two Ixchak. How they had remained unseen by the passing motorists— no one seemed even to have noticed the accident; there were no screeching tires, no one stopping to help—she did not know. Beyond the cluster of monstrosities around her she could see gigantic things above the tree line at the top of the hill. The long-armed, tusked giant was one of them, but another seemed to hang down from the storm clouds, all dark, wriggling tentacles. These were giant creatures of folklore and legend, gods and monsters, and they should not be here.

Ngaio averted her eyes.

Booted feet approached, squelching in the sodden ground. She shivered, sure it was a Vahrall and that her death had come for her. But when she looked up she saw the cruel eyes and rotting teeth of a Miquot demon as it crouched beside her. Its putrid yellow skin gleamed as the raindrops raced like tears down his face. The rows of finlike ridges on top of his head were darker than the rest of him and seemed strangely dry, in spite of the rain.

"Do you want to know why you still live?" the Miquot asked.

With a shriek of metal, the Vahrall demons began to tear the doors from the SUV and drag the other girls out.

Ngaio could only stare at the Miquot.

"For the moment, there is peace. But no more Slayers allowed, girl. Mark me well. There is one Slayer in the city and no others will enter until the gathering has concluded. Stay away, or you risk shattering the peace."

Staring at him, she had barely realized the other demons had begun to withdraw, moving up the hill and into the trees. In seconds even the Miquot was gone. Dori and the others had been moved a safe distance from the wreckage of the SUV and laid down, injured in the accident but alive.

Ngaio did not understand.

People began to stop. A man got out of his car, calling to her to ask if they were all right. Miraculously, it appeared that they would be. He had produced a cell phone and was barking into it, telling the police and ambulance to hurry.

Dori's chest had been crushed by the steering wheel, but she would heal. Slayers always did.

Except when they died.

"What do we do now?" Zamira asked as they waited to hear the police and ambulance sirens.

Ngaio shook her head. "Nothing. We call Buffy and we do whatever she tells us to do."

Zamira nodded. "I like that plan."

Over the course of his life, Giles had fallen asleep dozens of times in chairs, slumped over desks and tables in offices and libraries, and once—without a drop of alcohol as an excuse—on the floor of a antiquarian bookstore. He had long ago surrendered to the knowledge that a brief catnap of twenty or thirty minutes could reenergize him so that his research could continue. There had been times when closing his eyes for a few minutes had probably made the difference between life and death.

It was the longer naps that troubled him—the ones from which he woke with a tiny rivulet of saliva at the corner of his mouth or soaking into his shirtsleeve and with the imprint of the corner of a book or the smudge of ink from a scroll upon his cheek.

Not that such unease ever stopped him.

Buffy had phoned shortly after noon, tracking him down rather easily, and had caught him up to speed on the bizarre phenomena transpiring in Rhode Island. The situation would have provided enough of a puzzle were it merely that so many monstrous or demonic beings were showing up in a single city, but there seemed no escaping the logic that Providence was the destination of many of these migrating tribes of demons, and they each seemed to be sending some coterie of representatives.

Even more mysterious was the apparent lack of hostility and conflict among them. According to Buffy, whatever troubles the demons that had first arrived in Providence might have caused, they were no longer hurting anyone, or at least were going far out of their way to avoid it.

It seemed impossible. Some of the species Buffy had reported seeing on her patrol the night before were natural enemies. They ought to have been tearing one another apart.

Her report gave him a great deal to consider and a direction for his research. All of the books he had previously been perusing had been put aside and he had begun to search for records of demonic truces and gatherings that related to the information he'd discovered on migration patterns that morning and the previous day.

When the answer appeared, he felt like a fool. In the works of Arthur Conan Doyle, Sherlock Holmes had said that when you have eliminated the impossible, whatever remains, however improbable, must be the truth. Giles had made a terrible mistake. He had considered impossible something that was only wildly improbable.

Once he had rectified that error and felt sure he was on the right track, he had stretched and yawned, his eyes burning from reading and lack of sleep. Twenty minutes, he'd promised himself. Perhaps thirty. He had put his head down.

A hand jostled him gently.

"Rupert," said an intimate whisper.

Again he was jostled. "Rupert."

Giles became aware that his cheek felt numb. His mouth was dry and he closed it, licking his lips to wet them. He squeezed his eyes tightly closed and began to shift in his chair. How long had he been sleeping?

"Rupert."

He blinked several times, fully opened his eyes, and looked up to see Micaela Tomasi standing beside the research table. Her hair was long and unkempt and her clothes were rumpled. She looked quite a mess, but with her eyes bright and her skin deeply tanned from her time in North Africa, she seemed more beautiful than ever.

"Micaela," Giles said, pushing back his chair and standing. He reached out and crushed her to him, embracing her tightly. "It's wonderful to see you. I was so worried."

Micaela hugged him close, resting against him as though she had needed someone to hold her up.

"You were worried? Trust me, you were far from the only one."

He stepped back, held her at arm's length, and studied her. "You're all right?"

Micaela looked away. "As well as can be expected. Dyannah Neville and I were the only survivors."

"I heard. It's horrible. But you did survive, and I'm grateful for that."

She cocked an eyebrow. "I didn't know you still cared."

But Giles would not reduce their reunion to light flirtation. "How could I not? The past is the past, but true friends are rare, I find."

"As do I," she said. Micaela took his hands, stood on her toes, and kissed his cheek. "It's sweet of you."

Then the moment passed.

"I've been doing a great deal of research," Giles said. "And I think I may have determined the cause of all of this chaos."

"Yes," Micaela said, nodding. "I have a few ideas about that myself."

CHAPTER SIX

Faith hadn't slept much on the flight from San Francisco. Too many questions churned in her head. What the hell was Christabel de Tournefort up to, coming to Rhode Island, of all places? No way could it be a coincidence that Buffy was in the middle of something ugly in Providence and one of the oldest vampires in the world was on her way there.

The flight had been nearly empty, so she'd stretched out across a whole row in the back by the bathrooms—with their lovely aroma—but the extra room hadn't helped. Faith prided herself on being able to sleep almost anywhere, but she had her demons. Going back to New England troubled her. She wanted to feel excited about returning to her old stomping grounds, but the truth was, Providence was about as close to Boston as she wanted to get.

Too many bad memories there. Oh sure, she'd had some good times. But there had been nightmares, as well. If someone had asked her if she'd rather go back to prison or back to Boston, she'd have to think about it.

Yeah, all in all, Providence was close enough.

After a smooth flight, the pilot blew the landing, the plane bouncing and swaying a little as he tried to get her onto the ground on target. Then they were rolling along the tarmac. Impatient as she was by nature, Faith waited until the seat belt light was off, mainly to spite the jerk-offs who seemed to think that whatever they had to do was more vital than everyone else's business. When the captain made a point of announcing that you should stay in your damned seat, and you immediately got up and started grabbing your luggage, opening overhead compartments, Faith figured you deserved a suitcase to the skull. So when the grumpy-looking old guy diagonally across the aisle from her got exactly that, she grinned.

The wheels of justice were in motion.

When the light dinged off, she grabbed her duffel bag from the compartment above her head and started off the plane. No checked luggage for her. Faith traveled light.

She slung the bag across her shoulder and left the plane. The terminal seemed empty. Half of the lights were out and the maintenance staff was buffing the floors. Some of the shops where closed, metal grates pulled down in front of them. The whole state of Rhode Island seemed to close up shop by ten p.m.

At a small kiosk, she checked in and picked up the keys to the little Honda she'd arranged for in advance. With a flip of her hair to clear it from her eyes, she left the terminal, following signs for the parking garage where the rental company kept their fleet. Her car should be on the first floor of the parking garage, right next to the terminal.

Her eyes burned and her neck ached. She'd never been so happy to be off a plane. The night sky was cloudy and a light drizzle was falling, but Faith didn't mind. It was New England. Chances were good that the morning would bring bright sunshine and a ninety-degree day.

She heard the rush and roar of an airplane engine as one last flight took off. No matter how deserted the airport seemed, apparently some airlines were not quite done for the night. A bus chugged by, along with several cabs, but she stayed on the walkway to the parking garage and kept her eyes forward. When an old Ford in need of a paint job and a new exhaust system drove by, shaking and thumping with the rap song playing from its speakers, she bopped a little to the music. Most rap was ridiculous gangster crap, but some of the old-school stuff had musical integrity. She couldn't have explained musical integrity to anyone, but like so many other things, she knew it when she saw it. Heard it. Whatever.

Faith had the key to the car in her hand and the rental agreement stuffed in the back pocket of her jeans. Somewhere far off a car alarm started wailing. Shifting the weight of her duffel bag, she scanned the numbered parking spaces. The heels of her boots clicked on the floor, echoing off the concrete walls and ceiling of the parking garage. On one of the upper floors, tires squealed with a sound like screaming.

She spotted the car, a blue midsize thing, anonymous as hell. Anonymous was good.

Faith spun the keys on one finger.

The tire squeals died. In the moment after the sound went away, she realized she could no longer hear the distant car alarm, either. Then she frowned and stopped walking. She stared down at the toes of her boots, then took a few more steps.

No clicking of her heels. No echo. With a glance around, she focused on the sounds of the airport, but there weren't any. She couldn't hear buses or cars or an airplane taking off.

"What the—," she began, then cut herself off when she realized she could not hear the sound of her own voice. Even inside her head, the way you always did, she couldn't hear herself. "Hello?" she said, trying again. "What the hell is this?"

But though her lips moved and air flowed from her lungs, no sound came from her. The garage was completely silent. Impossibly quiet. Faith slipped the keys into her pocket and glanced around, bag swinging against her back as she moved. She tapped the toe of her boot on the concrete but did not make any noise at all.

How could there be no sound?

And just as she had the thought, a hissing static began in her ears. Faith winced and shook her head. She squinted as the static became louder. A rush of noise, it seemed to issue from inside of her and it only increased in volume. Scowling, she swore, and a burst of pain shot through her skull. Whatever noise she'd just made, it had somehow spiked the static's volume.

Frantic, she looked around, trying to figure out where the sound was coming from. Even her thoughts felt muffled, all other noise blocked out except for that hissing crackle. A tickle on her upper lip made her bring one hand up, and when she wiped at it and looked down, she discovered that her nose was bleeding.

Angry but not panicked—Faith wasn't the type—she started toward her rental car again. Maybe once she left the garage, the static would subside. She wondered if it had to do with the flight, if she'd screwed up her hearing somehow. But the moment the thought crossed her mind, she realized how stupid it sounded. Whatever this was, there was nothing natural about it.

Faith picked up her pace, running the last dozen feet toward the car.

Out of the corner of her eye she saw something moving.

She spun and there they were—slipping from between cars, gliding toward her, just a few inches from the ground. They were just as chalky white as Buffy had described them, dark pits for eyes and broad rictus grins that seemed to have been pinned back like dead butterflies. Their hands moved like lunatics conducting some asylum orchestra, and they never stopped floating, never stopped moving, grinning, staring.

The Gentlemen.

They were fairy tale creatures, Buffy had said. They'd come to

Sunnydale to steal and eat human hearts. Buffy had managed to destroy them, so this had to be a different group, somehow related to the others.

As Faith backed toward her car, staring at them, she saw other creatures slipping out from beneath cars, emerging as though they were boneless rodents, able to slip into any narrow space. They were lumbering, monstrous things, and she knew they had to be the Gentlemen's footmen—the ones who gathered victims so that the Gentlemen could harvest their hearts.

"Well, well," she started to say. "To what do I owe the pleasure?"

But she only made it through the first few words, and each one was an excruciating burst of screeching static in her ears. The pain drove Faith to one knee and she felt a dribble of blood begin to seep from her left ear. Swearing silently she shifted the duffel on her shoulder and stood.

The footmen raced toward her, jaws gnashing, capering almost like monkeys. Faith could barely look at them. Her eyes were on the Gentlemen, who glided toward her above the concrete, standing straight up and clad in preacher black. She'd seen the Irish Catholic life in Boston and met her share of priests.

Faith trembled. She couldn't remember the last time she'd been afraid, but some little-girl part of her, deep inside, saw these things and felt frightened.

Their grins never wavered. The sight of them made her want to scream, but she didn't dare.

Then the footmen attacked. Something snapped in Faith and she was in motion. The first one lunged for her. She caught his wrist, twisted her body, and hurled him at the windshield of the car behind her. The glass shattered without a sound. The Gentlemen came no closer, only grinned. Faith kept her duffel on her shoulder as she spun into a kick that cracked the skull of the next footman. He collided with a third and they both went down. Faith stepped over to the car and snapped off the radio antenna. When the next footman attacked, Faith began to beat the creature about the face and neck. It reached for her and she whipped at its arms until it stopping trying to touch her.

With a single kick, she caved in its chest.

All the while the Gentlemen only watched.

More footmen attacked. Fists and kicks flew. She fought them off, but as she did, she saw that the Gentlemen had begun to glide nearer to her. If anything, their grins seemed to have widened. Soon they would take her heart unless she did something to stop it.

Then it struck her. Moments before she'd thought this impossible. Now she realized that it was. The Gentlemen came to a place and stole away the voices of all the people so nobody could call for help when it came time to harvest their hearts.

They were vulnerable to sound, to the human voice. It didn't make any sense. How were these things even here, if the whole city hadn't had their voices stolen away? They weren't supposed to be able to blot out all ambient sound, only voices. And what had they done to her? None of this matched what Giles and Buffy had told her about the Gentlemen. Unless these things were something else, some variation?

Then she was pretty much screwed.

Which she would be anyway if she didn't do something.

A footman got a handful of her hair. Faith reached up and snapped his wrist. With his other hand he grabbed on to her duffel bag, but by now she was in motion. Her arm pistoned up and down and she pummeled the footman to the ground.

As the others moved in, she swung the duffel, knocking two of them out of her path. Faith raced for the nearest Gentlemen. His grin remained. He did not flinch or pause or even blink, only kept grinning, and she wanted to scream in fear and frustration and loathing. Her skin prickled with disgust, but she reached up and grabbed his head. She retched when he opened his mouth.

His black teeth were hideous, his breath stinking of rotting meat.

She tried to pull him down, but he was too strong. Faith shouted at him, but the scream only increased the static and she staggered back. Several of them surrounded her then, reaching for her, touching her, pulling at her clothes, and panic surged through her.

Glancing around for an exit, she saw the thing standing in the shadows between two cars. The static shrieked in her ears and Faith staggered, tasting her blood on her lips. But she had spotted it. The thing between the cars was some kind of demon with tiny legs and arms and a huge head that had been laid open like peeled fruit. A gaping hole existed at the center of its head, and Faith felt sure the static in her mind was coming from there.

Magick. The Gentlemen had stolen away sound, or this demon thing leeched the sound from around her, including her screams. All the cumulative noise of the parking garage seemed to funnel right into her ears.

Faith sneered and lunged for the demon. One of the footmen caught her ankle. Three Gentlemen grabbed hold of her arms. Together they began to drag her down.

She drove her fingers into the eyes of the nearest Gentleman. They popped with a disgusting sucking noise. Even with the gore from its ruined eyes running down its chin, the Gentleman continued to grin. The others reached for Faith, but she'd had enough. No way would this end well. There were too many of them—footmen and gentlemen and that disgusting split-faced demon.

Fury roiled in her gut.

If there was one thing Faith didn't do well—something she hated more than anything—it was running away. But she'd grown up hard and fast and had been in worse scrapes than this, and she'd survived by knowing when to get the hell out.

Now, for instance.

She swung her duffel, knocked down another Gentleman, then set off running toward the nearest row of cars. One of them was her rental, but there'd be no time to unlock the door, never mind get behind the wheel and start it up. As though dancing, she swept her right foot up into a kick that took the nearest footman under the jaw and then kept going.

Faith leaped up onto the trunk of a Cadillac, had time for two steps across the roof, and then dove through the space between the concrete barrier and the ceiling. She landed on the narrow strip of grass that surrounded the parking garage, dropped, and rolled into a somersault, trying to use her momentum.

The duffel's strap tangled around one leg, but she shook it loose and then sprinted across the street, bolting for the taxi stand in front of the airport terminal. A few cars were speeding along that pickup lane, headlights bright in the dark. The pavement was slick with the drizzling rain but she kept her footing.

She risked a single glance back and saw the footmen giving chase. In the opening of the parking garage's first level, in the deeper darkness there, she saw the marble-white grinning faces of the Gentlemen looking back.

The footmen scampered after her, hell-bent on delivering her to their masters. But the static had diminished almost to nothing and she could hear that distant car alarm still wailing. An engine roared somewhere close by. Tires hissed as they rolled across the damp pavement, kicking up a spray.

Faith reached the sidewalk. A single taxi waited at the stand, the driver standing outside the cab with a cigarette in his hand, looking bored.

"Drive!" she snapped at him.

He smiled, gave her a thumbs-up, and flicked the cigarette away.

Faith reached the cab, whipped open the door, and glanced up to see the first two footmen darting across the road toward her. She swore as she tossed her duffel into the taxi and knew she had just bought the driver the worst night of his life.

A bus whipped by, rattling like a subway train. It struck the footmen with a moist crack of bone and flesh. In the mist and drizzle and dark, and with the speed of the footmen, the driver hadn't noticed them in time. The rear lights came on and the brakes started to squeal.

Faith slipped into the cab and slammed the door.

"Where to?" the cabbie asked, checking her out in the rearview mirror. Guys were all the same. Faith knew she must look like a drowned rat, but all he wanted was a look at her wet T-shirt.

"Just drive," she said, unzipping her duffel and searching around inside. "Get out of here, and I'll find you the address."

"Will do," the driver said, already pulling away.

Faith turned around just once to see more footmen trying to keep pace with the taxi in the drizzling rain, and faltering.

She'd be all right—for now. Time to have a little chat with Buffy, figure out what was really going on around here. She'd have to come back in the morning for her rental car. Faith found the name of the hotel scribbled on a piece of paper in her bag and read it off to the driver. Then she slumped back against the seat, missing San Francisco.

So much for her trip back to New England. She felt just as welcome as she had when she'd left.

Xander drove along Blackstone Boulevard, searching for a place to park that would allow the car to go unnoticed for a while. It turned out to be more difficult than he'd imagined. Blackstone Boulevard was about two miles long, a separated road with a long strip of grass in the middle. During the day, he figured it was a nice place for a stroll, the sort of spot that might bring out dog walkers and such. At night it looked like a decent place to get mugged.

Plus there was the cemetery. People didn't like to hang around cemeteries after dark, even people who claimed they didn't believe in the supernatural. Skeptics were only one real fright away from running in terror most of the time. Xander didn't have skepticism as an excuse. He just didn't want to get killed and eaten.

Rules to live by.

Eventually he decided that the house under construction across the street from Swan Point Cemetery was as good a spot as any to risk getting towed. Not that he was worried about the car. The little Honda was a rental and it was on Buffy's credit card. If it got towed away, at worst it would be an inconvenience and an unexpected expense—for her. For him, though, coming out of the cemetery to find the car gone could lead to far more unpleasant circumstances—like being killed and eaten.

Hence, his rules.

Unfortunately it appeared he had little choice. After all of the weird they had seen the night before just wandering around Providence—demons outside a sports bar, drinking beer and laughing like a bunch of drunken baseball fans; a trio of freaky bat-men perched like gargoyles on the roof of the train station; and a small gaggle of goblins pouring out of the Providence Mall burdened with tons of shopping bags—all they really wanted were answers. Every time they'd tried to confront one of the demons or other monstrosities, they'd been left in the dust, scratching their heads, wondering what was going on. Nobody in Providence seemed to notice that the things that walked among them were not human.

Too strange. So tonight they had changed their tactics, and so far they had not been attacked. Xander thought maybe Buffy's reputation had preceded her. If he had horns or fangs, he'd damn sure run away if he saw her coming. But Buffy had disputed that suggestion, and had decided they were going to split up tonight. She had gone back up to the street where they'd nearly been killed by that freak sandstorm.

And Xander?

"Xander gets to go to the cemetery!" he said unhappily, voice low.

He popped the trunk on the rented Honda and glanced around at the house under construction. The place had its windows in, but no siding yet—just plywood walls. A big Dumpster sat on the property as well. When it was finished, the place would be a mansion. For now, it was just a ghost. Xander figured whoever was building the ghost would have asked the cops to keep an eye on the place just in case local kids tried to break in and use it as a party spot. If the cops found the car there, the tow truck wouldn't be far behind.

He'd just have to be quick.

In the light of the trunk he pulled out a map of the cemetery and studied it, searching for one grave in particular. From the trunk he removed a small penlight, which he stuck into his pocket, and a tire iron, just in case.

Watching for traffic, he raced across Blackstone Boulevard to the cemetery and then walked along the tall iron gate for about half a mile. When he stopped, he double-checked the map again, then clicked off the penlight. A car drove by without slowing down. As soon as it was out of sight, Xander started to climb.

Once upon a time going over that fence would have been impossible for him. Much as he would deny it, however, the years since he'd met Buffy had changed him. Losing his eye had only given a physical aspect to the changes that had taken place within him. Xander Harris had never had a lot of purpose or determination before he met Buffy Summers.

Yeah, you had both eyes back then, though.

With a smirk, he ignored the voice of the jester that never seemed to go completely quiet in his head, and kept climbing. Yeah, once upon a time he never would have made it over that fence— never even would have considered it possible. But he'd gotten good at a lot of things since those days, and the thing he was best at was not giving up.

He slipped twice. Banged his knee once and his forehead the

second time. Pulled a muscle in his back. To anyone watching, he would have looked like a buffoon.

But he got over the fence.

Dropping down on the other side, he ran to take cover in the midst of a copse of trees. Swan Point Cemetery was a hilly expanse of land traced through with narrow roads and dotted with stands of pine and oak and maple. Xander pulled out the penlight again and studied the map. He glanced around, finding his bearings based on two large tombs that were clearly marked on the page, and then he clicked it off and started moving through the darkness again.

A low mist rolled across the wet grass. It had rained lightly for most of the day and into the evening, but now the rain had ceased and only the mist and the damp remained. His sneakers and the cuffs of his jeans got wet quickly. The smell of wet grass filled his nose. It would've been almost pleasant if he weren't in the middle of the cemetery.

"Splitting up is stupid," he whispered as he hurried between tombstones. "Splitting up is always stupid."

He started up a rise, keeping to the shadows of trees and gravestones whenever he could.

Glass shattered up ahead. He heard someone laughing, a keening sort of giggle. There was a mental hospital not far away, he knew from reading up on the place, and he wondered if some escaped nutcase was wandering around the cemetery. Then the cemetery echoed with the loudest burp he'd ever heard, and Xander's face twisted in disgust. He had nothing against burps in general, but this one was revolting.

A burst of laughter followed, not from one person but from several. There came another pop—glass shattering. Then he understood: A bunch of teenagers, likely kids who on another night would be partying in the half-built house where he'd parked the Honda, were drinking in the cemetery. A few guys trying to ply girls with liquor. Or vice versa. Girls could take the initiative, manipulating the foolish male of the species with the ease and expertise of the black widow spider, and . . .

His social life had been appalling just recently.

Xander moved more slowly. Frowning, he tried to look at the map in what little moonlight came through the clouds, not daring to take out the penlight. He glanced around, again trying to get his bearings. If he was right, it seemed like the kids were partying almost exactly at his destination. For all he knew, they might be partying right on top of the grave itself.

He sighed. He'd come all this way just to have a look at the grave of H. P. Lovecraft, and now he was supposed to just hang out here and wait for a bunch of drunk-ass high school kids to wander off, when his rental car—Buffy's rental car—could be towed at any moment?

Beautiful.

Frustrated, he tried to think of some way to get the kids away from the grave. It occurred to him that he could get closer, find a spot out of sight, and start speaking in a spooky voice, trying to convince them he was the ghost of Lovecraft and was righteously pissed off. Somehow, though, he felt sure that kind of thing only worked in the movies.

Coming up here had seemed like such a good idea. The sandstorm had taken place on the street where the ghost of Edgar Allan Poe was reputed to wander with some frequency. True or not, some serious supernatural mojo had gone down there with whatever demon or monster had created that storm. It took a hell of a lot of power to break windows and scrape the paint off houses and cars.

And if Poe had drawn some supernatural attention, it only stood to reason that Lovecraft would as well. Buffy and Xander had both done a little local research. Lovecraft—by far a freakier individual than Poe—had been born on Angel Street, just a few blocks from the cemetery, and had lived there for years. Both of his parents had been patients at Butler Hospital, stuck in an asylum right down the street from his house. No wonder the guy had been such a lunatic.

Not that he was actually crazy. More than once they had gone up against things that seemed very similar to some of the old gods and demonic things from the mythology Lovecraft had written about. Giles had always said he figured the writer was only half mad, and that like so many people whose perceptions are out of the ordinary, he'd been able to tap into an awareness of the forces of darkness. In Lovecraft's case, though, he'd somehow tuned in to things more ancient and, to Xander's way of thinking, far more disturbing than mediums who talked to ghosts or exorcists who saw demons in people's souls.

These kids were partying at Lovecraft's grave.

Xander kept low to the ground and ran to a massive old oak tree, trying not to slip on the wet grass. He pressed his back against it, still wondering what to do about the high schoolers. He could smell something in the air, sweet and rich, but it wasn't pot. At least, he didn't think so. They were smoking something, though.

A high voice said something he couldn't make out and then more laughter followed. He rolled his eyes, but then froze. Something about the laughter bothered him. One of the voices was a kind of chuffing noise, like a horse sneezing, and another seemed too throaty, full of phlegm like some hacking smoker's cough.

Oh, crap, he thought, and he glanced around the edge of the tree.

He could only see the back of the tombstone and it was still fifty yards away, so he had to take for granted that it was Lovecraft's grave. But truly there was no doubt.

The revelers who were partying on Lovecraft's grave—drinking beer and whiskey and smoking something that hung heavy in the humid air—were demons. Several lingered at the edge of the crowd, a couple of Vahralls and a tall, stalklike thing that looked like some kind of plant. It had feelers that coiled like snakes in the air. He spotted a Fraxis demon and a couple of huge-bellied swamp demons covered in moss and mucus that might have been Matabiri, but he couldn't be sure as he'd never seen one outside the pages of a book.

Three hideous things stood up close to the grave, taller and broader than a man but otherwise humanoid except for the bulbous eyes and nests of tentacles that made up their faces. One of them thrust a bottle of beer into the midst of its twisting tentacle face and tilted its head back—tentacles gripping the bottle as it sucked down the beer. One of the tentacles hurled the empty bottle at Lovecraft's grave, and it shattered there.

A few hairy little demons with long tails darted over to the grave and started to eat the glass. One of them turned and began to urinate in a long stream onto the grave, and at last Xander understood.

Here was the final resting place of an ordinary man who had known what they were, who had seen the truth of the horrors that lay in wait for humanity just beyond the edges of their vision, and no one had believed him. Lovecraft had been the son of mental patients and people had thought he had a madman's imagination. No one had believed a word.

Whatever the demons and monsters were gathering in Providence for, some of them had taken a side trip tonight for a little revelry that served no purpose except to mock the ghost of a writer who had once tried to warn the world what lay waiting in the darkness. They'd come to taunt Lovecraft, to rub it in.

Xander wanted to step out from hiding, to run them off, maybe knock some of them around. But there were far too many of them, and others in the shadows, mere silhouettes he hadn't even tried to categorize. A small horde of demons, and what was he? Just one guy who knew too much for his own good, who wished he could warn the world but had learned hard truths that Lovecraft never had.

But the world didn't want to know what waited for it in the dark. People just wanted to close their eyes and pray that someone else would fight the monsters. That's why there were Slayers in the world. Xander might not be able to warn the world, but he could help keep it safe. Trying to bust up a party like this one wouldn't do anyone any good, except the demons, who might decide to have a little one-eyed-California-boy barbecue.

Which brought him right back to his number one rule: *Do not get killed and eaten.*

Carefully, he slipped away. He had no idea what to make of this scene, or how it fit in with any of the bizarreness they'd encountered over the past few days, and he had a feeling Buffy would be just as puzzled. His only hope was that she'd found something out tonight that could help them.

Since he'd met her, Xander had learned to hate mysteries.

Whatever had brought all of these demons together—and whatever was keeping them from tearing one another, and all of Providence, apart—it couldn't last forever. Even a fool could see that.

This thing would end in blood. Xander just hoped it wasn't his own.

Witchfinder Bors stood in the street and watched the dress shop burn, flames licking up into the darkness of the predawn sky. People began to emerge from apartments atop neighboring shops. Sirens wailed in the distance. He heard the worried Catalan chatter of the spectators, a language close enough to Spanish that he could make out some of what they were saying, but different enough that he had only gotten dirty looks when he tried talking to anyone in the city of Barcelona.

That was all right. He was leaving today. He'd finished his work here. Beautiful city, Barcelona, what with all the upscale shopping and the gorgeous old hotels, and the food and performers and masque shops on Las Ramblas. But he didn't like anyone looking down on him.

The weird thing about Barcelona was that the locals seemed

indifferent to his size—Bors was only four feet four inches tall, but sturdily built. No, it was his inability to speak their language that seemed to irk them.

So he stood in the growing crowd that gathered in front of the burning dress boutique, and he watched the glow of the fire reflected in their eyes. And he smiled, and he fantasized about locking each and every one of them in there with the blackening, melting mannequins.

Just as he'd trapped the witch.

When Bors had first left the shop, the fire already starting to blaze inside, the witch had been screaming. He had used herbal oils, salt, and a bit of charred bone to mark lines in front of the doors and windows, muttering the incantation that would trap the witch inside.

Now, though, the screams had stopped. The fire roared, beginning to spread to the buildings on either side of the dress shop. Bors grinned as he watched the flames and listened to the cracking of beams and the shattering of glass blown out by the heat. One of the women on the street screamed and that made him grin wider.

If he'd done the job earlier in the evening, there would have been many more bystanders to watch in fascination. People loved fire. They loved to watch things burn, even though most of them would never admit it. Bors never hid his passion for the flames.

The sky continued to lighten. Dawn would arrive soon.

Sirens grew louder and then cut off sharply, and he could hear the roar of the engines of the emergency vehicles. Firefighters would put the blaze out soon, but by now the witch would have melted just like one of the boutique's mannequins. Bors wished he could go into the shop and have a look, but not this time.

He slipped the charred bone from his pocket and dropped it, crushing it underfoot. If the police stopped him now, all they would find was oil and salt, and he would claim they were for a meal he planned to cook today. The bone would go unnoticed until long after he had departed Barcelona.

Letting his head loll back, he enjoyed the warmth of the fire. A woman sniffed at him and moved away, shooting him an ugly look. Bors ignored her.

A hand touched his arm. Irked, he turned to see Malik standing beside him. The black-clad warrior had begun to grow a beard. Bors approved. Malik had always been too handsome and the stubble on his cheeks made him look properly grim.

"Come away now, Bors," Malik said. "We've work to be done."

Bors frowned. "The fire—"

"There will be others. Always others."

Bors took a deep breath, then nodded and reluctantly allowed himself to be led away. If Malik said there was work to be done, Bors knew it would be the sort that gave him pleasure. Witches were his preferred prey, but other creatures of magick burned just as well, screamed just as loudly.

Even darkness could burn.

CHAPTER SEVEN

With a distant church bell tolling the midnight hour, Buffy saw the demons emerge from a sewer grate—tossing it back with a clang—and begin to trail two women who must have been walking home from a party. Drunk as they were, they still ought to have noticed the three lumbering Charnel demons—monsters whose bodies were constructed from human corpses—following them down Benefit Street. Yet, once again, as in other cases she and Xander had seen in the past two days, the demons seemed all but invisible to ordinary people.

People who weren't looking for them.

Buffy moved through the dark, avoiding the splashes of light from lampposts. Her hair was tied back and she wore a dark jacket, despite the warm August night. The demons might be invisible, but she was not. If there was trouble and some of the people living on Benefit Street looked out their windows, all they would see would be a young blond woman. She didn't need a visit to the local jail, especially not when she was trying to figure out just what the hell was going on in Providence.

Whatever it was, one thing seemed certain—it was huge. The idea that a little corner of the world like Providence, Rhode Island, could draw this much supernatural attention seemed absurd until she wondered where else all of these monsters would gather. Why not here?

Obviously, they agreed.

Buffy picked up her pace. The demons hung back, not getting too close to the stumbling, drunk women, who laughed together at something that probably wouldn't have been funny had they been sober. The demons laughed as well, if that sound—a kind of explosive crackle—could be called laughter.

Whatever these things were, they weren't anything she'd seen before. Their bodies were made of some kind of stone, but were pitted with holes from which red fire flickered, burning endlessly, as though inside they had only furnaces. The way the fire burned made Buffy think of volcanoes, and that got her thinking that their bodies might be made of lava rock.

Not that it mattered. They were on fire, and made of stone, and they weren't going to be easy to stop. She'd called in plenty of Slayer backup, but none of the others had shown up yet. Buffy would make do. She was used to being on her own. But the cavalry would have been nice.

The Charnel demons began to catch up to the drunken women, who seemed to be trying to figure out if they had passed the house that was their destination.

Time to go, Buffy thought.

She took off in a sprint, arms pumping, racing toward the demons, focused on the holes that pitted their bodies, the fire roaring up from inside. Lava men. How the hell did she fight lava men?

The drunken women staggered up to the front door of a house, one of them pulling out her keys with a jangle of metal.

Buffy leaped into a flying kick at the back of the nearest demon. The impact sent a jolt up her legs, but the demon staggered and then went down hard, spurts of fire shooting from the holes in its body. Off balance, Buffy could only fall. She hit the street, rolled, and tore off her jacket as she stood, wrapping it around her right hand. Hitting these two would hurt. Her ankles were singed from the kick.

The two Charnel demons still standing turned toward her. Buffy swore, blinking in surprise. They didn't have faces. Or, rather, where their faces should have been were only featureless rock slabs shot through with those fire vents. Flames burned inside those holes, but none of them looked like eyes.

Somehow, though, they could see.

One of them moved. Buffy dropped into a defensive stance, but the demon surprised her by running away.

"Fleeing. There's something you don't see every day," she said. "At least, not until after the butt-kicking."

But the others weren't running away. The one who'd stayed behind but hadn't been hit yet seemed to waver, uncertain. But the lava demon on the ground stood up, hands and knees and feet scraping the street with a rasp of heavy stone, and it came at her.

"That's more like it," Buffy said. "I've had enough of all the nonviolent evil. Been wanting to hit something."

With the jacket wrapped around her fist, she took a step forward and threw her weight behind the punch. Lava rock cracked, connecting two of the fire vents and making the flames jump higher from the demon's broken face. One of her knuckles might have broken. Buffy shouted with pain, and then with frustration as her jacket lit on fire.

She threw the burning coat to the ground, then faced the two lava demons in a combat stance.

"Thanks a lot, pyro. That's the only jacket that went with this top."

Where the third one had run off to, she didn't know. Beyond the remaining demons, she saw the two drunken women finally get the door open and stumble inside. Somehow they'd been unaware of the whole fight, and Buffy didn't think they'd been blinded by beer goggles.

"So, we have a fight here, or are you two candy-asses gonna scamper like your friend?"

Candy asses. She'd been spending too much time with Faith. Soon she'd be saying "wicked."

The Charnel demons started to shake. The fire that rose up from the holes in their stony bodies burned higher, sparking geysers from the vents in their faces. Red, molten lava flowed like tears from those holes.

Then they came for her.

"About time," Buffy said. She wasn't going to get any answers from these demons, but if she kept patrolling, kept causing trouble, eventually she'd drag down a more talkative nasty.

One of them lunged. Buffy knocked its hand away—burning her arm—and then shot a kick at its chest, shattering stone. Liquid lava poured out onto the pavement, but the demon did not fall.

Buffy hesitated. "Okay, possibly not the smartest fight I ever picked."

The gust of wind came out of nowhere. She staggered, nearly going down, and then the sand swept around and past her as though purposely avoiding her. It started as just the wind and grit, and then the sand struck like a wave, passing by Buffy and enveloping the two lava demons. It swirled around them in twin cyclones that ground their heads away in seconds. Fire flickered in the midst of those twisting funnels of sand and wind, and then was snuffed out.

When the sand retreated, gusting back the way it had come, chunks of rock fell to the ground and shattered. Nothing else remained of the demons.

Buffy turned to find a sandstorm behind her, a cloud of spinning wind and sand that billowed and pulsed in a controlled sphere. Within that sphere stood the silhouette of a man, the very same creature she had come back to Benefit Street in search of. Through the sandstorm she could make out bright white eyes like the glare of the sun and a humanoid body as perfectly sculpted as Michelangelo's *David*.

He was beautiful.

"Not sure a thank-you's appropriate, since you almost did the same thing to me the other day. Make it up to me. Tell me who you are, and what's happening here. And if you say 'something wonderful,' I'm going to have to kick your ass."

The sandstorm churned and billowed as though with the inhale and exhale of the creature's breath. There was something hypnotic about it. Buffy couldn't stare directly at the man's eyes, but didn't mind having to look at his body instead.

"I am a demon of the desert," a voice said, sounding like the rasp of sand across the pavement. "And you have made a mistake, Slayer. Do not disrupt the peace. You have a vital role to play in the days ahead, and I would not see you harmed before that time has come."

Buffy cocked one hip and gave her head a small shake. "That's great, thanks. Do you take classes in vague? How 'bout some elaboration?"

The sandstorm collapsed, the wind dying, and the sand showered to the pavement just as it had done before. Then a breeze picked up and the sand skittered slowly along Benefit Street, disappearing into the night.

Buffy sighed. "And yet another first date with a hot, mysterious guy where I end up more frustrated than ever."

Tired and sweaty, with stinging burns on her arm and ankle, she kicked at the scorched remains of her jacket and started back to the hotel. Half a mile later she found a cab. Providence wasn't New York City, but it seemed to have more taxis per capita than L.A., at least.

She gave the driver a decent tip, mainly for not staring at her in the rearview mirror, and made her way up to her room, pleased to find that her momentary fear that she'd left her key card in her burned jacket pocket was unfounded. But when she'd gotten into her room and kicked off her shoes, Buffy halted halfway to the bed.

There were voices coming from Xander's room. He wasn't alone.

Warily, she padded to the connecting door and raised a hand to knock. Even as she did, a knock came from the other side. It startled her and then she rolled her eyes, feeling foolish.

"Buffy?" Xander called through the door.

She unlocked it and pulled it open. Xander stood there in jeans but barefoot, his T-shirt on inside out. The patch over his eye drew her focus, as it always did, and probably always would.

"Hey! I thought I heard you coming back. We've got company."

Before Buffy could ask, Faith appeared from behind Xander and moved up next to him. Her pants were copper red and zipped up the side, and her boots were killer. The spaghetti strap tank she wore left little to the imagination. She looked damn good, which made Buffy feel even more a wreck.

"Well, well, look what the cat dragged in," Faith said with a grin. That same old Faith grin that always seemed to say she knew more about what was going on in your head than you did—maybe more than you wanted to know.

"You talking about me, or yourself?"

Faith glanced heavenward, then at Buffy again. "Me? I look fine, B. You, on the other hand, look like you've been in a real scrape."

"You could say that."

Faith shrugged. "Me too. But I guess I came out of it a little better off."

Xander held up both hands. "Ladies, let's not bicker. There's plenty of me to go around."

Buffy couldn't help it. She snickered. Faith did the same, and then the ice was broken. Shaking their heads at Xander's delusions, the two Slayers came together. Faith put out a fist and Buffy bumped it with her own. So much ugliness had passed between them that there was always that bristling wariness when they came together again. But they were allies now, and had been for a while. Whatever bitterness or resentment had once been there had not been forgotten, but it had been set aside.

"So what happened to you?" Faith asked her.

"You first," Buffy replied.

"No, no," Xander interrupted. "Me first. I already told Faith the story and I'm on a roll."

So Xander began, and the three of them exchanged stories until they had caught one another up on all of the evening's exploits, leaving them all more baffled than they'd been when they began.

"There's more," Faith said afterward.

"I can't wait," Buffy replied.

But Faith wore a grim expression, and a frisson of uneasiness went through Buffy.

"What is it?" she asked.

"I got in touch with some of the others. I'm not the only one who got ambushed on my way into town. Every Slayer you asked to come to Providence has had a welcome wagon waiting for them, and the hospitality is sorely lacking. Adrianna told me their car got rolled. Dori was driving. She and Ngaio are in the hospital. So are a couple of others."

All the humor had left Xander's face as well. With the patch and the grim set of his jaw, he looked old. No trace of the laughing boy he'd once been remained. He was all soldier now.

"Any casualties?" he asked.

"Not that I've heard," Faith said. "But I'm the only one who's gotten through."

Buffy thought on that for a minute, then got up to pace the room. There were no answers yet, and it didn't seem like throwing

Slayers into harm's way without any idea of what they were up against was a smart solution.

"So far all the demons and monsters have been peaceful, even with me—except the ones I went after tonight. They're trying to keep all of the other Slayers out of Providence? All right. We let them."

Faith cocked her head. "You sure that's a good idea, B?"

"As good as any. Right now we want answers. Giles and Willow and . . ." She paused, remembering Tara. The resurrection still unsettled her, but she didn't want to have to explain it to Faith just yet. "They're due in tomorrow. So we wait, and we see if they can get a better handle on this puzzle than we can."

"You're the boss," Faith said.

A moment of awkwardness passed between them. Buffy hadn't always been the boss. There was a time when Faith had usurped that role. She hadn't wanted the job, had sort of gotten it by default, but it had happened. The truth was, she'd done it well.

"Excellent," Xander said. "Does that mean sleep and breakfast come between now and more monsters?"

"You're in heaven," Buffy said, smiling.

"Only if I stay here while you two change for bed."

Faith arched an eyebrow. "Change into what? You know I don't wear a stitch to bed."

Buffy shot her a look. "You do if you're sleeping in here."

Xander sighed. "A young man's dreams, crushed under the cruel heel of reality." He looked at Buffy. "You want me to make some calls, tell the other Slayers not to try to get into Providence right now?"

"Yep. But tell them not to wander far, just in case we need them."

Faith flopped down on the bed.

"Need them? Come on, Buffy. It's you and me. Ain't nothin' we can't handle."

Willow's eyes were itchy and her mouth felt dry. Her muscles ached in places she hadn't known she had muscles. In spite of all that, she felt exultant just to be off the airplane. She and Tara had woken up early and made it to the airport in Athens that Friday morning just in time for their flight, then tried to nap while crossing the Atlantic. They'd flown into JFK Airport in New York, then switched to a small puddle-jumper flight to T.F. Green Airport in Providence.

It felt like they hadn't stopped moving for days.

How strange, then, to arrive in Rhode Island on a beautiful summer afternoon. Back in Athens it would be quite late, the city swathed in darkness. But here the sun shone brightly and Willow couldn't help but be happy.

"I feel like I'm coming out of hibernation," she said, pulling her wheeled suitcase along behind her.

Tara had only a small carry-on that Willow had bought her in Athens, filled with a few days' worth of clothes. She took Willow's hand and smiled.

"Me too. But more literally."

Willow felt a shiver of real joy go through her as she squeezed Tara's fingers and smiled at her. What a gift she had received, this second chance. As a little girl, she'd felt bliss often enough to know that it existed. But growing up tarnished a child's ability to feel bliss, so she knew how precious it was, what she felt now.

Whatever came their way, it wouldn't matter, as long as she could have Tara with her.

"You're ruminating again," Tara said as they walked through the baggage area and toward the exit.

"I'm musing—on the return of my muse. That's you, in case you weren't sure."

Tara bumped her hip against Willow's. "It better be me."

Willow grinned. The electronic doors swept open at their approach and they went out onto the sidewalk. Taxis and buses and cars and hotel shuttles went by. Police officers and airport security directed traffic and sent double-parkers on their way. Passengers were hugged by the people who'd come to pick them up.

It all still felt like a dream. Like heaven.

Willow faltered, her fingers slipping away.

Tara turned to look at her, eyes full of the same openness and empathy that Willow had fallen in love with in the first place.

"What is it?" she asked.

"Nothing. Let's just—"

"Willow."

With a sad smile, Willow relented. She glanced away and then forced herself to meet Tara's gaze. Her girlfriend deserved that.

"When Buffy was dead," Willow began, "and I brought her back, she said she'd been in . . ."

She stopped, unable to say the word.

Tara reached out and touched her face, caressed her cheek, lifted her chin. "Heaven?"

Willow nodded. "Were you . . . did I pull you out of—?"

"No," Tara said quickly. Then slowly, more firmly. "No." She set down her carry-on and pulled Willow to her. "It couldn't be heaven without you."

Tara kissed her temple and tucked Willow's hair behind her ear, then gently kissed her there as well. Willow felt Tara trembling against her and was overwhelmed yet again. How could her heart be so full? How could the scars of her grief simply have vanished?

A deep sense of contentment spread through her. Reluctantly, they parted. Tara picked up her bag. Willow still had a grip on the handle of her wheeled suitcase. They turned together to walk toward the taxi stand and nearly collided with Rupert Giles and Micaela Tomasi.

From the way Giles only stood there, staring at them, Willow thought he might have been a gape-mouthed, wide-eyed statue, erected on that spot decades past for pigeons to roost on. Micaela seemed confused, looking back and forth between the astonished Giles and the two young witches.

"Giles!" Tara said excitedly.

But the man only glanced at her, confusion and hurt in his eyes, and then stared at Willow.

"What have you done?"

Tara flinched, and Willow glanced at her and saw the way the words pained her. Her face flushed with anger.

"It's not what you—"

"What else could it be?" Giles snapped, his voice echoing off the windows of the terminal and the passing cars. People stopped to look at them.

Micaela touched his arm. "Rupert?"

Giles shook her off and approached Willow, ignoring Tara as though she were not even there.

"After all you've been through, the promises you made, the people who put themselves out for you when you didn't deserve absolution for the things you did when magick had gotten the better of you, I'll ask you again, Willow: What have you done?"

Giles glanced at Tara, his face falling with despair.

Willow felt fury raging inside of her. The temptation to do magick—to do him harm—was great. But Giles was right about one thing: She had made promises to him and to Buffy and to the coven of witches who had taught her to control her darkest impulses and to use magick only for positive ends, and not because she *needed* it.

Taking a deep breath, she put a hand flat on his chest.

"Giles, listen," Willow said, staring into his eyes, making sure he was focused on her and only her. "I didn't do anything. Not really. Kennedy and I fell apart. I went to Athens, and I met a witch unlike any of the ones we know. Catherine Cadiere. Does the name mean anything to you?"

Giles shook his head.

Willow shrugged. "She's older and more powerful than any witch I've ever met. She knows magick that pretty much nobody else has remembered for centuries, and she said she sees something in me, offered to work with me. Bringing Tara back . . . it was her gift to me."

She'd said the words with all her heart, knowing he had to see reason, had to understand that she had not broken her promises. Willow had not let the darkness tempt her again.

But Giles only shook his head. His upper lip curled in revulsion. He turned to glance at Tara, and there was pain in his eyes before he shifted his gaze to Willow again. The hydraulic brakes on a bus squealed and a car horn blared. Somebody swore loudly. A baby was crying not far away.

"You really see it that way? As a gift?" he said. "Haven't you learned yet that nothing comes without a price? Magick costs us, Willow. This Catherine woman, if she's that ancient, she'll know it better than you or I. Magick costs. I hate to think what this will cost."

He turned to Tara. "Is it really you?"

Tara had begun to cry. Her eyes were red and tears streaked her face. Willow wanted to hit Giles for making her cry, wanted to punch his lights out. But now Giles reached for Tara, and she went into his arms and the two of them wept together.

"I missed you so much," Giles said.

"You've got a f-funny way of showing it," Tara whispered.

Giles could only smile then, but his anguish did not disappear. "You'd become the heart of us, and we hardly realized it until you were gone."

"I missed you too," Tara said.

But then Giles was stepping away from her and picking up his suitcase. Micaela gave his upper arm a squeeze—not the touch of a lover, but the supportive gesture of a friend—and looked at Willow and Tara again.

"It appears our destination is the same," Micaela said. "Perhaps we should go on to the hotel. Rupert's already called ahead to let Buffy know we've arrived."

Willow nodded. Tara wiped away her tears and smiled at her, but there was a kind of veil across her eyes now. She bore the burden of Giles's doubts, and Willow knew they would both be haunted by the words for some time to come. Part of her wished they had stayed in Athens and just reveled in their reunion, never letting the outside world intrude upon their bliss. They'd found their little piece of heaven in that pristine hotel in a grimy neighborhood in Greece's capital city. Willow was determined that, when the situation in Rhode Island was resolved, they would hide away together again and reclaim that peace.

"Let's go," she said.

The cab ride was tense. Giles sat in front with the driver while Micaela joined Willow and Tara in the back. The gorgeous Watcher—whose onetime betrayal Willow had forgiven but not forgotten—struck up a polite conversation with Tara about Athens and their long travels. Willow remained mostly silent, fidgeting in her seat and looking out the window, doing anything to avoid looking at Giles. Not that it would have mattered, as in her few glimpses of him all she saw was the back of his head as he stared out the windshield.

At the hotel, Willow started to get her money, but Giles paid the taxi driver before they got out. She didn't argue. It hurt her to feel so frozen out by him, but if the tension compelled him to pick up the fare, that was fine with her.

The driver unloaded their bags and they went into the hotel together, leaving the pleasant heat of the August day for the air-conditioned lobby. The hotel received them warmly. Willow felt at home here. How strange for the brainy little small-town girl to have come to look at checking in to a nice hotel as a homecoming. But she traveled so much these days that all of the hotels she stayed in had sort of blended into one for her.

"We'll check in, see if Buffy's about, and meet in, say, half an hour to exchange information and decide upon a course of action?" Giles said, looking at her.

Willow nodded. It was the first time he'd spoken to her since they had hailed the taxi. "It's a plan."

The four of them walked toward the front desk, where velvet ropes defined a queue for check-in. There was no line, but one guest was in the midst of checking in.

Oddly, Tara recognized him first. She reached out and tugged at Willow's shirt. Willow glanced at her, saw where she was staring, and looked again at the guy standing at the front desk. She blinked in astonishment, wondering how she could not have known at first glance that it was him. Perhaps it was simply that she had not seen him in so very long, and that running into him here, at this time and in this place, seemed so incredibly unlikely.

Short guy, spiky red hair. First love. The only boyfriend she'd ever had, before she realized what she really wanted was a girlfriend. But she'd loved him, just the same.

Giles was the one who said his name.

"Oz?"

The woman behind the counter had just given him his key card and he'd bent to pick up a big, heavy-looking duffel bag. Now Oz turned, only slightly curious, as if someone calling out his name in a hotel lobby in Providence, Rhode Island, were the most ordinary thing in the world.

He saw them coming toward him, Giles and Micaela, Willow and Tara. Willow felt sure she saw a flicker of something in his eyes that betrayed his laconic nature, some surprise or possibly regret or that melancholy that had been such a part of him when they'd last parted, and when he'd seemed to have become so wise.

Oz only smiled.

"Hey," he said.

"Hey," Willow replied.

A long, awkward moment passed.

"I presume you're here to see Buffy," Giles said.

Oz cocked his head. "No, actually. Just checking in. Is Buffy here?"

"This can't be a coincidence," Micaela said to Giles.

"Perhaps we should all go up together," Giles suggested.

Oz waited while they all checked in and Giles asked for Buffy's room number. Tara ended up next to Oz in the elevator. He looked at her, nodding to himself.

"What?" she asked.

"You look good. Kinda radiant."

Tara nodded. "I was resurrected a few days ago."

Oz arched an eyebrow. "That'll do it."

CHAPTER EIGHT

When the knock came on the door to Buffy's hotel room, she tossed aside the remote control and hopped up from the bed. Xander and Faith had gone out to pick up some Chinese food for dinner. It was early, but they were headed out into the city again tonight and Xander insisted they eat before trying to intimidate the demonic tourists into giving them some answers.

"You better not have forgotten my dumplings," Buffy said as she opened her door.

Willow and Tara stood in the hall.

Tara's face lit up with her lopsided grin. "Now, how could we ever forget your dumplings?"

Buffy had known they were coming, just not when. And Willow had told her about Tara and Catherine Cadiere and how it had all happened. Still, she realized that Tara's return had not been real to her until this very moment.

"Um, Buffy? Letting us in at some point?" Willow said.

Only then did she realize she'd been staring. Buffy gave Willow a hug and then let her pass. Then Tara was standing right in front of her, breathing and alight with the calm, self-effacing sweetness that had meant so much to them when she was alive.

Buffy took a long, shuddering breath. "I'm not usually at a loss for words. Usually, there's a long, rambling kind of thing that only half makes sense and that somehow people seem to understand anyway. The rambly babble. Which I'm kind of doing right now."

"It's good to see you too," Tara said.

Buffy looked her up and down. Tara had always been mousy and shy, somehow able to disappear into the back of any crowd or even vanish in the midst of a conversation, retreating inside of herself. That had changed. There was something almost regal about her now.

"You seem different," Buffy said.

A sadness touched Tara's eyes. "So do you."

Buffy looked away. How to tell Tara that after her death everything had become so much darker, had seemed so hopeless. She had not given a lot of thought to the idea of Tara's death being the trigger—though it certainly had been for Willow—but now that she had returned, it did feel like some vital part of their puzzle had been found.

Tara gave her a hug.

"It's a good omen, you coming back," Buffy said.

"I hope you're right," Tara whispered, voice too low for Willow to hear. "Goddess, I hope you're right."

Buffy had nothing to say to that—certainly nothing to say while Willow was in the room. For her part, Will seemed to bristle with excitement, giddy as a birthday girl. Buffy was thrilled for her, and a little bit jealous. She hadn't felt that way in forever, or so it seemed.

"Xander and Faith should be back in a few minutes," Buffy said, closing the door behind them.

"Faith?" Tara asked.

Willow smiled. "Yeah. You've got some catching up to do." She glanced at Buffy. "Haven't given her the lowdown on a lot of the current stuff yet. We've been otherwise occupied."

Buffy smiled. "I'll bet you have."

"Giles is here," Tara said. "And that Watcher, Micaela. They'll be up in a minute."

"It's about time," Buffy said. "With you guys here, maybe we can finally figure out what flavor of chaos we're up against this time."

"And Oz," Willow added.

Buffy frowned. "Oz. Didn't see that coming. I mean, it's always good, but—"

"He didn't even know you were here," Willow said. "He said something about a bunch of werewolves getting together."

"Them too? Wish I could say I was surprised."

Another knock came at the door. Giles and Micaela arrived, and Oz showed up a few minutes later. There were greetings and reunions all around. As awkward as some of the relationships in the room were, Buffy felt good about them all being there with a shared purpose. Any discomfort would be set aside for now, and maybe by the time they'd sorted out the chaos, it would be forgotten.

While they were all talking, Buffy heard the door opening in the room next door. Xander and Faith had returned with the Chinese food. The door slammed shut and then there came a rap at the connecting door between the rooms.

Buffy opened it.

"Here we go," Xander said as he started through the door with a big brown paper bag, steaming with delicious aromas.

He froze and looked around at all the people jammed together in the single hotel room.

Faith peeked over his shoulder and raised her eyebrows.

"Wow," she said. "We're gonna need more spring rolls."

• • •

It turned out that the restaurant delivered. A menu had been stapled to the bag, so Buffy ordered more food—a lot more—and while they waited for it to arrive, they shared what Xander and Faith had already bought. Xander whimpered with every teriyaki skewer that ended up in someone else's mouth.

Stories were shared, until they all knew what the others had experienced in recent days, including the attacks on Slayers attempting to enter Providence, Buffy's run-in with the demon of the desert, the sandstorm on Benefit Street, the nonviolence on the part of the demons, the death of the archaeological team excavating in Morocco and the rebirth of Kandida, the strange migration of demon tribes and old gods, and Oz's visit from the old wolves who'd asked him to come to Providence.

By the time they finished, the rest of the food had arrived, and Xander was happy.

"It's obviously all connected," Buffy said, glancing around at her friends, all of them gathered close in that small room. "What I need is for you guys to tell me how."

Giles and Micaela exchanged a glance. He reached up and took his glasses off and cleaned the lenses on his shirt. Buffy felt better just seeing him do that. They had known each other for a very long time, and she understood that it meant he knew something.

"We believe we have the answer," he said, settling his glasses back upon his nose.

"It's the Dark Congress," Micaela said.

Giles glanced around at them expectantly.

"If you're confused by the sea of blank looks," Buffy said, "let me be the first to say, the dark *what* now?"

Faith sat on the corner of the bed. "You're saying all these demons are from Washington?"

Oz nodded thoughtfully. "Actually, that explains a lot."

"No," Giles sighed. "They're not politicians—"

"So you're talking some kind of demon orgy here?" Xander asked.

Micaela made a little tsking noise with her tongue. "Not that kind of congress. Actually, the political analogy isn't entirely wrong. It's a gathering of ambassadors."

Another pause.

"Another wave in the sea of blank faces," Buffy said. She crossed her arms and leaned against the armoire, looking at Giles. "Maybe you should start at the beginning."

"Right, then. The beginning," Giles said. "Throughout history, all the races of demons and dark gods and monsters gathered once every hundred years to resolve conflicts among them. Even the most hostile and belligerent demonic races realized that war among themselves was not conducive to their efforts to eradicate humanity from the globe."

"Sounds sensible," Willow said.

They all looked at her.

Willow turned to Tara with a sheepish look. "From the demons' point of view, I meant."

Tara patted her hand. "We know."

Willow grinned.

Micaela picked up the tale.

"There were a number of demonic species that had no trouble sharing the world with humanity, some who even preferred the idea that humanity should control the Earth. If human beings were exterminated and the demons rose again to the prominence they'd had in prehistoric times, those more peaceful races would themselves be exterminated or subjugated. To them, also, the Dark Congress was a welcome event."

"All of these ambassadors gathered together," Giles went on, "to determine the course of their future in the Earth dimension and decide on the efforts they would put forth to battle what they perceived as 'the plague of humanity' that grew stronger with every passing year. As we've said, this centennial event was called the Dark Congress."

Faith leaned forward. Bed springs creaked under her.

"Okay, back up a second. If you're the peace-loving demon tribe, I get why you'd want to take part in this thing. If there's a forum or whatever where they can talk out their differences, make truces, all that political crap, then you're less likely to get eaten. But if you're the kind of demon who digs bloodshed and maybe eating human hearts, and these peaceful demons stand in the way, why bother with the Congress at all? Why not just eat whoever stands in the way?"

Micaela nodded. "It *has* nearly come to that in the past. But the politics of demons are intricate. If the demons who enjoy the status quo and those who want to live in peace join forces with the non-demonic supernatural creatures in this world to halt the belligerent forces' attempt at conquest, the war would tear the world apart, and there is no way to know which side would win. The flesh eaters and human haters know this, and fortunately the cooler heads among them prevail. Unless they can sway the others to their thinking—or at least extract from them a promise not to interfere—an attempt to destroy humanity or take over the world would be likely to fail."

Buffy sipped from a bottle of water. "So every Dark Congress is about this issue?"

Giles crossed his arms. "Well, historically it has been the undercurrent of every gathering. But records show that the ambassadors who come to each Congress come with a host of issues to be resolved or aired in front of the gathering."

"Just like human politics," Xander said. "Everybody has an agenda."

"Precisely." Giles nodded.

Faith threw up her hands. "All right, we get the gist. But here's my big question. We've been fighting the nasties all this time and now you tell us there's this web of relationships that connects them all, right? So how come we've never heard of it?"

Micaela's expression grew dark. "You haven't heard of it

because the last Dark Congress took place in the second century B.C. The conflicts that were brought to that Congress were never resolved. Instead, they ignited an internecine war that drove wedges between the various demon races that have lingered from that time until now."

Tara spoke up. "Why? What happened?"

"It all began very simply," Giles replied. "Kandida, the great North African river demon, was among those who argued in favor of the status quo. Her kin enjoyed the worship of humanity and the presence of humans, though many of them enjoyed killing and sometimes eating people. They enjoyed their status as gods and demons. The desert demon Trajabo and his ilk despised the river demons and wanted to exterminate humanity from the world. Among their own kind, Kandida and Trajabo were two of the most respected of those who kept the peace. But they fell in love."

"Their union created a storm of hatred and fury," Micaela said. "Think of Romeo and Juliet. Kandida and Trajabo represented different regions, different breeds, different philosophies. When they came together they began to try to persuade all of the ambassadors to the Congress that the time had come for an answer to the ultimate question once and for all, a final consensus on the future of the world. Their kin despised one another. The desert demons thought Kandida would influence Trajabo to her way of thinking, and the river gods believed Trajabo would sway Kandida to his own philosophy. Neither could afford such a defection.

"The two sides hated each other, but on one thing they could agree: The love between Kandida and Trajabo would never be allowed to survive. The lovers were attacked, Trajabo scattered among all the sands of the desert, and Kandida nearly killed, and magickally entombed in the bank of the river Sebu, in Morocco."

Giles continued. "the Congress was torn apart. War erupted among the demon races, clans, and tribes, among the monsters. The old gods were dying out anyway, and took refuge. It seemed reasonable to presume that there would never be peace among them all again, as there would never be another Dark Congress."

Buffy stared at them both. It seemed almost too much to take in, but she had followed it all, and she understood.

"Your dig in Morocco," she said to Micaela, eyes narrowed. "You set Kandida free."

"By accident," Micaela replied. "But yes."

Willow pushed her hair away from her eyes. "Then the desert demon Buffy ran into, the one who created that sandstorm—"

"Must be Trajabo," Giles said. "We can only presume that somehow Kandida was able to summon him in the desert, to gather his essence together even after two thousand years and more."

Xander had lost all trace of amusement. The soldier he'd become had retreated when faced with this gathering of old friends. But Buffy saw the gravity return to him now.

"So they've called the Dark Congress to session," Xander said. "That explains all of the insanity that's been going on here. But that brings up a pretty fundamental question. Why here? Why Rhode Island? I mean, it's nice and all, but"—he shrugged—"not getting the allure."

Faith shot him a look. "Did you just say 'allure'?"

"Pretty sure I did."

Everyone else was staring at Giles and Micaela, waiting for the answer.

"We're not entirely certain," Giles said. "What we do know is that there was a Hellmouth here once—"

"On Benefit Street," Buffy interrupted.

"No," Micaela said. "At least, we don't think so. Unless there was more than one, it seems you were mistaken about the location."

"More than one?" Tara said in a small voice. "H-how could there be more than one Hellmouth in one city? I don't like the sound of that."

"Have you done much reading about Providence?" Xander

asked. "I can see it. This place has been riddled with stories of supernatural occurrences. I'm not just talking ghosts. Look at Lovecraft's stories."

"Yep. I've read that stuff," Oz said, nodding. "If half of it's true, this place could be like supernatural Swiss cheese—but not as tasty."

"That's not far off from the theory Micaela and I were developing," Giles replied, then shot a glance at Oz. "Though we suffered an appalling lack of food metaphors in our version. Regardless, it stands to reason that without a currently open Hellmouth anywhere in the world, they've come to the place where the dimensional barriers are the thinnest, or have suffered the most frequent . . . perforation."

Buffy shook her head. The smell of Chinese food that still filled the room was getting to her. "So you're saying they've called the Dark Congress in Providence because it kinda feels like home."

"Or as close to home as they'll get," Micaela replied.

"And they're here to discuss their plans for the future and the fate of the human race, possibly to make peace, and if they make peace, that could mean they all join together in one huge army to erase humanity from the face of the Earth?" Buffy said.

"That sums it up rather neatly," Giles said.

Willow perked up with a hopeful look. "Or they could, y'know, not. After what the Congress did to them, maybe Kandida and Trajabo won't cooperate with that really unfriendly plan. I mean, love conquers all, right?"

"That's one possible outcome," Micaela said politely. "But I think we need to be prepared for the other."

Faith stood up. "Have any of you even thought about how many nasties there are in this city right now? If they wanna have their big happy demon reunion, no way are we gonna be able to stop them."

"Not with our fists," Giles said, "so we must attempt diplomacy."

"Oh yes, 'cause we're excellent at that," Buffy replied.

Micaela took a step into the center of the room and looked around. "We've got to find out where the Congress will actually take place and try to make contact with as many ambassadors as possible—peaceful contact. If we can locate Kandida and Trajabo, it's possible we can influence them, but at least we can find out what their intentions are."

"And then we'll know whether or not to panic," Xander said. "Great plan."

Buffy's brain hurt. Too many thoughts. Too many questions. She turned to Oz.

"You know," she said, "none of this explains why those were-wolves wanted you to come here. I mean, good to see you and everything. Been too long, blah, blah, blah. But what's the deal with that?"

Oz shrugged. "Pretty sure they want me to be an ambassador for the full-moon crowd."

They all stared at him.

"That could be useful," Giles said. "You didn't think to mention this before?"

"Nobody asked."

Faith strode along the street, edgy as a junky looking for a fix. She knew the truth wasn't too far off from that. Her fingers curled and uncurled, ready to form into fists. It had taken her some time, but Faith had learned not to lie to herself; she was itching for a fight.

"It's getting to me, too," Buffy said.

Faith glanced at her, arching an eyebrow. Once upon a time she'd have doubted that. Buffy had seemed like Snow White to her, all perfect and shiny, and maybe sometimes she'd acted that way too. But over the past couple of years they'd both learned that nobody was perfect. A lesson learned all too well.

"My body just reacts, y'know?" Faith said. "All the baby-eating, blood-sucking bastards in this town and none of them'll stand and fight. I just want to hit something."

"Me too. But every time one of them gets a whiff of us they take off like scared rabbits."

Faith grinned. "They should. But that's not the point."

"No, it's not," Buffy replied, all seriousness. "They're avoiding us like we're walking cootie machines. But they tried to keep you out and they've driven off all the other Slayers who've tried to get into the city. So why not attack us? Throw us out of town?"

Faith kicked a beer can that had been left standing beside a newspaper machine. Drops of beer sloshed out onto her jeans and her boot.

"Damn it," she muttered, shaking her leg once. She stomped on the can, crushed it flat.

"Feel better?" Buffy asked.

Faith smiled. They walked side by side along the sidewalk. An electric sign in front of a bank gave the time as 10:17 p.m. and it felt like they were wasting their time. It had been an hour since Faith had bothered to look at street signs. She had no idea where they were in Providence, but by design they had headed to one of the uglier neighborhoods in the city. Faith had rarely been so troubled that a visit to a dive bar, where hard-muscled, swaggering guys would buy her a beer and adore her, wouldn't cure what ailed her.

Friday night in the bad part of town. An Irish pub up the street had its door propped open, people spilling out onto the sidewalk, and music blaring from inside, some kind of bluesy, honky-tonk stuff that put a smile on her face. The sound of laughter and clinking glasses reached them, and Faith was in her element.

Several of the people on the sidewalk weren't people at all. Nobody else seemed to notice.

"So you're thinking this is witchcraft? The way the demons blend in with the crowd?"

Buffy nodded. "I'm thinking. Has to be."

"Never seen magick on that scale without some massive demon invasion attempt or dimensional breach," Faith noted.

"Me neither. It's supersize mojo. The family value meal bucket of mojo."

Faith glanced at her. "You hungry or something?"

Buffy shrugged. "Nope. Just a metaphorin' girl."

With a shake of her head, Faith kept on down the street. Buffy seemed comfortable at her side. It would be easy to start thinking about it as seeming like old times, but those old times were too complicated and too dark to look back on with much fondness. Yet, as much as she and Buffy still butted heads, Faith knew that together, nobody had a chance in hell of beating them. And that felt good.

Which got her thinking.

"Tell me again why we don't just call in the cavalry?" Faith asked as they approached the Irish pub. Glass shattered inside, followed by a round of applause. The place was rocking.

"Overkill," Buffy replied.

Faith stopped and turned to look at her, forcing Buffy to halt as well.

"We've identified over a thousand new Slayers in the past three months. What've we got signed up and training now? Three, four hundred? We should bring them in here like the National Guard. The demons haven't started destroying the place yet, but if the Dark Congress creates a truce and they throw in together to try to take down the human race, having the troops in place seems like a pretty reasonable frickin' plan to me."

Frowning, Buffy met her gaze fiercely. "They're not ready, Faith. Most of these girls, you'd be throwing them to the wolves. Never mind that all we'd be doing is agitating the demons, who—in case you've had enough head trauma that it's screwed up your short-term memory—don't want Slayers in Providence."

Faith took a breath and threw up one hand in surrender. "All right. Your call—for now."

They started along the sidewalk again. When they'd come within a dozen feet of the front door, one of the demons who stood in front of the plate-glass window of the Irish pub saw them and his beer slipped from his hand. The glass shattered on the sidewalk. The two others out there with him looked up, saw his alarm, then spotted the Slayers approaching. How they recognized her and Buffy right off the bat Faith didn't know, but they rabbited.

Faith tensed to chase them, but Buffy caught her arm. "Let them go. There'll be more inside, and they won't have anywhere to run."

Turned out she was right.

The place was crowded. When Faith wanted to have a good time, she loved a crowd. Sweaty, smiling people all dancing and grinding and crashing into one another—there was joy in that kind of abandon. But tonight she was working, and when she was on the job, Faith hated such situations. Moving through the pub, it was all she could do to control her urge to start swinging her fists.

They found a Miquot demon at the bar. Others vanished into the shadows of the pub or took off in search of a back door, but the Miquot—under some kind of glamour that must have made him look human to those whose minds would not accept the supernatural—stood flirting with a redhead with a killer body.

"Eeew," Buffy whispered.

"Pretty much my thought. Only I'm not sure 'eeew' would have been my word of choice."

The Miquot tipped back his beer and took a long swig. Faith moved up on one side of the demon and Buffy on the other side. It was weird being able to see the strange fins on his head—like that dinosaur, the stego-something—and his yellow skin, when obviously the other women in the pub saw something else entirely. Faith shoved one of them out of the way.

"Hey!" the blonde protested.

Faith silenced her with a look.

The redhead gave Buffy a harder time. "Who the hell do you think you are?" she said, her voice shrill, full of attitude.

Faith would have knocked her on her ass. Buffy only smiled and said something about needing to talk to the Miquot about something she might have caught from him. Her doctor had told her to advise all of her partners to get checked out. The redhead shuddered and moved away, upper lip curling in disgust. She didn't actually say "eeew," but she didn't need to.

"Nicely done," Faith told her.

"Thanks," Buffy replied.

The Miquot had set down his beer and now he glanced back and forth between them, eyes wide and nervous. He started to fidget, and tiny beads of sweat had popped out on his leathery forehead.

"This is the kind with the knives that come out of their arms, right?" Faith asked.

"Yep."

"That's somehow gross and cool at the same time."

The Miquot took a breath, showing the filthy, sharklike teeth in his mouth, then got up from his stool. He tried to slip away from them, but Faith took one arm and Buffy the other, and after a moment he relented with a sigh. They let him go.

He took another sip of beer, but said nothing. They had discipline, all these vermin. Faith had to give them that.

Buffy leaned in close to him. "Two questions. Easy ones. Where is the Dark Congress convening? Where do we find Kandida and Trajabo?"

With as much dignity as he could muster, the Miquot sat up straighter on his stool. He stared at the mirror behind the bar and did not so much as glance at either of them again.

"Kill me if you wish. I will not fight you. And I will not answer any of your questions."

Buffy sighed, then gave him a friendly smile. "I won't kill you just for not answering." She nodded toward Faith. "But she will."

The Miquot did not tremble at the thought of death. He lifted his chin farther, as though exposing it in anticipation of some blade or other weapon.

Faith caught a glimpse of movement behind Buffy and said her name. Buffy turned just as the redhead swung a beer mug at her head. She blocked, then punched the other woman in the side of the head hard enough to knock her over. The redhead took a stool down with her and started swearing so savagely and colorfully that even Faith was impressed.

"We should go," Buffy said.

"This night is turning into Suck City."

Buffy didn't argue.

Faith led the way through the crowded pub. One guy tried to block her in, maybe thinking he'd insist they wait for the police to come. Faith cleared him off with a smile. It pleased her to no end that she had the ability to suggest such a variety of things with nothing but a smile. Sometimes it was about flirtation—sometimes about pain.

Out on the sidewalk, she didn't even slow down to wait for Buffy. Her itch to hit something had worsened dramatically.

"Faith," Buffy said, catching up.

"This is lame," Faith said, still walking away from the pub. "What are we accomplishing?"

"We're doing the job that needs to be done," Buffy replied. "The solution isn't always just hammering away at something until it breaks."

Faith laughed. "Tell that to the babe you just decked back there."

Buffy had no reply for that. Both frustrated, they strode along the street, away from the Irish pub just in case the police had been called.

"Notice anything weird about that place?" Faith asked.

"Yeah. Still no vampires."

They'd talked about it half a dozen times that night. It had not seemed important to Buffy when she and Xander had been on their own amid the growing chaos in Providence, but with the stories Giles and Micaela had told about the Dark Congress, and Faith's run-in with Christabel de Tournefort and Haarmann in San Francisco, they'd agreed that the absence of vampires had to be important somehow.

"They've gotta be planning something," Faith said. "Maybe sabotage. Or a coup, or something."

"What makes you say that?"

"I don't know. But you don't get vampires as ancient as Haarmann and de Tournefort—master vampires—coming out of hibernation or whatever for the first time in a century or two just to party. They're not in Vegas playing Texas Hold 'Em."

"No," said a voice from the shadows of an alley. "No, they're not."

A shiver of excitement went through Faith. Automatically, she and Buffy turned their backs to each other, ready for combat. A figure emerged from the shadows, almost a living shadow himself. Others dropped down from the roofs of buildings and several darted from the spaces between parked cars.

Vampires. As though summoned by Faith's words.

"Good evening, Slayers," said the one who'd spoken first, a European by style and accent, though it was impossible to tell what nation. "If I might say, it's lovely to feel wanted."

"You've been following us since half an hour after sundown," Buffy said, rolling her eyes. "Please. You don't actually think we didn't know you were there?"

Faith shot her a curious look. If Buffy had picked up their presence, she hadn't said anything. For her part, Faith hadn't noticed a thing, but she was not about to admit that.

The vampire faltered, surprised by her attitude.

"We were meant only to follow. But Slayers, well . . . you're irresistible."

"All the boys say that," Faith replied.

Buffy glanced around. There were slender, beautiful vampires, aged things whose flesh had begun to change to reflect the appearance of the demon inside, and huge bruisers, built for battle.

"We want to know where the Dark Congress will convene, and where to find Kandida and Trajabo," Buffy said quietly. She reached around behind her and pulled the stake that had been sheathed against the small of her back. "And we'll have answers."

"Nice," Faith said, producing her own stake. "Finally something to dust."

The vampire hissed, baring his fangs. He started for Faith. In the same moment the others began to move in.

Something shrieked above them. Faith risked a glance up and caught a glimpse of wetly gleaming wing as something hideous swooped down from the darkness. In the single moment that it came into the light, she saw jaws like those of a crocodile snap shut over the vampire's head, tearing it from its roots and snapping its spine. The headless leech exploded in a cloud of dust, and then the demon beat its wings and took once more to the night sky.

A sewer grate exploded upward and clanged onto the street. Tentacles thrust out and dragged two screaming vampires beneath the city.

A blade flickered past Faith's face, coming within inches of slicing off her nose. It struck a vampire in the forehead. The wound wouldn't kill the bloodsucker, so Faith ran toward it, ready to finish it off, but then a huge thing lumbered from the shadows of the same alley—a flopping, bulbous demon that left a snail trail of mucus behind it. A whiplike tongue shot from its mouth, punctured the wounded vampire in the chest, undulating and digging and searching, and then it retracted, dragging the leech's black heart with it.

Buffy and Faith backed into each other.

Faith glanced at her. "What the hell?"

"Yeah. Pretty much," Buffy replied.

The demons swarmed in. The blade that had nearly cut Faith had come from the Miquot they'd rousted in the bar. He attacked another vamp.

"Unclean filth!" the Miquot snarled. "You don't belong here."

Then the surviving vampires turned tail and bolted, and the demons set off after them.

In moments the two Slayers were alone again on the sidewalk.

"Is it just me," Buffy said, "or did we kinda leave our big Chinese food powwow earlier with the idea that we were starting to have a clue what was going on around here?"

"It's not just you," Faith assured her.

"And now?"

"Back to no-cluesville."

"I'm thinking about buying a condo in no-cluesville," Buffy said. "Makes more sense than renting all the time."

A breeze kicked up, blowing grit from the road into their faces. Faith squinted and turned away. Tiny bits of sand stung her cheek.

"What the hell—," she began.

Buffy tapped her on the shoulder. Faith glanced up, saw the direction of Buffy's gaze, and forced herself to turn into the wind, shielding her face as best she could from the sand. What approached them looked like a small tornado, dark with soil. The twister's howl grew louder as it moved toward them. Where the pavement had already been cracked, bits of the street were torn up and flung away from the howling sandstorm. Faith ducked as a fragment flew past her head.

There were two figures in the center of the twister, clinging together. Buffy had told Faith about Trajabo, but this time the demon of the desert had not come alone.

Faith swore loudly, shouting at the demon to get rid of the wind. When the gusts ceased suddenly and the churning storm collapsed into a scattering of sand so that the street looked like a beach, Faith felt relief. But she did not attribute the end of the small tornado to her pleas or Trajabo's courtesy. The demons had arrived.

Wrapped around the golden-eyed desert demon was another creature. This demon had green hair and pouting slashes on her throat and sides that could only be gills. Her eyes were enormous and damp, reminding Faith of Japanese cartoons, and her fish lips were full and stretched around the sides of her face in an eternal, gaping grin. She wore a long, black satin dress that looked as if she'd stolen it off a department store mannequin, but her visible skin had diamond-shaped scales in a cascade of colors.

"I am told you have been searching for me," Kandida said, her voice stilted, as though she uttered words she did not herself understand. "That is helpful, for there are things we must discuss."

The river demon glanced pointedly at Faith. "Once *she* is gone."

Faith bristled. For a moment she had hoped she and Buffy might get out of this without a fight. But now she wanted one.

CHAPTER NINE

Xander took Oz to Lovecraft's grave and found another party in progress, or perhaps it was simply an ongoing bash that would last for the duration of the festivities surrounding the Dark Congress. As they worked their way across the cemetery, Xander found himself pleased that the ruckus was still going on. He would have felt foolish dragging Oz all the way out there to end up sitting alone in the graveyard.

Not that he felt awkward with Oz. He should have, no question about that. The little guy with the spiky red hair and the taciturn manner had never been a brilliant conversationalist. Oz tended to speak only when he had something to say, whether it be out of necessity or some wry observation. In that way, he and Xander were polar opposites. But they also both had a history with Willow. Xander had been her best friend all through childhood, never allowing himself to realize that Willow loved him until the worst possible moment, when they kissed, unaware that they were observed.

Oz had taken it pretty well. Xander's girlfriend at the time, Cordelia, not so much.

But that had been years ago, and these days Willow had no interest in guys at all. Water under the lesbian bridge, as far as Xander was concerned. Still, had anyone asked him—not that anyone could have predicted he and Oz would visit Lovecraft's grave together—he would have guessed hanging with the wolfman would be uncomfortable as hell. Instead, it was just the opposite. They'd known each other a long time, and if they had never truly been friends, they still had a shared history. That meant Oz didn't have to deal with the fumblings of someone trying to make conversation, and Xander knew what to expect as well. None of the romantic entanglements of the past seemed to matter at all either. It all seemed to have happened in another age, and almost to other people entirely.

"This way," Oz said as he moseyed along a line of trees, taking what had to be the long route to get a closer view of the demon revelry. He never seemed in a hurry, even when he ought to have been. Words like "sidle" and "mosey" and "meander" seemed to have been invented for Oz.

"Kind of the long way," Xander pointed out.

Oz nodded. "Gotta stay downwind."

"Right. Werewolves stinky."

He didn't want any of the demons to catch his scent. Xander hadn't even thought of that last night, but then again, the scent of a human in the cemetery wouldn't necessarily draw attention. The pheromonal stew that the typical werewolf probably gave off, on the other hand, would give them away.

Together they moved along the line of trees. Xander stayed low and went swiftly, careful on his feet and ready to defend himself if the necessity arose. He reached a tall marble and granite crypt and paused to wait for Oz, thinking about the old story of the tortoise and the hare. But Oz arrived only a step or two behind him.

"What do you think?" Xander whispered, glancing around one side of the crypt. The demons at Lovecraft's grave were capering and laughing. A terrible smell came downwind to them and Xander wondered how many of them had relieved themselves on the gravesite. His nose wrinkled and he thanked the Powers That Be that he didn't have Oz's wolfy senses.

Oz shrugged. "You're secret agent man."

Xander thought about it a moment. He had a dagger in a sheath at his back. Now he pulled it out, sheath and all, and reached up to hide it on the edge of a granite ledge that ran around the top of the crypt.

Then he paused and took a few long breaths. He squinted hard. The empty eye socket ached, but he pushed the deep, dull pain away.

"They're not killing anybody with the Congress in town," Xander whispered. "Plus, you're supposed to be an ambassador, right? So we crash the party, see what we can find out."

"Kinda doubt they'll buy you as a demon," Oz said.

Xander smiled, but felt no humor. "Maybe a pirate, right? But yeah, that's my point. No pretending. No more sneaking around. We just ask. Not much of a plan, I know, but what's the point of strategy if we know they're not going to try to eat us?"

When Oz didn't reply, Xander glanced over to find the stubbly-faced wolfman watching him.

"What?" Xander asked.

Oz cocked his head, one eyebrow raised. "You've changed."

"You mean because I'm not clowning around all the time?"

"I'm gonna say the clown's still there," Oz said, "but not so much with the babbling and jokes."

A shriek of demonic laughter carried across the graveyard. A night breeze went through the branches and something rustled the leaves of the nearest tree. Xander hoped it was just some nocturnal squirrel or a bird up past its bedtime. He took a peek at the cemetery dance going on by Lovecraft's grave, but nothing had changed. Bottles were strewn across the grass. A demon with a crack in its skull—inside of which flames burned brightly—tilted back a liquor bottle and poured dark liquid down its throat.

"I still babble. Ask anyone. But not so much from the terror anymore."

Oz made a small, contemplative sound. "So nights like this don't scare you anymore?"

Xander did not face him. He kept his focus on the demon revelers. "I'm terrified on a regular basis. It's automatic—kind of like breathing. But there's no upside to it. When things get ugly, the only way to make it to sunrise alive is to do the job."

"See, that's pretty much what I mean," Oz said. "When did it become your job?"

Xander turned to look at him. "The day I met Buffy. I just didn't know it then. What about you, fuzzy? You're here too, and you've been gone for ages. This isn't your job."

Oz nodded. "Yeah. Pretty much a werewolf, though. It'd be easy to say I got dragged into it, but I'm not totally sure I believe in coincidence anymore. The wind blows us around, and we land where we land."

With a laugh, Xander shook his head. "I'm not the only one who's changed. That's about the most I've ever heard you say at one time. What's up with that? You on some philosophical journey or something?"

"Pretty much."

Xander grinned. That reply seemed more like the Oz he knew.

A death cry tore across the warm night. Xander turned and peered once more around the side of the crypt, wondering if one of the demons had turned on the others. Whatever truce kept them from killing humans in Providence might not apply to other demons. Or maybe all the drinking had led someone to take things too far.

The hideous scream devolved into a choking gurgle.

Oz moved behind Xander for a better view. He tensed, as though about to rush toward Lovecraft's grave. Xander put up a hand to halt him. At the gravesite demons and monsters had started to shout and chitter in a language that hurt Xander's ears. The towering creatures whose faces were masses of tentacles drew together, glancing around for some unseen enemy. A winged monster took flight from a branch that its weight had nearly pinned to the ground. The vulturelike thing started to flap upward in an odd, lazy fashion, almost in slow motion.

A dark figure appeared as though from nowhere, stepping out from some kind of night cloak. Grim and bearded and wielding a sword that gleamed ghostly in the moonlight, he ran at Lovecraft's grave marker, put a foot on the stone, and launched himself into the air. The sword whistled in the dark, cleaving the vulture thing in half. Blood showered down upon the revelers and the two halves of the corpse struck the ground wetly.

There were other screams, but only a few. These were not helpless children, but demons, some of them creatures of heinous evil and savagery. A chorus of anger filled the night and they charged at the swordsman. He moved with inhuman swiftness, severing limbs and saturating the soil of Lovecraft's grave with the blood of monsters.

Tiny missiles like antique perfume bottles sailed end over end in an arc above the demon revelers, first two, then three more in rapid succession. Only one hit the ground and shattered harmlessly. The other four hit demons and exploded in a burst of hellish fire, like some kind of supernatural napalm. Xander smelled burning flesh and fur instantly.

A small man—a goblin or a human barely over four feet tall— appeared from his hiding place behind a heavy marble headstone. Xander figured he'd hurled the bottles, but now he had some kind of small ax, a double-bladed thing that he swung with deadly skill.

The branches swayed again in the tree where the vulture thing had roosted. A man dropped down from the limbs, dark-haired and broad-shouldered, strong enough to snap someone in half. None of them said a word as they continued the slaughter. More of the demons tried to flee. A stunningly beautiful red-haired woman in a summer dress came walking toward the melee as though she were out for a stroll in the park. The only thing that gave her intentions away was her sword, and then she, too, began slaying demons.

Oz and Xander watched the massacre in breathless astonishment. How had this happened? They'd come only to talk, but there would be no answers today if the four killers finished their work. Even so, Xander did not even consider trying to intervene.

Then Oz started out from behind the crypt.

"Hey!" he said.

Xander swore and hauled him back by the T-shirt. "What the hell are you doing?"

His eyes were too narrow and his teeth too sharp, as though he had been about to wolf out. "I can't watch this. They were here in peace."

"Yeah," Xander whispered, staring at him. "Tonight. Most nights they'd be cutting us up into little bitty pieces. Human tartare. I don't like watching it, but you can't get in the way. You're one of them, remember? You're not human. These guys aren't playing."

Oz hesitated, and in that moment of silence between them, Xander realized that the screaming had stopped. There were no more roars or snarls or curses uttered in guttural demon tongues, no shrieks of fear or agony.

Only the two of them were behind the crypt, but Xander could hear the breathing of a third person.

"Crap. He's right above us, isn't he?"

Oz glanced up with remarkable nonchalance. "Yeah. Guy with a beard. All bloody. Sword."

Xander could smell it now, the stink of the blood of a dozen different breeds of monster and demon. Something dripped onto his shoulder and he wished he could make himself believe a pigeon had just anointed him.

Oz grabbed his shirt and jumped away from their spot behind the crypt, practically dragging Xander across the ground, a reminder of the strength of the werewolf. The blood-soaked warrior, whose beard was only thick, dark stubble, dropped from the roof of the crypt.

"Pitiful!" the swordsman snarled, advancing on them, though he kept his sword point lowered, angled out to one side. "Look at the two of you, cowering back here! What is wrong with you? Those maggots were tainting this holy ground with their presence, with their pestilence, and you do nothing? You simply stand idle while evil is at hand? You disgust me!"

Xander scrambled to his feet, shook loose from Oz, and took a step toward the swordsman.

"Hey, back off, Jack Sparrow. You think you're something special, slaughtering a bunch of dumb monkeys who aren't supposed to fight back?"

He glanced at the ledge of the crypt's roof, where he'd left his dagger. The swordsman flung it at him, sheath and all, and the knife thunked to the dirt. The message was clear. Xander could pull the dagger if he wanted to, but sword boy felt pretty confident it wouldn't do him any good.

The huge, broad-shouldered monster hunter came out of the trees to the left of the crypt. The little man and the gorgeous redhead marched around from the other side, where they'd scattered the pieces of two dozen night beasts across the cemetery grounds.

Oz growled.

Xander shot a quick glance at him and knew it was time to get out of the way. Oz didn't stand a chance against all four of them— not after what Xander had just seen them do—but he had better odds than a one-eyed, unarmed man. Oz began to change. Fur sprouted on his flesh and his bones cracked and popped as they reasserted themselves. Fangs lengthened as his jaws extended.

The werewolf stood hunched over, halted halfway between man and wolf.

The towering Asian man rushed toward Oz, hatred etched upon his features. He reached around behind his back and drew a long dagger that seemed almost blue in the moonlight, but Xander knew from the glint of intent in the silent man's eyes that the blade was silver.

"Tai!" snapped the bearded swordsman. "No!"

The silent warrior froze. His chest rose and fell in deep breaths and his eyes gleamed with malignance.

The little man laughed softly.

"He dislikes loup-garou," said the woman, her accent French, her voice as sultry as her form. Xander would have found her a great distraction if his life weren't in peril.

"Tai," the swordsman said, the name now inflected with warning. "You cannot. This one is allied with the deathless Slayer. He is a hero, just as we are."

As we are. Xander stared at him for a second, doubting anyone so bloodthirsty could have pure motives, but in the man's eyes he saw only grim purpose and perhaps nobility. These people were monster hunters. Hard as it was to accept after the massacre he had just witnessed, it was obvious that they did think of themselves as heroes, and on most days that might well be true.

With a deep exhalation, the silent man sheathed his silver dagger. Tai might not like werewolves, and might be even less fond of the idea that he and Oz were on the same side of the war against the darkness, but he backed away from them.

With a soft growl, Oz shapeshifted, resuming his human form.

"You have a name?" Xander asked, focusing on the swordsman, who was obviously the leader.

"Malik," the swordsman replied with a nod of his head. "Tell the Slayer—the Summers woman—that we will speak soon about what must be done."

"Yeah. I'll pass that along," Xander said.

Malik scabbarded his sword and turned away. He and Tai and the other two—the redhead and the little man—merged with the shadows and slipped away into the darkness, almost as though they themselves were wraiths.

"Well," Xander said after a long moment had passed, "that was interesting. Most places you'd have to pay good money for that kind of entertainment."

Oz glanced at him. The edges of his mouth twitched up in the hint of a polite smile and then he started back the way they'd come. Xander followed. Scaling the fence around the cemetery did not get easier the more frequently he did it, but Xander found it did become more annoying. He hoped never to have to visit Lovecraft's grave again, at least not at night—preferably not during the day, either.

Once again, the car remained where he'd left it in front of the half-finished house. As Xander pulled out of the dirt drive, a man walking a dog shined a flashlight on him. Probably a curious neighbor. Xander was glad to be gone before the guy resorted to calling the police. The dog barked wildly and strained at its leash, but the guy held on tight.

If the dog was barking at Oz, he didn't seem to notice.

They spoke very little on the drive back to the hotel. It was a pattern for them. Xander did not think there was much to be said until they had Buffy and probably Giles in a room. Figuring out who Malik and his buddies were would fall to them. Even so, he replayed the scene of carnage from the cemetery over and over in his mind, searching for any clue to the identity of these newcomers. The one thing he and Oz briefly agreed upon was that Malik and the others seemed human.

All of these thoughts were racing around his mind as Xander pulled the rental car into the garage beneath the hotel. They'd gone down to the third level, and he was scanning for a parking space when Oz stiffened in the seat beside him.

"Back up—fast," Oz said, glancing calmly over his shoulder.

Xander looked in the rearview mirror and knew it was too late to back up. The ramp leading back up to the next level had been blocked by a pack of werewolves.

"I love this city," Xander said. "I'm moving here. Or at least being buried here."

More werewolves slipped out of the shadows between cars. Several leaped up on top of cars and SUVs. Car alarms started going off.

"That's good. People will come."

Oz shot him a look that questioned his intelligence. "That's not good. People come, they get eaten."

"That's bad," Xander replied.

"Thanks for that, Egon." Oz turned to him, one eyebrow arched.

The werewolves began to move in around the car. Xander knew they could tear the doors off easily. Again he glanced in the rearview mirror.

"So do we try ramming them?"

"We won't get far."

"Okay, Mr. Optimism. What's your plan, then?" Xander asked.

The car began to rock slightly from the weight of the werewolves pressing up against it. The air conditioner was running on low, and Xander twisted the knob to shut it off. The stink of musk permeated the inside of the car.

Then the wolves by Oz's window separated to reveal a muscular guy with shaggy blond hair and a scraggly beard. He looked like some kind of cowboy, only without the hat. Xander decided he had seen too many movies.

"Who's this?" Xander asked, voice in a whisper though he knew with their keen hearing, the wolves would catch every word.

Oz frowned. "Just another wolf. Put it in park."

Xander sighed and did as he asked.

Oz rolled down the window. "You guys mind getting out of the way? We're trying to park here."

The shaggy man bent to peer in at Xander, then focused on Oz. "Mr. Osbourne, why haven't you scented us out? You have been here quite long enough to have located any of the packs represented—"

"Pretty sure I mentioned? I'm not part of a pack. You said if I came here, I'd find some answers as to what you're up to. I'm finding them. Figured you'd show up eventually, let me know what you have planned."

The shaggy blond growled in a voice so low that it was almost a purr.

"As I told you in Portland, you have been chosen to be an ambassador of the lycanthropic community—"

"Because I know the Slayer," Oz interrupted.

"That, and because of your discipline. You have reined the beast more successfully than most. It is often said that in politics, cooler heads prevail. We will send two ambassadors. I am the first. I sometimes succumb to my temper. It would be helpful to have you as our second. You agree?"

Oz hesitated.

Xander leaned over and smiled through the open window at the shaggy man. "He'd love to. He's honored. That means you're not eating us, right?"

The shaggy man never took his eyes off of Oz, who finally nodded.

"Good," the other wolfman said. "the Congress begins tomorrow at dusk. Rest—if you can."

Then he shapeshifted, his fur blond but streaked with a rust color. The wolf trotted between two cars and vanished into the shadows, and then the others bolted, running up the ramp to the next level and otherwise disappearing into cars and stairwells.

Xander let out a long breath and put the car in drive, cruising for a parking space. Only when he had shut off the car and stepped out, dropping the keys into his pocket, did he turn and stare at Oz over the roof.

"Well, at least we know when it starts."

Oz nodded. "There's that. It might even help if we had a clue about where the big shindig is supposed to go down."

Xander slapped his forehead with an open palm. "I really don't like this city."

"Maybe it's just politics you don't like."

Tara held Willow's hand as they walked along Prospect Street on College Hill. The neighborhood of antique homes was remarkably well preserved, and with the warm lights on inside and the moon and stars above, there was something incredibly charming about the area. They could have been living quietly in a place like this, away from the bloodshed and the monsters, if fate had been kind to them.

The thought brought a sadness to Tara's heart and she pushed it away. She wouldn't do that to Willow. Surrendering to melancholy would be unfair. Willow squeezed her hand and Tara glanced at her, smiling shyly.

It felt almost as though they had come here only to stroll hand in hand and be in love. Tara would have given anything to make that the truth. Instead, though, they were doing something she would never have imagined in a million years.

Tara and Willow were hunting witches.

Finding them had been remarkably simple. In a city this old, with its Puritan history, there were sure to be witches, and of course there would be witches sent as ambassadors to the Congress. Willow had come up with the idea and Tara thought it perfect. In fact, it was so obvious, Tara wondered why she hadn't come up with it herself. They had used the computer in the hotel's business office to do an online search for tarot readers, magick stores, and occult bookshops in Providence and made a list of the ones that seemed the most, well, sincere. Beginning with Roberta's Bell, Book, and Candle, they'd gone inside and begun looking at books and herbs, talking between themselves, making it obvious that they were witches and in the city for the Congress. At the third stop—the second had been the office of a tarot reader who had gone out of business—they'd been interrupted by an excited fortyish witch who seemed almost giddy with anticipation of the Congress.

Willow had guided the conversation expertly and soon discovered the name and address of the most revered witch in Providence, the leader of a coven respected throughout New England, and whose membership dated back to the Mayflower. Tara had found herself a bit troubled by Willow's talent for deception, even for a good cause. It brought back difficult memories.

Now, though, she refused to dwell.

They enjoyed the summer night and the smell of spicy food cooking in a restaurant they passed. They had done a good deal of walking, but Tara did not feel tired. Instead, she felt energized as they walked up Prospect Street, studying the front of a row of town-houses in search of the home of Margaret Hood.

When they found it, Tara started toward the front door.

Willow tugged her hand back and pulled her in close for a soft kiss. They studied each other's eyes a moment, and Tara blushed at the passion she saw in Willow's gaze, then glanced away and tucked her hair behind her ear. But then Willow kissed her again, and any trace of shyness evaporated. When they broke off the kiss, Tara was breathless.

Hand in hand, they went up the steps of the brownstone and rang the bell. Tara could hear music playing inside, a jazzy little something that reminded her of Madeleine Peyroux. Of course, she hadn't been around for a while, so perhaps it was a brand-new CD from Madeleine. She'd have to check that out.

The bell received no immediate response, so Willow rang it

again. After a few seconds, footsteps could be heard from within, a woman's heels on hardwood floor. They heard the lock being drawn back, and then the door opened inward to reveal a lovely woman of perhaps forty-five with chestnut hair and beautiful skin.

"Yes?" the woman asked, an almost mischievous sparkle in her eyes.

"Are you Margaret Hood?" Willow asked.

"I am, sister," the woman said.

"My name is Willow Rosenberg. This is Tara Maclay." Squeezing her hand, she nodded at Tara. "We were hoping to ask you a few questions about the Dark Congress."

The woman glanced down at their clasped hands, then up at Tara. She smiled kindly.

"That's why we are all here," she said, stepping back from the door to allow them entrance. "Come in. And please, call me Maggie."

"Thank you, M-Maggie," Tara said, surprising herself by stuttering a bit. The woman's presence, the powerful magickal aura surrounding her, was both warm and intimidating at the same time.

The townhouse had been decorated with antiques and fresh flowers, and Tara felt as though they were stepping back in time. Maggie's home was pristine. She could almost believe the witch had lived in this place since the era when the elegant homes of College Hill had been new.

Maggie led them down a short corridor toward an arched doorway. Excited, enthusiastic voices drifted out to them—the voices of women with purpose. Through the archway they found themselves in a living room—Tara wondered if parlor were a more accurate word—that seemed also to have been transported to the present from some bygone era. Women were gathered in the room, sitting on chairs and sofas or standing in front of the windows, some quietly perusing the bookcases. They seemed a wonderful assortment of women, many facets of the feminine, with complexions of various hues, some smooth with youth and some lined with age. Some were dressed with immaculate sophistication, others with a kind of dark wildness that struck Tara as post-post-Goth.

They had only two common elements. Each of those women emanated a sense of confidence, and each of them fairly seethed with magick. This could not be Maggie Hood's coven. It seemed clear that many were from out of town and some were strangers to one another. They had come for the Congress.

"Sisters," Maggie said, entering the room, "we have new arrivals."

The witches all turned at the sound of her voice, and that was when Tara and Willow noticed the silver-haired woman in the shadows by the bookshelf at the back of the parlor.

"Catherine?" Willow asked.

There could be no mistaking her. Catherine Cadiere had an ageless radiance and emanated magick more powerful even than Maggie Hood's.

"You know each other?" Maggie asked, a flicker of confusion upon her face.

"We do," Catherine replied, glancing around at the others. "Sisters, meet my apprentice, Willow Rosenberg. Her lover is called Tara."

One of the witches—a slender, twentyish girl with Romanesque features and purple hair—studied Tara closely.

"But she's a cat," the purple-haired girl said.

A shudder went through Tara. She felt the feline in herself, knew that she could transform at any moment, but most of the time she tried not to think about what Catherine Cadiere's magick had made her, or the fact that within her soul was the spirit of the cat that had once been Catherine's familiar, just as Tara now was Willow's.

"She's a witch," Catherine said, "but also a witch's familiar."

A ripple of unease went through the room. At first Tara did not understand and thought they did not want her there. But when she glanced at Maggie Hood and saw the way she eyed Catherine, she realized that the other witches were troubled by the spellcraft involved. Tara wondered if they were wary or simply jealous.

"Well," Maggie said, "both of you please come in." She gestured for them to join the group. "I don't recall Catherine's ever taking an apprentice before, Willow. You must be something special."

"Oh, she is," Tara said, almost defensively. Sometimes she found it difficult to stand up for herself, but championing Willow felt as natural as drawing breath.

Whatever conversation had been going on when they arrived was dropped. All the focus had turned to Willow and Tara and Catherine.

"She is extraordinary," Catherine agreed. "I had only just begun to mentor her when the Congress was announced. In truth, I'd left them both in Greece and had not expected to encounter them here." She glanced at Willow. "But you're quite enterprising, aren't you, darling?"

Tara flinched at "darling." It might have been an old-fashioned term of endearment, a somewhat belittling, diminishing word, as though Catherine spoke to a child, or it might have suggested something else. Before she could decide which, Willow had begun to reply.

"Always have been. It's a big part of my charm."

The women laughed politely.

"Willow tells me they have some questions about the Dark Congress," Maggie announced.

Catherine smiled. "Of course they do—and about Kandida, I suppose."

All of the witches seemed to warm to her instantly at the mention of Kandida.

"Come in and join us," Catherine said. "And we shall speak of many things."

Room was made on a sofa for Willow and Tara to sit together. A tray of grapes, cheese, and crackers was on the coffee table, but Tara could not bring herself even to nibble. When wine was offered to them, she took a glass only to avoid being perceived as rude to their hostess.

Maggie Hood began by telling them the tale of Kandida and Trajabo, most of which Tara and Willow already knew. It diverged from the version Giles had told them only in that it was more elaborate and filled with examples of the great wisdom of Kandida as a member of the Dark Congress. She might have been a river demon who preyed on humans, including children, but the witches seemed willing to overlook that fact due to her diplomatic acumen. Tara thought it seemed quite like human politics.

"Kandida's return could mean a great peace unlike anything this world has ever known," Catherine said, picking up where Maggie had left off. "Or it could be the harbinger of the destruction of humanity."

"Kind of a big variable there, don'tcha think?" Willow said.

Catherine smiled. "Resurrection is never simple."

She did not so much as glance at Tara, but she may as well have.

"It would have been better, I suspect, for Kandida to remain imprisoned in the riverbank for eternity. With the Congress shattered and the creatures of darkness set against one another, they were disorganized. But her return has convinced both her betrayers and her allies to convene, which means there will be debate, and there will be voting."

The purple-haired girl, whose name turned out to be Alice, chimed in.

"Many demon tribes want to live peacefully among humans. Others want to return to their own, dark dimensions."

"Yes," Catherine said, hushing the girl with a look. "But there are those who want to tear the world apart—to remake it in their image, or to destroy it entirely. Those who desire the latter, of course, want it for themselves, not to share with the others."

"Yet Kandida is a powerful orator, loved and respected for her wisdom and ferocity by those ancient enough to have known her then," Maggie Hood went on. "If she can gather the ambassadors together and broker a treaty, she can guide the Dark Congress to peace. The ancient records say she wanted demons to live at peace in the shadows of the human world. If the Congress votes to support her, humanity will be safer than it has been in thousands of years."

"And if they vote against her?" Tara asked, glancing nervously at Willow.

Catherine Cadiere smiled. "If they vote against her, darkness will consume the world, and humanity will be slowly exterminated."

Willow's eyes widened. "Well, she's got my vote."

CHAPTER TEN

The Hotel Kensington had a lounge, but it was mainly a business travelers' hotel, and by Friday night those patrons had usually already left for home or had turned in early so they could get up and catch a plane. The guests who were ordinary tourists had better places to spend Friday night than the lounge in their hotel. Therefore, as midnight approached, the Hotel Kensington's lounge would normally be empty. The bartender wasn't even on duty anymore, which frustrated Giles, because at the moment a drink would have been more than welcome.

"Obviously, you didn't leave," Giles said, looking at Faith.

Faith scowled and leaned back in her chair, sprawled there in her carefree tough-girl style. "Damn straight. I wasn't going anywhere."

"They've been keeping all the other Slayers out of Providence," Buffy explained. "But they made it a point not to kill any of the girls."

"Yeah. Nice of 'em," Faith muttered.

Buffy glanced at her. "I told Kandida if she wanted to talk to me, Faith was staying. She'd already gotten past their little blockade, and that was that."

Micaela had gotten a scotch and soda before the bartender had disappeared, and she'd been nursing it for an hour. She sipped the melted ice at the bottom of her glass.

"I'm not sure I understand," she said, setting down the now-empty tumbler. "We wanted to find her. Yet you essentially told the river goddess you weren't interested in talking to her? Couldn't Faith have gone back into the bar for a few minutes or something?"

Faith shot her a dark look and seemed about to say something regrettable, so Giles stepped in.

"I'm sure Buffy simply read the situation," he said. "That's always been one of her strong suits."

"That's me," Buffy agreed. "But yeah, it was pretty obvious Kandida wanted to talk to me as much as I wanted answers from her. Trajabo didn't say a word. All we heard from him was that creepy noise of the sand blowing across the road."

Xander coughed to clear his throat. "Okay, we get it. They let Faith stick around. Can we fast-forward to what the Wonder Twins actually said?"

He and Oz were leaning against the bar. Willow and Tara were sitting together on a cushioned bench that ran along the opposite wall, with Faith, Buffy, Giles, and Micaela seated in chairs around two small lounge tables. They had all gathered within the past hour, trickling in two at a time, each with their own stories of the evening's events. They had already detailed their particular adventures, including Xander's troubling account of the encounter with Malik and his companions. Micaela planned to begin researching Malik that very night.

Giles had asked Buffy to wait until the others had already spoken so they could all have a clear picture of what they were dealing with, and so pertinent details would not be lost in the shadow of the interest they all shared in the appearance of Kandida and Trajabo.

Buffy had turned her chair around and crossed her arms over the back. "Kandida told us that the Congress starts tomorrow night at dusk, but you guys have all confirmed that—Oz with the mysterious wolf guy, and Willow and Tara with this Cadiere witch."

She glanced at Willow when she said the last part and Giles saw something pass between them. Evidently, Buffy was not convinced of the benevolence of Catherine Cadiere any more than Giles himself was. He found that a comfort. And if Willow noticed the extra emphasis that Buffy put on the word 'witch,' she did not protest.

"Thing is, according to Kandida, the Congress can't start until they've appointed an arbiter," Buffy went on.

"Which is what again?" Xander asked.

"Like a referee," Willow explained. "Someone to settle conflicts peacefully."

Faith snickered. "Yep. And they want Summers to do the job. She'd have been my first choice too. Settling conflicts without resorting to violence. That's B, all right."

Buffy rolled her eyes. "Pot, kettle, yadda yadda. But Faith's right. They want me to do the job."

"For God's sake, why?" Giles asked.

"Thanks for the vote of confidence."

"No, Rupert, think about it," Micaela said. "The choice makes perfect sense. Inevitably, there are going to be arguments that could turn the Congress into anarchy. If they all agree to abide by an arbitrator's decisions, they'd have to have someone of a supernatural nature, who understands but is not afraid—someone who could impose order but whom all of the members of the Congress could agree is not beholden to any of them. The Slayer is the only logical choice."

Buffy sat up straight. "Time out. I didn't say I wanted the job. And anyway, I'm not the only Slayer around these days, remember.

There are plenty of us to choose from, but they're keeping everyone else out. So why me?"

Oz didn't even look up when he spoke. "Because you're special."

"Aren't I?" Buffy said, framing her face with her hands. "Seriously, though."

"I'm not serious?" Oz said, turning toward them all. He'd been creating some kind of architectural structure on the bar using plastic stirring straws, which now collapsed. "The wolf who tracked me down—the other ambassador, I guess—he called you the 'deathless Slayer.' This isn't exactly a surprise. You're not like the other girls, Buffy."

He concluded with a slight raising of the eyebrows that in someone else would have been a wry grin.

Tara laughed softly.

"All right," Giles said, "you're to be the arbiter. They've banned all other Slayers from the city for the duration of the Congress—"

"Except Faith," Buffy cut in. "She gets a special exemption."

"Oooh, and a gold star," the dark-haired Slayer said, upper lip curling. "I had to make a vow not to interfere—cross my heart and hope to die, that sort of thing."

"If any of the other Slayers even try to get in, Kandida says her enemies will use it as an excuse to claim that the truce of the Dark Congress has been broken," Buffy said. "Could lead to all-out war among the night tribes, destruction of humanity as we know it, all the good apocalypse-type stuff."

Faith sat up and looked around, spread her arms to include them all. "Meanwhile, the rest of us have been given a job to do— our own little assignment."

"Which is?" Xander asked.

"The vamps aren't invited either," Faith said. "No surprise, right? We'd kinda sussed that out already. But the demons and monsters and the old gods or whatever, they think of the vamps as second-class citizens. No vampires allowed. Naturally this pisses the leeches off. It's our job to track down any vamps who've slipped in and get them out of town."

"Who the hell do these two demons think they are?" Willow asked. "Giving us assignments."

Faith shrugged and leaned back in her chair. "Doesn't matter to me. I came here in the first place because of de Tournefort and Haarmann. You're talking some seriously ancient bloodsuckers. I'm happy to take 'em off the map."

"Not sure that's a solution," Buffy said.

"What's troubling you?" Giles asked.

Buffy reached up and pulled out the rubber band that had been holding her ponytail in place, then shook out her hair. "You mean other than everything? Pretty much everything else. But here's my question: Why do they even want a Slayer around? Why invite me? Okay, yeah, dark origins and supernatural powers, but it's not like I'm a demon. I've spent plenty of time skinny-dipping in the lake of evil, but, hello? Still not evil."

"Slayers have wallowed in darkness for centuries, but only rarely succumb to it," Giles replied.

"That's a comfort. Thanks," Buffy said. "But okay, putting aside what this does to my self-image, how do we agree to a truce with pretty much all the evil in the world, just let them get together in this city like comic book geeks swarming San Diego? Shouldn't we at least try to take advantage of this? Take them down?"

"How?" Xander said. "You going to nuke Providence?"

"It's a thought," Faith muttered.

"You can't!" Tara said.

They all looked at her. Giles smiled. Ever the gentle one.

"There are all kinds of demons that aren't evil. You know that. Never mind witches and werewolves," she said, putting up her hand, "right here."

"Okay," Buffy said, "nukes are out. But shouldn't we do something?"

Tired and frustrated, Giles removed his glasses and let them dangle from his fingers.

"I'm afraid there's little we can do. If we try to bring in reinforcements, chaos will result. And even with all the new Slayers you have gathered and begun to train, the odds would be against us. We would be in the midst of a civil war with dozens, if not hundreds, of different factions all fighting against one another. And there is the population of Providence to consider. The truce that is part of the Dark Congress has forestalled any bloodshed thus far, but there would be death on a massive scale, not only in this city, but across the state as the battle spread.

"No, the Dark Congress will happen. We must cooperate, at least for the moment, and pray that the outcome does not put humanity in jeopardy. If we're very fortunate, Kandida's wisdom will influence the Congress to a decision that will lead to security for the Earth and the human race, rather than devastation."

Silence followed his words as the gravity of their situation truly set in.

Strangely, Oz was the first to speak.

"Wow. When you say it, things almost seem bleak."

Two hours later, Faith crouched in the darkness behind an enormous, rusty blue Dumpster while Oz quietly scaled the chain link fence behind her. Xander hadn't been so stealthy coming over the fence, but he'd done all right—better than she would have expected. The Miquot—Ryvak—came last and was the quietest of all. Oz and the Miquot took up position behind a massive yellow backhoe loader, a piece of construction equipment that in this case had been brought in for destruction.

"School's out," Xander whispered beside her.

Faith did not look at him. "I'm guessin' it's been out for a while."

The John J. Harrod Elementary School had been closed down for some time if its appearance was any indicator. Weeds grew up through cracks in the parking lot and many windows had been broken and then boarded up.

It was just the kind of place vampires loved to nest.

"You buying this?" she asked, glancing back at Xander. She didn't like to look directly at him. The eye patch bothered her, which was weird, because Faith had never been squeamish. Maybe it was because of all of them, Xander was the one she always thought would stay free of the taint of darkness that had touched everyone else.

"Why not?" he replied. "Yeah, the Miquot could be running a game, if he's one of Kandida's enemies. But you said he was part of the group that ran the vampires off earlier tonight. Whatever his politics, he's obviously on board with the whole no-vampires-allowed thing."

Faith nodded. That had been precisely her thinking, and it was why she had brought Oz and Xander back to the Irish pub where she and Buffy had run into vamps earlier in the evening. Dunphy's—as the place was called—had been closing up when they arrived, but a few stragglers had waited out last call, and they caught up with the Miquot as he left the pub. A little buzzed, but far from drunk, Ryvak had been more than willing to help. When he found out they'd been in touch with Kandida, he had even apologized for being so short with the Slayers earlier.

The apology seemed a little much to Faith, but she was just going to have to accept it. All she wanted from Ryvak was for him to walk her through the demon skirmish with the vampires earlier that night. But once they started following the trail of the vamps who'd fled from the attacking demons, it had been simple enough for Oz to track them. The enhanced senses of a werewolf came in handy—especially the ability to follow a scent—but Faith wouldn't have wanted them. Living with the stink of people and their cities would drive her insane.

Oz's sniffer had led them to the school. She glanced over at him now and the little guy gave her a thumbs-up. The scent was strong here.

"You ready?" she asked Xander.

He had a fire ax that they'd taken from the hotel, and a couple of stakes as backup tucked into his belt, one at each hip.

"Would've been nice to have Willow and Tara along. A little mojo wouldn't hurt, especially if those master vamps you keep talking about are inside."

"Nah," Faith said. "De Tournefort and Haarmann have lived this long because they're not brave or stupid enough to hang out with the minions. The ancient ones always hide away until they're ready to strike. Besides, I think Willow and Tara could use a little postresurrection down time. This is nothing we can't handle."

Xander frowned. "We could all use a little down time. I don't get why they—" He stopped and his eyes widened. "Ooh. Right. Never mind."

"So, ready?" Faith asked.

"I'm never ready. But I'm dumb enough that it doesn't stop me," Xander replied, almost proud.

Faith raised a hand and signaled to Oz and Ryvak. The Miquot went first. Oz ran after him, not changing yet so that the vampires wouldn't catch the werewolf scent, which would be much stronger when he went all furry. Xander and Faith came out from behind the Dumpster, and then all four of them were rushing the front of the school.

Faith hit the front steps at the same moment as Ryvak. She sprinted to the top and shot a side kick at the double doors, right between the handles. Wood splintered, metal tore, something cracked, and the lock gave way along with the chain that had held the doors closed from the other side.

The Miquot did not even wait for her. He was through the doors before they finished swinging open, plucking a bony blade from the flesh of his left arm. There were three vampires on guard just inside the doors, and Ryvak took one down with a blade to the eye almost immediately. The vampire screamed and fell. The other two moved to stop him from attacking, but Faith arrived at the same moment. She snatched a leech up in her left hand and plunged a stake into his heart. The vampire exploded in a cloud of dust that swirled in the wind blowing through the open doors and skittered across the floor.

Ryvak grappled with the third vampire as Faith staked the one who lay on the ground screaming about his punctured eyeball. Then the Miquot tore one of the posts from the banister and rammed its splintered end through the heart of the vampire attacking him, and the guards were gone in a gust of summer wind.

The doors lay open to the night, the breeze, and the starlight, but Oz came through the window instead. Glass and the boards that had been put over the window to ward off vandals and local kids shattered as the werewolf crashed into the school. Whoever put up the boards hadn't counted on monsters. Through the open door of the empty classroom to their left, Faith saw that Oz had shed his human skin and gone full-on wolf. With a snarl, he lunged at something in the shadows of the dark room. Vampires swore and attacked the werewolf. Faith could hear bones cracking. Oz would be fine.

Footsteps trammeled on the floorboards above them and Faith looked up to see four or five vamps starting down a nearby staircase. Two of them looked hideous the way that old vampires often did, some of their demon essence showing through the human shell they wore. The other three were young females, beautiful and fit. Vampires only recruited the fit and the beautiful.

The first vamp down the stairs had a killer body and dressed like a truck-stop hooker. Whatever beauty she'd had went away the second her face morphed into the true countenance of the vampire, the beast within. She drew back her fangs and leaped from the fifth step, swift enough that Faith couldn't get her stake up in time.

They went down hard on the wood floor, rolling. Faith used the momentum against the vampire, twisting her as they rolled, and shattered her skull against an iron radiator in the foyer. Staking the girl was just an afterthought, and she was up and moving away before the dust of the vampire's remains had settled to the floor.

Ryvak had another vamp on the ground. The Miquot was using a jagged, bony blade taken from his arm to raggedly and messily decapitate the vampire, even as two others pulled at him. One tried to sink its fangs into his throat, but Ryvak twisted around and plunged the blade into its heart, then easily plucked another from his own arm.

Neither of them was dead yet, so Faith moved in to help.

Then she heard Xander shouting from the back of the school, and swore under her breath. They'd agreed that he would watch the back door for any vampires who tried to take off, but no matter what war wounds he carried, there were only so many bloodsuckers an ordinary guy could take on.

"You got this?" she asked the Miquot.

"Go," he said.

Faith met Oz in the hallway. The werewolf crashed through a second classroom door, slid on the wooden floor, claws digging up the boards, and careened into the wall. He spun, snarling at her, yellow eyes gleaming in the dark. But then his nostrils flared as he scented her, and he turned to race down the hall toward Xander's shouts for help. How many vampires the wolf had killed, she didn't know, but there were bloody gashes on his back and spots of blood on his fur.

They hit a T junction intersecting the main hallway with a corridor that ran the length of the back of the school. To the right hung open a metal door that Faith assumed led to the basement and the boiler room, precisely where the vamps would've slept during the day. Even as she glanced that way, several came up from below.

Oz took down the first one, driving the vampire to the floor. The werewolf bit its head off and the husk of the body burst into a shower of burning ash. Oz coughed, then sneezed. His huge, lupine body shuddered like a dog shaking off a bath, and then he stood on his hind legs and fell on a second vampire, tearing into it.

Faith dusted the third one.

Xander shouted again from the back of the school. Faith left Oz to deal with the last vampire and ran down the hall in search of the door. She felt the warm August breeze moments before she saw the metal emergency doors that led out into the school yard. One of them hung askew on its hinges, the other still locked.

Faith found Xander in the school yard surrounded by half a dozen vampires. Even as she emerged from the school, the grim-faced Xander swung the fire ax he'd stolen at the nearest vamp, a tall, muscle-bound thug. The movement was so abrupt and unpredictable that the vampire wasn't ready for it. He tried to get his hands up to block, but only succeeded in losing two fingers as the ax blade struck true, lopping off the vamp's head as easy as Xander might have split logs in his backyard.

Oz bounded out the emergency door behind Faith, corded muscles rippling under his fur as he stalked his prey.

"About time. I was starting to think you weren't coming," Xander said.

"We had to clear a path," Faith told him. "Didn't figure so many of 'em would run for it."

"Our reputation precedes us," Xander replied.

One of the vampires lunged at him, but Xander buried the ax in its chest and whipped out one of the stakes he was carrying. Faith and Oz moved in. There were five vampires remaining against the three of them—bad odds for the vampires.

"Keep one alive," Faith said.

Xander sighed. "You ruin all my fun."

A couple of minutes later, the final vampire lay on his back on the ground with Faith kneeling on his chest and Oz growling, slavering jaws only inches from the vampire's head.

"Christabel de Tournefort," Faith said, leaning toward the vamp, a slim male with ragged blond hair and long sideburns, like some kind of grunge rocker who didn't know the nineties were over. Her hair brushed his face as though he were a lover and not an enemy. "Tell me where she is, and you can run."

The vampire's face reverted to its mask of human smoothness and its golden eyes returned to normal. "I . . . I don't know. No one knows except her personal guard. Even if I did, it wouldn't be worth my life. What she'd do to me . . ."

The vampire averted his gaze, expecting the stake to come down, crack his rib cage, and pierce his heart.

The Miquot came out of the school.

"All clear?" Faith asked him.

Ryvak nodded. "All those inside have been destroyed. He is the last."

"Good." Faith stood up and gestured for the vampire to do the same. The vampire rose, glancing around at them with a curious caution. Oz snarled, but did not attack.

"You're letting me go?"

Faith smiled. "With a message. Tell Christabel and Haarmann that they're to stay out of Providence. No vamps allowed. If one of you fang boys gets caught within the city limits—or I hear about you hunting outside of town—you're all dust."

The vampire sneered, then caught himself and gave her a wary, apologetic look. "She won't listen."

"Then all we're giving you here is a head start," Xander said. "But deliver the message."

He stepped away from them carefully, taking a few slow, deliberate paces toward the drive that led out to the front of the school and the road beyond. When he truly believed that they were not going to follow, the vampire ran.

Only when Faith had thanked the Miquot and Ryvak had departed, leaving the three of them alone in the school yard, did Xander speak again.

"This feels pretty strange, don't you think?" he asked.

"What? Playing enforcer for a bunch of monsters?" Faith said. "Yeah. Freakin' peculiar. The only upside is that I know Christabel's not going to listen to threats from us. She'll be getting into the mix, which means I still get a chance to kill her."

Faith turned to Xander and Oz, enjoying their confusion.

"Hey," she said, "a girl's gotta have her priorities straight."

Buffy didn't mind running errands once in a while. It gave her a chance to get away from the others, clear her head. The coffee in the hotel sucked badly, so she had offered to run out to get caffeine for everyone and some doughnuts for Xander. You could take the boy out of Sunnydale, but you could never take the Sunnydale out of the boy . . . or something like that.

Saturday had started off warm and had only gotten hotter. It hadn't been this steamy since the day Buffy and Xander had nearly been scoured by the sandstorm on Benefit Street. They had been fortunate with the weather. Not today.

Of course, Buffy had only Giles's word on how the day had started. She hadn't crashed until nearly dawn and had slept until almost eleven o'clock in her air-conditioned room at the Hotel Kensington. Giles and Micaela were already starting to talk about lunch and Willow and Tara were on board with the idea, but at noon Buffy and the others were just getting their heads on straight, and a caffeine dose was required.

The hot as hell August day meant *iced* coffee, though. She carried a stack of two trays, eight drinks all together, ice sloshing in the Dunkin' Donuts cups. The bag of doughnuts was clutched in her right hand and dangled under the coffee trays.

It felt odd to have nothing to do, but unless some kind of chaos broke out before nightfall, Buffy would not be needed until dusk, when the Dark Congress began. Giles and Micaela had found a record of a small Hellmouth opening beneath the State House up on Smith Hill, the domed landmark right in the middle of the city, so the mystery of where the gathering would take place had been solved. Faith and the others had rousted the vampires last night, the demons were still not harming the residents of Providence, and the magick that kept them from being seen had held up.

The calm before the storm, she thought as she balanced the trays of iced coffee against her. Then she admonished herself. There was no way for her to know what would happen. It might all go perfectly.

Unfortunately, Buffy could not believe that it would. Her own experience told her otherwise. But they had to try.

Two blocks from the hotel she came to an intersection heavy with traffic. The pedestrian light glowed red, and cars and trucks rumbled by. She waited at the curb for the little walking man to light up so that she could cross the street.

A man stood on the opposite corner, watching her with interest. Buffy sized him up instantly. Tall and strong, dressed in a white button-down shirt and black pants—clothes crisp and new—he stood out among the more casual pedestrians waiting to cross the street. His dark hair seemed a bit wild, swept back from his face European-style, and his thin scruff of beard gave him a roguish air.

She couldn't take her eyes off him.

"Excuse me," someone said irritably from behind her, and Buffy realized that the walk signal had changed.

As she stepped off the sidewalk, a broken curbstone shifted underfoot and she stumbled. Carefully, she kept her grip on the trays of iced coffee, glancing away from the man for a moment. When she looked back up she saw that he had not moved from his spot on the other corner, almost as though he was waiting for her.

Then she knew. Xander had described him well enough.

Malik.

He had a smoldering, dark, broody look that reminded her of Angel—or of how she imagined Angel must have been in the old days back in Europe when he'd been the evil Angelus.

Enough of that, she thought, her brain going in all the wrong directions.

Buffy ignored Malik and walked right past him. The hotel was a block and a half away. The tall man caught up with her in just a few strides.

"You cannot walk away, Miss Summers. I saw the recognition in your eyes. You know who I am."

"Kinda looks like I'm walking away," she said.

Malik grabbed her arm. Buffy swayed toward him to keep from dumping all eight coffees onto the sidewalk and then twisted around to face him.

"You make me drop these coffees, I swear you'll sing soprano the rest of your life."

He held up his hands. "It is not my desire to fight you. The Powers would not approve. In any case, I believe we are here with a shared purpose."

Buffy frowned. The Powers? As in the Powers That Be, the cosmic sentience that had manipulated her life and the lives of so many others? The Powers might have chosen Champions—the way they had chosen Angel—to fight in the war against the darkness, but their methods left something to be desired. Cosmic sentience made for poor people skills.

A light switch clicked on in her head.

"Wait, you're saying you're a Champion?"

Malik opened his hands as though in surrender, and he smiled. "Of course. Surely you didn't think we were some band of marauders who hunted monsters for our pleasure, like some perverse big-game hunters?"

Buffy arched an eyebrow. The thought had occurred to her. But this made much more sense. Xander and Oz had described the way that Malik and his motley band of companions had fought, and she had felt sure that they had supernatural abilities, or at least some kind of enhancements. They weren't ordinary humans, that was certain.

"All right. Let's say I believe you," she said, moving in closer to the office building to get out of the way of the pedestrians passing by. Malik moved with her.

"You said you think we have the same mission, or whatever. Gotta say, I don't see it. I heard about the way you slaughtered those demons last night. I've never gotten my jollies out of being the Slayer—all right, maybe 'never' is a strong word, but you get the point. Sounds to me like you and your buddies were having way too much fun. That's not the way I operate. Never mind the fact that you could have started something that would have broken up the Congress, and nobody wins in that scenario."

Malik's expression darkened. It only made him sexier, as far as she was concerned. She wished he weren't such a hottie. Made it hard to focus.

"I don't understand. You intend to let the Dark Congress proceed unopposed? The Powers have sent my allies and me to destroy the Congress. It must be done."

Buffy shook her head. "The Powers can get another puppet. They just like messing with our heads. Think about it. We don't have the firepower to take on all the demons in Providence, not even with you and your band of Merry Men. Too many innocents will die—"

Anger flickered across Malik's face and his eyes widened. His nostrils flared as he moved in closer, trying to intimidate her physically.

"And how many innocents will die for every creature you allow to escape? This is an opportunity for extermination that has not come along in hundreds of years. Only a coward would not take advantage of it."

Buffy narrowed her gaze. She didn't like to be crowded and she sure as hell didn't like being called a coward.

"You want to watch your tone with me, Boy Wonder. In fact, you should walk away now. I'm not with you on this, and I'm not taking orders from the Powers. I'll take that a little further. I don't trust the Powers, but even if I did, I've only got your word that you're here working for them."

Malik went very still, his expression flat. "You think I speak lies? I was born more than eight hundred years ago, in Turkey. For centuries I have served the Powers, seen the way the world changes depending upon which people take their advice and which do not.

"You are a fool," he said. Then he seemed to remember who and where he was and he stepped back, reining in his temper. Malik bowed to her. "Should you regain your senses, we stand ready to aid you in this crisis."

Buffy stared at him, trying to remember why it was she had felt so attracted to him. Just then, thinking about the slaughter of the night before, the man only looked ugly. Malik and the other Champions he traveled with had not bothered to sort out which of the demons at Lovecraft's grave might be allies instead of enemies. Clearly, to Malik there was no difference.

The urge to dump all the coffee she was carrying on him was suddenly very strong. Had it been hot, she might have done it. But iced coffee didn't have the same effect.

"Stay out of it, Malik. The Powers are manipulative as hell, but they ought to know better than to light the fuse on a powder keg like this. If you try to interfere or attack the Congress in any way, then it's gonna be me you have to kill next."

Malik seemed to contemplate that a few moments longer than Buffy would have liked. "I will consult the Powers. You have my allegiance, as Slayer, and I would not like to be your enemy. Perhaps your involvement is enough to control the tide of fate here, and the Powers will alter their instructions. I will hope that is the outcome. Any other would be tragic."

Without another word, he withdrew, turning and heading off along a side street and eventually vanishing in a group of people at the next intersection.

The ice was melting in the plastic cups. Buffy turned and started again for the hotel, but her thoughts lingered on the smoldering, arrogant Malik. With all the monsters running around Providence, and the vampires already causing trouble, a bunch of zealots for the Powers That Be were the last thing she needed.

CHAPTER ELEVEN

The white marble building atop Smith Hill had been completed in 1901, designed by the architectural firm of McKim, Mead, and White to be the Rhode Island State House. As in many such buildings, the two wings were a natural split between the legislative branches, with the senate chamber and offices in one wing and the house chamber and offices located in the other. In front of the domed structure between the two wings, the architects had placed an entrance rotunda complete with stone staircases grand enough to represent the high ideals of government.

In the history of that august structure, certain events had been actively forgotten. Nowhere within any official record would one find reference to those few months when a Hellmouth opened beneath it, closing only with the death of Lovecraft on March 15, 1937. Coincidence was possible, of course, but unlikely.

As he entered the rotunda and looked around at the marble and the pillared porticoes, Oz wondered if the Hellmouth had been sealed by Lovecraft's death—if he'd somehow been connected to its opening in the first place—or if he had died as a result of his closing it.

That stray thought fled and was instantly forgotten as he glanced around the rotunda. Just inside the entrance and thronging the stairs, flowing up and to the right, apparently into one of the legislative chambers, were more breeds of nightmare than he had ever imagined existed in all the world. Of course, he was only a werewolf, not a Slayer or a Watcher. Even Xander and Willow, with their long association with Buffy, would have been able to identify dozens of the creatures he saw. To Oz, however, they were only a rippling ocean of monstrosity and horror.

There were shambling things that left wet, sticky trails on the marble, humanoid demons of many varieties, things with tentacles or horns or vast, gaping mouths full of hooked teeth. But there were many things other than demons as well. There were childhood bogeymen and creatures of myth, cadaverous ghouls and grinning phantoms and thick-headed ogres. There were tall, elegant creatures so breathtaking in their beauty that they had to be among the deadliest of those gathered, and figures so cold and dark and ominous that merely glancing at them was enough to make Oz shudder with uncharacteristic fear. There were old gods, practically wraiths, from a dozen pantheons, now long forgotten.

There were no vampires, of course.

And there were no weapons allowed.

Oz had thought that part a bit ridiculous. Most of these creatures were living weapons, himself included. And that was the thought that had been resonating in his mind ever since Xander had parked the car in front of the State House. They had picked up a second rental during the day and the eight of them—Giles and Micaela, Buffy and Faith, Willow and Tara, and Xander and Oz—had found parking spots a couple of blocks away, an hour before dusk.

The horrors had already gathered around the building. There

should have been humans as well, both on the streets and milling around the State House, going about their business. But either through magick or intimidation, they had been kept away. With all of the cars parked on the street, he imagined that some of the offices were occupied by men and women who were either oblivious and kept that way via magick or terrified and hiding under their desks. However they'd arranged it, representatives of the Dark Congress would have the State House to themselves.

Buffy had exchanged some final words with each of her friends, particularly to wish Oz good luck and remind Faith that she wasn't to enter the building under any circumstances unless she wanted to start a supernatural cataclysm. Faith made her usual protests, sneers, and curses, but it seemed clear to Oz that she had matured over the years. She would not risk the world for her own pride.

When it seemed clear she could think of no other reason to procrastinate, Buffy went into the building. The nightmares moved out of her way, creating a passage for her to go up the stairs and through the massive doors into the rotunda. Oz, on the other hand, had waited dutifully, certain there would be some kind of announcement. The others had waited with him, but no one spoke much. They all seemed to hold their breath. The stakes had been high in other cases they'd dealt with, but never had any of them been so completely immersed in the world of demons, of monsters, and of darkness.

Willow and Tara had not clung to each other physically, but both of the witches continued to return to the other for reassurance, unconsciously touching hands or brushing shoulders or simply exchanging looks. Oz would always have love in his heart for Willow. Once upon a time she had meant the world to him. But he had no regrets. All he wanted for them now was happiness.

At last a signal was given, and then the monsters began to flow up the steps. He nodded good-bye to his companions. Giles muttered some final advice but Oz barely heard him. The fact of his participation hung over him as a heavy shadow. Buffy had balked at her own inclusion—a Slayer had powers whose origins were tainted with darkness, but she was no monster.

Oz, on the other hand—no one would argue that a werewolf was anything *but* a monster. He perceived himself as a pretty ordinary Joe, a guy who loved his guitar and the rapport of a club gig, who loved pizza and Pop-Tarts and those hazelnut chocolates people tended to give only at Christmastime.

Just a guy.

Now he stood in the rotunda of the Rhode Island State House as ambassador from Werewolf Nation, and through that act alone all of his illusions and rationalizations were stripped away. Standing there was a confession. He wasn't just the guy who loved his guitar—not just some ordinary Joe, quiet most of the time but deftly capable of finding a few right words when the moment called for it.

The horrors flowed around and past him, chittering and muttering and tersely debating as they herded toward the legislative chamber where the very future of humanity would hang in the balance, and Daniel Osbourne was one of them: the Wolf.

Oz could not deny it. He had caged the beast and gained the discipline never to be monstrous, but he was a monster, or they would never have let him through the doors.

"Are you ready, pup?"

The voice seemed a growl in his ear. Oz turned, the hair on the back of his neck standing up, and found the shaggy blond man behind him. The guy seemed like a throwback from another era, some kind of mountain man or grizzled Scottish clansman.

"Pup?" Oz said. "You know how to make friends."

The shaggy man arched an eyebrow. "You prefer your given name?"

"Not really. They call me Oz."

The werewolf nodded. "All right. And I am Sharpe."

"That's your name?" Oz asked.

Sharpe smiled, revealing wicked fangs. "It's what they call me. Shall we go in?"

Without waiting for an answer, he forged ahead into the sea of monsters, and Oz followed.

Giles and Micaela had retreated across the street from the State House. Willow, Tara, Xander, and Faith remained in the midst of the crowd of supernatural creatures that gathered outside the building like Romans waiting for the cardinals to choose a new pope. This seemed ill-advised to Giles, but he knew that his young friends were beyond his influence now. And perhaps their intrepid nature was warranted—for the moment.

"This is unwise," he said, staring at them, standing there in the midst of the demons and dark beasts.

Micaela laughed.

Giles looked at her askance. "What is it that you find amusing about this? About any of it?"

She dipped her chin, blond hair falling down to frame her face, and gazed up at him with her eyes cast deeply in shadow.

"Honestly, Rupert . . . 'unwise'? That's the best you can do? This is potential suicide, not only for Buffy and Oz, but for all of us, as well. So the witches and the others mingle with the horrors. What of it? Nothing will happen to them unless the Congress completely implodes, and if that happens, do you think being across the street is likely to make us somehow safer than they are? If we're worried about that, we should be far, far away from here."

Giles blinked, brows knitting. "I'm not just leaving Buffy and Oz in there—"

"Of course not," Micaela said, lifting her chin so that the moonlight washed over her lovely face. "I'm only pointing out that if the worst happens, we won't have very long for regrets."

He glanced again at the others, across the street at the foot of the steps in front of the State House. Faith fairly shook with energy, her hands clenching and unclenching, stretching her shoulder and neck muscles like a prizefighter just before the bell. Xander kept glancing around at the creatures that surrounded them. Once or twice he held the glare of some demon a few moments longer than necessary, as if to prove he was not afraid. Willow and Tara stood side by side, calmly holding hands. But the demons gave the witches a wide berth, perhaps sensing the power than emanated from them. Not far away there stood a large group of rather ordinary-looking women of various ages. When Willow waved to them, Giles knew they must be the coven and associates of Maggie Hood.

On either side of the State House and behind it, things hung in the sky or lumbered nearby, gigantic creatures whose true visages only appeared when seen peripherally. Giles tried not to look upon them directly, regardless. He knew what their presence meant. If the Congress shattered and went to war, only a fool would think he had any chance of survival. Micaela was right. They would not have long for regrets.

Surprised at the depth of feeling in him, he glanced back at her.

"Given we may not have a moment later . . . I'm glad you're here with me."

"So am I," Micaela said. "No regrets."

On the dome of the State House, Kandida stood and gazed down upon the pilgrims who had made the journey to honor the purpose of the Dark Congress. Thousands had gathered below, and there were several thousand more in and around the city of Providence. She hoped that the name of the city itself stood as a good omen. This world seemed stagnant to her, in its way not very different from the centuries she had lingered in her grave, awaiting the moment when she and Trajabo could be reunited.

But the world had staggered into motion again. the Congress had done that. If she had her way, the humans could continue with the illusion that they controlled this world and this dimension, but there were many, many others. Together, the Congress could create alliances among those dimensions, a confederacy of monsters and myths of the human world with the demons from a hundred hells. The way would be open for so many to return to their own nether realms, and perhaps they would stop encroaching upon one another's territories. Those who wished to live peacefully among the shadows of the human world could do so, and those who had always preyed on humanity would be able to continue, so long as they did not risk exposing the existence of others.

Kandida wished for all of these things, but she had known throughout her life that wishes were not easily fulfilled. Still, Trajabo had wished for her to return to him, and here she was, so perhaps wishes were worthwhile after all. Whatever happened, the important thing was for the Dark Congress to decide together, to work together to determine their fate.

Trajabo caressed her throat with his rough fingers. She turned and gazed into his eyes, which were the indigo of the desert sky at night. In them she saw the depth of his love for her. Had her captivity lasted for an eternity, he would have waited for her.

She dipped her head toward him and their lips brushed. Kandida shivered. As much as she longed for the water, wishing to immerse herself even now in the nearest river, the rasping of the sand on her flesh made her shudder with pleasure.

With a knowing glance, Trajabo gave up the humanoid form he usually wore. On a wind of his own summoning, he stretched himself out and around her, brushing her greenish flesh, the sand whispering against her like the gentle-then-rough clasp of a lover. Kandida let herself relax into the grip of the swirling sand. Oh, how she had missed the passion of his touch, the heat of the desert in his caress, warming her to her cold bones. The wind danced around her. Trajabo moved with her. If he let her go, she would have tumbled from the dome of the building, but he buffeted her with wind and sand.

Kandida moistened her lips with her tongue, a dry rasp in her throat.

"We'd best go inside," an intimate voice said in her ear.

Teasing her, the sandstorm abated. Trajabo took form again, standing beside her. She gave him a look of admonition for arousing her that way and then expecting her to concentrate. The demon of the desert only smiled at her.

"Shall we?" Trajabo asked.

Kandida batted at him playfully. Then the seriousness of the task before them loomed and she sighed.

"Let us descend," she said.

The wind whipped at Trajabo again, seconds of erosion turning him into a churning sandstorm. Somehow without scouring her flesh, he lifted her up with the desert wind and the two of them slipped from the dome of the State House. Trajabo carried them on that wind down to a window in the cupola just below the dome. They had left the window open for just that purpose.

Inside, the sand sifted and became Trajabo once more. He kissed her hand, but now Kandida's mind was elsewhere, already rushing ahead to the challenge ahead of them. Her cold heart thumped in her chest as they wended their way along a back stairwell and then into the corridor that led to the meeting chamber of the State House. Trajabo led her to a small room just off the chamber but away from the hall where some of the ambassadors would no doubt still be lingering.

"Shall I have a look?" he asked.

Kandida nodded, gesturing toward the door that separated the small office from the meeting chamber. "Yes. See which of the newcomers have seated themselves with our enemies—with our betrayers."

Trajabo hesitated. His indigo eyes gazed upon her with profound sadness. It would have been so much simpler for both of them, Kandida knew, if they had never fallen in love. There were demons of desert and ocean out in the meeting chamber, and many others. Deepwater monstrosities and earth diggers, lake serpents and cave trolls. And their tribes, on both sides, and yet Kandida and Trajabo had lost all of their kin when they fell in love. Whoever had been responsible for nearly killing her before—and Trajabo's relations had made certain he thought her dead, had driven him off into the vast desert for centuries until her resurrection had led him back to her—surely were here.

"Any of them could be our enemies," Trajabo reminded her.

Kandida nodded, but made no reply. She could not argue with the truth.

Anxious, she rose and went to peer through the partially open door herself. The voices of the ambassadors were a low, rumbling chatter. The marble floor clacked with the footfalls and hoofbeats of demons. The massive room was a vast menagerie of creatures, some of which she had never seen before. Kandida wondered if new species of demons had slipped into the human world in the centuries of her absence, if new hells had been discovered or merely grown ambitious. Other faces were familiar and she felt a wave of spite pass through her.

There were nursery bogies and hunched giants and ogres, mugwumps and Black Dogs, dragon men and merrows, oni and kaia, Scythian demons and Rou Shou. Kandida saw shambling shuggoths and Gorlug the Doomed, with chains of human souls still weighing him down, tethering him forever to this plane of existence. She recognized Mr. Hideki, whose entire body was composed of writhing maggots, and the shimmering oil-black musculature of Squamancus, the leeching demon. Among the serpent demons and horned Baalites were those who seemed entirely human. Those were the demons she worried least about—the ones who had adjusted to living among humanity. They would be unlikely to stand against her. They were also the most insidious, the most evil, the most cunning. These were her allies now. It saddened her.

In the midst of the Congress stood a single figure none seemed willing to approach. Cutty Dyer stood seven feet tall, but would have been taller if his body had not been hunched and contorted. A water demon, Kandida's English kinsman was more bloodthirsty than she had ever been. In the days when her kin had despised her for falling in love with Trajabo, Cutty Dyer had not spoken against her. Kandida had always thought this was because Dyer was not truly a water demon. A lurker, he lived beneath a bridge in Somerset, England, and caught and ate those children foolish enough to walk the bridge alone at night. Though his blue-tinted flesh and wide eyes gave him a physical resemblance to some water demons, the child-eater seemed little more than a bridge troll to her.

Whatever his loyalty, he could not express it now. Cutty Dyer was the speaker of the Dark Congress. He had taken an oath to remain objective, to facilitate discussion and only to express opinion when it came time to vote.

Dyer stood hunched in front of the podium on a dais at the front of the meeting chamber. In a chair only a few feet away sat the Deathless Slayer, who had been chosen as the arbiter of the Dark Congress. Kandida and Trajabo had recommended and recruited Buffy Summers, but Cutty Dyer had approved the decision beforehand. He had thought the choice inspired, whereas Kandida and Trajabo had thought it only careful.

"Take your seats now!" Dyer shouted to the others. "Quiet, and take your seats. Night has fallen. The Dark Congress is in session!"

They did as he instructed them. The speaker threw his arms wide, head still hunched so that he had to roll his eyes upward to gaze around at the assemblage.

"As ordained by a majority of the Congress prior to this gathering, I stand as speaker," Dyer declared, his voice deep but with a kind of whistling rasp, as though he could not catch his breath. "Seated beside me is the arbiter I've appointed for the Dark Congress, Buffy Summers. She is answerable only to the speaker, and in the execution of her duties has my entire authority."

A murmur of dissent went through the chamber. The Slayer's expression was impassive, which pleased Kandida. The Summers girl was a formidable creature—the perfect choice for arbiter. Though most of the ambassadors had learned of the choice over the course of the day, for others it was news. They did not seem pleased with the idea, but they could do nothing about it. Kandida knew that, given time, they would adjust. The Slayer had to abide by the rules of the Dark Congress. There would be no violence in the meeting chamber. Regardless of how evil she might believe some of the participants to be, she could do nothing to any of them as long as the Congress was in session.

"We are all grateful for this opportunity," Cutty Dyer announced to the ambassadors. "Destiny has returned Kandida to us, and to Trajabo. Through their union, we hope to at last find the peace that has eluded us for eternity."

Trajabo slipped between Kandida and the door, sifting like sand through that opening.

"The time has come for me to enter," he said.

Kandida only nodded and watched as he refashioned his body, the powerful, lithe desert demon. Heat emanated from his core and she shivered with pleasure as he went past her.

When Trajabo entered there came another round of displeased muttering. Kandida studied the faces and mouths of the Congress and marked several as enemies of the couple. She had waited for everyone to enter and now she hesitated. Kandida would be the first to speak, the first among equals, here in the Dark Congress. She had no higher position than her fellow ambassadors, but those chosen to address the gathering would find their voices heard, if not always listened to.

The speaker began her introduction. Kandida watched Trajabo take his seat. She studied Dyer's face, then Buffy's, and she surveyed the entire chamber, wondering where the future would take them.

Something shifted in the air in the antechamber. Kandida frowned and glanced around, but the gloomily lit room was empty. Another glimpse of the quickly settling meeting chamber told her that the speaker had just called her name. Somehow she had missed it.

The water demon began to step through the door separating the office from the Congress.

Again something moved in the shadows. Figures loomed out of the air, dark silhouettes, and light glinted off of metal. Kandida tried to move, but some enchantment held her fast. Dark figures rose up around her.

Kandida began to scream.

CHAPTER TWELVE

The scream brought Buffy to her feet. Surrounded by hunger and evil and cruelty, she had been tensed for a fight and her nerves had been jangling with alarm. But the terrible, mournful cry of pain and anger that came from behind the door tucked away to the far right side of the meeting chamber still startled and unsettled her.

Though she had seen Trajabo come through that door, it still took her a moment to realize whose voice now echoed from the marble and the wooden seats, whose scream now brought nearly the entire assemblage to its feet.

Trajabo exploded into a flurry of whirling sand like a vampire bursting into a cloud of dust. The little sandstorm flowed in a funnel of wind toward the door, tearing it from its hinges as the demon of the desert crashed into the room. It seemed the storm itself cried out then, the sound like the whining of a drill deep inside Buffy's skull.

The echoes of the scream were still resounding from the walls of the chamber as the sandstorm blew back through the door. This time there lurked a figure at its center, a dark silhouette whose arms and legs hung akimbo like a marionette whose strings had been cut.

Buffy held her breath, knowing what had happened, understanding immediately that something had to be done. She moved to the podium on the dais, right beside the Speaker of the Dark Congress, and she watched as the whirlwind of sand began to slow and coalesce as the demon of the desert drew it back into himself.

Trajabo stood at the center of the Congress chamber, holding the corpse of Kandida in his arms. The river demon hung there, and at first she almost seemed asleep or unconscious. But as Trajabo knelt and laid her out on the marble, Buffy saw the enormous hole in the center of her chest. She saw that the turquoise fluid that spilled down Trajabo's chest and spattered the floor was not water, but the blood of a demon.

Murder, Buffy thought. *But not just murder—magick, too.* Someone had torn out Kandida's heart. Buffy had paid attention when Giles and Micaela told the story of the river demon. The last time the Dark Congress had wanted to get rid of her, they'd had to get her as close to dead as they could, then bury her in the riverbank with a talisman to keep her from being resurrected. But Buffy also knew dead when she saw it, and this time Kandida was dead. This had been no ordinary murder. Whoever had done it had some powerful magick to burn, and knew exactly how to take Kandida down.

Not murder, then—assassination.

"Hogboon!" Trajabo shouted, his voice like the scrape of stone upon stone.

It took Buffy a second to realize that this nonsense word was a name, and by then Trajabo was in motion. The demon of the desert raised his hands and seemed almost to blow across the chamber. He rose up and over the first few rows, moving diagonally and landing in one of the aisles.

The creature whose name he had invoked stepped forward from a cluster of allies—stone demons and trolls and something made of earth—and stood defiant in front of Trajabo. The thing called

Hogboon was a little gray-fleshed man with eyes like flat rocks and bits of dirt that clung to his clothing.

"At last she's dead!" Trajabo said. "You stole my love away for so long that none remain who worshipped her, and now you've murdered her. Are you content at last?"

Hogboon did not so much as shake his head in denial. He simply stared at Trajabo.

"I did nothing," said the little gray man.

"Savor the moment. Perhaps it will sustain you in death!" the demon of the desert shouted.

Someone lunged from the aisles, holding up long-fingered hands to halt Trajabo's rage. Some kind of water demon perhaps, but astonishingly beautiful—or she would have been, if not for the rubbery white flesh that made her look as though she had drowned and spent weeks under water.

"You must stop!" the water demon shouted. "Kandida wished for nothing but this Congress. Would you destroy it now, making her death meaningless?"

Trajabo hurled her away from him. "Traitorous whore! Her death is meaningless, Rusalka! the Congress means nothing without her. You conspired with them again, and now you've all gotten what you wanted. The threat of peace is gone! You can have your war and hatred for eternity, and it begins now!"

He stalked toward Hogboon. The two troll ambassadors pulled the gray man backward and moved to stop Trajabo. The demon of the desert lunged at them, his body transforming into a blinding sandstorm, a whirling funnel of gray that swallowed the trolls up in its midst. From within the churning sand there came shouts of surprise and pain and then the sand released them.

All that remained of the trolls were there bones, which fell to the marble floor with a clatter.

Trajabo went for Hogboon.

Buffy reached him first.

The speaker had started to instruct her the moment that Trajabo and Hogboon had faced off against each other in the aisle. But Buffy did not need instruction. Her pulse thundered in her temples as she leaped from the dais, jumped over the corpse of Kandida— unable to avoid glancing at the gaping hole in the river demon's chest, where her heart should have been—and ran at Trajabo.

Whether she could have any effect on the demon of the desert, she had no idea. Certainly, he had more solidity at some times than at others. But she had to try.

Buffy passed right through the churning sand and driving wind that in that moment Trajabo was composed of. She screamed as his power scoured her flesh. A moment or two later and perhaps the flesh would have been stripped from her own bones, but her timing was perfect. Instead of striking Trajabo, she went through him and struck Hogboon, dragging the little gray man down and tossing him into the midst of the various demons and nursery bogies and werecreatures that had clustered around.

She rose, blood seeping from a thousand tiny abrasions on her skin.

Trajabo had reformed, and now he glared at her. "How dare you?" he demanded.

Buffy winced in pain, but kept her gaze locked with his. "How dare I what? Throw myself in front of a speeding train? You think I want to get in the middle of this? Uh-uh. My idea of a good time involves ice cream and sappy movies. Or possibly Rice Krispies Treats."

The demon fumed, indigo eyes wide with maddened rage. "What are you babbling about?"

She barely heard the words over the growing roar of anger and shock from the Congress. Kandida had been murdered. Trajabo had just killed the two troll ambassadors. the Congress was about to come apart completely, and with all the monsters in Providence, the entire region would soon be a smoking crater.

Buffy had to think fast.

"Babbling. I do that. It's my . . . thing. My babbling thing," she managed. She shook her head, trying to clear it as she was jostled from all sides by abominations. Totally skeeved, she took a step nearer to Trajabo, not breaking eye contact with him. "What am I babbling about? Your selfishness."

His eyes were wild, roving around as though in search of some explanation for her audacity. "My selfishness?" he screamed. "My . . . did you not see what just happened here? She is dead! After all this time, waiting, keeping my faith, keeping her in my heart, Kandida is dead and we'd only just begun to build our love again!"

"I know—"

"What do you know of love?" the demon spat. Hot desert wind flowed from him and her scrapes stung.

Buffy's expression darkened and her heart went cold. "I know." *About love, and pain, and loss,* she thought. But she did not speak those words out loud. She only repeated the phrase. "I *know.* But that drowned chick you just decked isn't wrong. This isn't what Kandida would have wanted. You're going to destroy the Congress, if you haven't already."

"And what would you have me do?" Trajabo demanded.

Already others had begun to move closer to him as though they might drag him down to make him pay for his crimes. How they would attack, Buffy could not guess. But she knew it would go badly.

"I am the arbiter of the Dark Congress," she said. "You heard the speaker!"

She said this last part so loudly that her words echoed off of the marble, so that even above their insinuations and grief and pitiful mutterings, the entire Congress could hear her.

"I'm the arbiter, and I will solve this problem. I'll find out who murdered Kandida, and I'll bring them before the Congress to pay for what they've done."

Silence reigned in the chamber for several long seconds.

Then Cutty Dyer, the speaker of the Dark Congress, arrived at her side. The old demon moved slowly.

"The arbiter is correct. She will bring the killer to the Congress for justice, or there will be no Congress," Dyer said, glaring at Trajabo. "Do you agree?"

At first Trajabo said nothing.

Dyer turned in a half circle to include the entire chamber in his question. "Is there anyone among us who disagrees?"

No one spoke a word, which surprised Buffy. She suspected if there were any other trolls in the room, they would have debated the decision, but both troll ambassadors were dead.

Dyer turned once more to Trajabo. "Do you agree?"

Trajabo's expression crumbled. He glanced back down to the center of the chamber, where Kandida lay in a pool of her own turquoise blood. Slowly he turned his gaze upon Buffy.

"For her sake, in her memory, I will give you until dawn. After that I will take vengeance in my own way."

Buffy nodded once and turned to where she'd seen Oz and the blond, shaggy werewolf ambassador.

"Oz, let's go!" she called.

With a sheepish expression, as though his mother had shown up to excuse him early from school, Oz trotted over to her.

Buffy glanced at the Speaker. "Seal the building. No one in or out except for him or me."

Then she ran up the aisle, Oz trucking along beside her. The guards on the doors stepped aside. She banged them open and raced into the corridor and past the locked offices toward the rotunda, already thinking two steps ahead. She had very little time and thousands of suspects.

"Penny for your maelstrom of confusion," Oz offered.

"There was magick, for sure," she said. "Willow's new buddy, Catherine Cadiere, she's a freakin' powerful witch. A wicked witch, if you want to get all Faithy about it. And she wasn't one of the witch ambassadors, so she could have been in there. But that's only me being suspicious and paranoid.

"Could've been vampires. Could've been any of those demons, the ones who wanted to break Kandida and Trajabo up way back in Flintstone times. Could be that Malik guy. Could be Hogboy—"

"Hogboon?"

"Yeah. Him. Trajabo sure seemed to think so."

Buffy ran with Oz down the stairs to the rotunda. She stopped with him in front of the main doors, where the guards watched them with concern. Then the two demon guards glanced past her, and Buffy turned to see Cutty Dyer at the top of the stairs behind her, gesturing to the guards to let them go.

The doors were opened for them.

Buffy moved in close to Oz to make sure he was the only one who heard her. "Get Giles and Micaela to dig up anything they can get on Malik and his hunting party. You, Xander, and Faith go track down de Tournefort and the other vamps. Find out if they're involved in this. If they are, bring me back at least one to admit it in front of the Congress, and dust the rest. And tell Willow and Tara my fears about Catherine. I want to know if the wicked witch had a hand in it."

Oz frowned. "You want Willow to interrogate her new mentor?"

"You have a better idea? Mojo versus mojo."

Oz gave a small shrug and a nod.

"You heard them. We have until dawn. I'm staying here. Gonna see who had the most to gain by this. But on the outside, you've all got to make sure none of the factions out there uses this as a reason to start a war."

"You don't ask for the small favors, do you?" Oz said.

Buffy smiled. "I'll buy you Pop-Tarts."

"That's not fair, considering my passion for the Pop-Tart and all."

"Everyone has their Scooby Snacks. Pop-Tarts are yours."

Oz cocked an eyebrow. "On my way."

She watched him go out the doors, into the milling, mumbling crowds that swarmed around the State House in the night. Then the guards closed the doors behind him, and Buffy was alone in the midst of the Dark Congress, tasked to find a murderer amid a gathering of monsters.

Without hesitation, she raced back to the steps.

Night had only just fallen, but already the morning seemed far too near.

Oz stood in front of Dunphy's Irish Pub with Faith on his left and Xander on his right. The car was parked across the street and Oz had been reluctant to leave the air-conditioning. Danger was in the air, and blood, and the wolf inside him was very close to the surface now. Most times he could control it almost completely. He had spent months learning to accept the bestial heart as part of himself. But sometimes the wolf felt separate from him, still, and stronger.

The heat made it worse.

"This place is getting to be a habit for us," Faith said. She and Oz had been to Dunphy's just the night before.

Oz nodded. "A bad habit."

Music floated from the open door of the pub like a ghost, a slow, lovely dirge by the Perishers. The smells of food and human bodies and stale beer emanated from the place, swirled around by the lazy ceiling fans. It was the sort of pub Oz would've loved to play, if it weren't a watering hole for demons and night beasts. Dunphy's was a dive, sure, but a much better class of dive than Willy's back in Sunnydale, or any of the other places Oz had found monsters congregating to get drunk and hook up over the past few years.

"You guys bring me to the fanciest places," Xander said. He scratched at his cheek, right below his eye patch. Oz wondered if the patch irritated his skin. "So, what's the plan?"

They had originally been heading to the school where they and the Miquot, Ryvak, had found the vampire nest. But they'd cleared that nest out, and Oz had thought all along that the plan made no sense. Vampires could be real numbskulls, but from what Faith had said of Christabel de Tournefort, that didn't seem to be the case here.

Xander had been the one to suggest they try Dunphy's. Back in Sunnydale, Willy had always had the skinny on what was going down in monster town. It stood to reason that the bartender at the pub might have an inkling of where the vampires were hanging out in Providence. When the Congress wasn't in session, he probably had vampire clientele. He'd have heard things.

That was the logic, at least.

Time to find out if Xander was right.

"No plan," Faith said. "Plans have a way of sucking."

She went through the open door and was swallowed by the beer smell and the mournful music. Oz glanced at Xander and shrugged.

"She's not wrong," the wolf said.

They followed Faith into the pub. A television over the bar showed the Boston Red Sox playing a night game somewhere, but the sound was off so that the music piped through the sound system in the pub could be heard. The intense scrutiny of the patrons of Dunphy's made Oz's skin prickle. He felt the wolf bristling inside him.

"This place is a barrel of laughs," Xander said.

Oz did not reply. The three of them approached the bar together. There was no sign of the Miquot they'd earlier befriended. A couple of Vahrall demons sat on stools on either side of a woman who might have been a succubus or a prostitute. Oz had to guess the former, because a prostitute who looked that good wouldn't waste her time in a place like Dunphy's.

Faith went up to her. "Take it into the alley out back, honey. We've got business."

The succubus smiled sweetly, reached out, and touched Faith's lips in a gesture so flirtatious that Oz heard Xander sigh.

"For you, anything," the succubus said. She was playful rather than afraid.

Faith cocked her hip. "You're in over your head, girl."

The succubus raised both hands in a gesture of surrender, then slid from her stool and reached out to take the Vahralls with her, clasping each one by the hand. The demons stared at Faith as if they desperately wanted to start something, as if they would've given anything to tear her apart. Oz thought it was fortunate for them that the Congress had forbidden any such contact.

"Hey, reggae," he said to the dreadlocked demons. "It's not worth it. Go have fun."

Xander glanced at him, that single eye so expressive. "Reggae. That's good. I was working on a Predator joke, but not really getting anywhere."

One of the Vahralls snarled at Xander and began to puff up, trying to intimidate them. The succubus didn't want that kind of trouble. She tugged on her two friends and they moved away from the bar.

Once upon a time Xander would not have been able to resist the urge to volley some kind of parting shot in their direction. But time had wised them all up, and he controlled the urge.

The bartender—a fortyish guy, short but with thick arms and the puglike features of an Irish boxer—had watched the entire exchange. Back in Sunnydale, Willy would have been whimpering by now. Not this guy. He came down the bar, put both hands on the smooth wooden counter, and leaned over to fix them with a hard look.

"You guys are bad for business."

Xander slid onto a stool. "Well, you better get us out of here fast, then."

The little pug crossed his arms. "What do you want?"

Faith slid between two stools and leaned against the bar, getting close enough that the guy had to have her scent, human or not. Up close, Faith was hard to resist. Xander had once referred to her as "walking, talking sex," and Oz didn't argue.

"Kind of place you run, I'm gonna guess you get all types in here," Faith said. "When they're not too scared to come to town, bet you get some vampires in here."

Oz watched the bartender's face. His eyes narrowed, just slightly.

"They come in sometimes. Don't mean I want 'em here, but I don't turn 'em away."

Faith glanced around. Oz surveyed the pub as well. The humans, demons, and other things in Dunphy's seemed to have gone back to whatever conversations they were having before the trio walked in. But they'd be listening if they could.

"Where would they go outside the city limits? Is there a regular place, an old house or something, a nest? If there are out-of-towners around, where would they go?"

Oz expected the grim man to refuse to answer the question. Instead, he scrunched up his face.

"Don't know of anywhere out of town. In Providence, yeah. But I don't know a damn thing about anything else."

"There's gotta be something," Faith said, smiling. But her smile held nothing friendly or humorous.

"Otherwise you're a pretty crappy excuse for a bartender," Xander added. "Bartenders listen. It's the first thing you learn, before you mix a drink."

Faith glanced curiously at him.

Xander shrugged. "What? I took a course."

The bartender relented. "I might know a place. Used to make candy there. Mints or something. I've heard some things."

Oz stepped nearer to Xander and Faith. "How do we find this place?"

With a shake of his head, the bartender gave a small chuckle. "You guys got a death wish, but if you're that hot to get your necks sucked, just follow Ogden Street out of the city. You cross the Tillbrook Bridge, it's right there on the hill. Hard to miss the place."

Xander glanced at Oz and Faith, then looked back at the bartender. "Now pretend we're from out of town."

The man rolled his eyes. "What, you want me to draw you a map?"

"Actually," Faith said, "that'd be good."

While the bartender sketched on a napkin, Oz looked around at the demons gathered in the pub.

"Word's going to reach this place at some point," he said. "I'm thinking soon. If we were loitering around here when the news broke, we might learn a few things."

Xander leaned back on his stool. "I'm pretty pleased not knowing what evisceration feels like, actually. I'll pass on that."

"We don't know how they'll take the news," Faith argued.

"I'm gonna say not well." Xander crossed his arms.

"Safe bet. But who's going to want to be the one to go against the Congress? We've got till dawn before the bad stuff happens."

"He's right," Faith said. "We could both benefit from someone being here."

Xander glanced back and forth between them. "Why are you both looking at me?"

Oz and Faith kept looking. After a few seconds he huffed and reached into his pocket for the keys to the rental car. Tossing them to Oz, he turned and ordered a beer.

The bartender handed Faith the napkin on which he'd scrawled the map and asked Xander for his ID.

Less than twenty minutes later, Oz and Faith were driving out of the city on Ogden Street, looking for the former Charlotte's Candies factory.

Just like the bartender at Dunphy's had predicted, the place wasn't hard to find. The factory was a darkened hulk sitting on a hill just outside the city limits, past the bridge whose name Oz had already forgotten. A long driveway led through some thick woods up to the factory. A heavy chain hung on a gate, blocking the way, but Faith broke the lock with a quick snap and they swung the gate open, then drove up the hill.

The sign for Charlotte's Candies had been ruined by the passage of time. The loops that should have formed the double *t* in "Charlotte" had fallen at some point and the *s* hung askew. The second word had been so rotted by weather that it was unreadable, save for the first letter. Both capital *C*s were twice the size of the other letters and had somehow retained the pink paint they had once been coated with. Even in the moonlight it was clearly pink.

Once upon a time Oz and some of the others who'd helped Buffy back in high school had used everything from Super Soakers filled with holy water to flashlights with a cross painted on the lens to fight vampires. But Oz didn't need any of that stuff. The occasional stake came in handy because it was expedient. Other than that, the wolf could do his own killing. That was one of the things Oz had had to accept when he admitted to himself that he and the beast within were not two separate creatures, but one and the same—that sometimes the up-close stuff, the times he could turn himself loose, were pure bliss.

"You ready?" Faith asked after Oz killed the engine on the rental car and the headlights went out.

Oz watched the Slayer slip on her jacket and make sure there were stakes hidden in each of the sheaths she'd sewn into the lining. When she was done, she glanced up at him, her eyes asking the question again.

He nodded.

They opened the doors simultaneously, glancing around, waiting for the ambush that had to be coming. No way had they broken the lock and driven straight up to the front of the factory without alerting the vampires to the fact that they were coming. If there were any leeches here, they would have posted guards.

Still, nothing moved except the wind in the trees and the occasional flutter of wings from a night bird.

Oz and Faith walked together up to an oversized door set into the cold, featureless industrial face of the factory. She turned the knob and it opened. Unlocked. The Slayer pushed the door wide and stepped inside, but Oz paused on the threshold.

"What is it?" Faith asked.

His nostrils flared. "Charlotte made mints, apparently. The smell's pretty strong."

Strong enough to hide the scent of anything else that might be waiting for them inside.

Faith hesitated a second.

A vampire dropped down on her from above, just inside the door, screaming something Oz did not understand. A loud hiss, like a nest of vipers, came from deep inside the factory, and he saw golden eyes gleaming in the darkness. Many, many eyes.

The sound of running came from behind him and Oz turned to see several vamps rushing at him from the trees that lined the factory's long drive. Their faces were ridged and pinched with the evil visage they all had when the bloodlust was upon them.

Ashes spilled on the ground by his feet, the remains of the vampire who'd fallen on Faith.

Oz turned his focus to the ones rushing at him from the woods. He opened his arms as though to embrace them, fingers lengthening into claws, and he smiled as his jaw elongated. The fur burst through his skin with a horribly itchy sensation. Their scent overpowered the minty candy smell now. With the stink of vampires in his snout, he threw back his head and howled.

Oz let the wolf off his leash.

• • •

Giles stood at the window of his hotel room, looking down on the busy shopping district below. The air conditioner rattled as it blew cold air up at him, rippling the sheer curtains that he'd opened only wide enough for a glimpse outside.

Behind him, Micaela Tomasi sat on his bed, talking on the phone to Rory Kinnear, the branch director for the Watchers Council back in London. Even just this brief period with the two of them alone in his hotel room made Giles flush with the memory of their dalliance. Ever since he had discovered her true motivations—for which she had long since redeemed herself—he had told himself that he could never overlook the past enough to engage in any future relationship with her.

With her there in his room, perched on the edge of his bed, blond hair a bit unruly, he wondered if perhaps he had previously been both hasty and unfair in his condemnation of her.

Men were simple creatures. Giles had long since discovered that awareness of his gender's flaws did not excuse him from them. Rather than make a fool of himself with Micaela—particularly during such dire circumstances—he focused on the view outside the hotel room window and listened to her end of the conversation with Kinnear. It was clear that Micaela did not think the branch director quite as much of a buffoon as Giles did, but that higher opinion did not improve the man's competence. Long minutes passed as he made several calls, keeping Micaela on hold all the while; Giles was grateful that she'd used a calling card provided by the Council.

At last the call ended and Micaela hung up.

Giles turned to face her. She leaned back on the bed and stretched her neck, legs crossed like a femme fatale from a Humphrey Bogart movie. The fact that this pose was unconscious made it all the more alluring. When Micaela opened her eyes and saw the way he was looking at her, she blinked in realization, blushed a bit, and then stood up. She wore a shy smile, and she had never been shy.

"Anything from Kinnear?" Giles asked.

Micaela walked past him to the window. "Yes." She peered out, craning her neck in both directions. "No sign of the apocalypse yet?"

"Buffy appears to have things under control with the Congress, for the moment. Are you going to tell me what Kinnear said?"

She turned to face him, quite close now. The memory of other such intimate moments threatened to distract him.

"Sorry. Just a lot on my mind," she said. And was there some small irony in her smile? He thought perhaps there was. "Kinnear phoned around. Ted Hastings says there are dozens of references to Malik in the journals of the Watchers over the years. He's definitely a Champion for the Powers."

"Any luck identifying the others?"

Micaela hesitated a moment, then walked away from him. She went into the bathroom for a glass and opened the four-dollar bottle of sparkling water that sat on the nightstand, filling her glass.

"That's not as simple, apparently. From Oz and Xander's description, the big one's easy enough: Tai. Specializes in were-wolves, but also a Champion. The dwarf is Bors, a witchfinder. The other could be one of several Champions, but Hastings said he'd wager it's a demon hunter named Simone Beauvais."

As Micaela drank sparkling water, Giles took a deep breath. He shook his head and leaned against the small desk near the window.

"Right. That's them off the list, then," he said. Aside from the demons who had allied against Kandida and Trajabo all those centuries ago, Malik had been his prime suspect. "It must be someone in the Congress."

"Why so quick to let them off the hook?" Micaela asked.

"The Powers would never allow this. Not that they would object to the killing, even by assassination, of a demon. But they're the Powers That Be, Micaela. They know about fate. With what's at stake here, the kind of powder keg this whole thing has become . . . the Powers would never condone it."

"Okay, but it still could be vampires, or that Cadiere witch. And if it isn't Malik, maybe we can get his help. God knows we could use all the help we can find right now," she said.

Giles nodded. "Four Champions? Their priorities might be different from ours, but they can't turn their backs on something like this."

He started for the door.

"Where are we going?" Micaela asked.

"The market. There are a few things we'll need for a locator spell. Now that we know they're legitimate, magickally tracking Malik and the others shouldn't be at all difficult."

He paused and looked at her. "Of course, I'll rely on you to do the spell. You have a far greater facility for magick."

Micaela gave a small bow. "Your wish is my command."

Giles hurried out of the room with Micaela in tow, trying not to let his imagination make more of those words than she'd put into them. The time they'd had together—he'd thought of it as a dalliance before, and that was all it had been. Maybe one day, they'd dally again, but that was a thought for the flight home, when the crisis had passed.

When they'd survived to see the sun rise.

CHAPTER THIRTEEN

The cinnamon cat found a window open in the back of Margaret Hood's townhouse. From the rear porch, the cat could just reach the frame, and her claws were sharp enough—magickally sharp—to slice the screen. After making a hole for herself, there in the moonlight behind the townhouse, the cinnamon cat slipped through the torn screen and landed in the kitchen sink with a soft, whispery noise, claws clicking on the stainless steel.

The cat—the witch's familiar—paused to listen for any cries of alarm. Margaret Hood led her own powerful local coven. It stood to reason that she would have some mystical defenses in place. But after several seconds without any response to her home invasion, the cat stepped up onto the counter, padded to the end, and dropped soundlessly to the kitchen floor.

Old-time jazz played quietly in another room.

Tara Maclay moved through the kitchen, becoming more and more comfortable in the body of the cat, and turned into the corridor that led toward the front door of the exquisite townhouse. As she did, she heard the doorbell chime.

Willow had arrived at the front door.

The cat pressed herself against the wall in shadows. She stood quite still and listened, and her attention was rewarded by the sound of someone rousing herself in a room off to the left—the same room in which the jazz still played.

The cat watched, anxious, breathless, as the slender, silver-haired woman emerged from the archway that led into the back parlor. It was the same room where Willow and Tara had met the witches who had gathered in Margaret Hood's home in preparation for the Dark Congress. Maggie Hood was one of the witches chosen as ambassador to the Congress, so she wasn't home at all, and they had seen only a handful of witches gathered outside the State House to witness the momentous occasion.

Catherine Cadiere had not been among them.

Willow and Tara had both suspected that she would be here, awaiting the outcome and holding court. The other witches seemed wary of her, but respectful. They treated her with both distance and deference. But tonight Catherine seemed to be alone, for the chiming of the doorbell had not disturbed anyone else. Nothing stirred. No sound came from within the house except for that jazz, the echo of the doorbell, and the footsteps of Catherine Cadiere.

But the silver-haired witch—that elegant, sophisticated woman—did not go to the door immediately. Tara heard her pause, and a moment later the sound of something being dragged across the floor of the foyer and into the living room, out of sight.

The doorbell chimed again. Willow was growing impatient.

The cinnamon cat grew curious. Tara remembered the old saying about what curiosity could do to a cat, but she could not help herself. Silently, she padded into the rear parlor, where a small, stained glass lamp provided the only illumination, a garish wash of multicolored light.

At first glance she thought all the witches in that room were dead. Women were sprawled on the sofa and in every chair. One olive-skinned, well-dressed woman had slid down so far in her chair that her skirt had been rucked up nearly to her hips. Purple-haired Alice lay on the floor, right cheek against the carpet, a bit of drool at the corner of her mouth. Staring at her, Tara realized that the witches were not dead. They were unconscious.

It could only be witchery. Magick had caused all of them to fall into some kind of sleep or trance state, and from the look of them, Tara felt sure it was nothing they had participated in willingly. Narrowing her cat eyes, she realized the odd glow around them was not merely due to the stained-glass lamp. They all had a pulsing aura of silvery light.

Voices came to her from the front of the townhouse.

Willow!

Panic seared her heart as she realized that Catherine had let Willow in, and that whatever the ancient witch had done to these women, she would not want it discovered. Frantic, Tara forced herself not to imagine what might happen next. The cinnamon cat darted back into the hallway and slunk toward the foyer.

"You're not suggesting I had anything to do with this?" Catherine said, a dark edge to her voice.

From the shadows, the cat watched Willow's face. She saw so many conflicting emotions there. This woman had given them back the love that had been stolen from them, the destiny they deserved. She had seen the potential in Willow and wanted to share with her centuries of wisdom and knowledge.

But that turmoil left Willow's face after a moment, replaced by steely resolve. *Goddess, how can I love anyone so much?* Tara thought, studying that face.

"I'm not saying anything of the kind, Catherine. But someone murdered Kandida, and there was magick involved. Witchcraft seems a safe bet. I came to find you because if any of the witches who've come for the Congress would have that kind of magick, I kinda figured you'd know about it."

Catherine brushed the words away with a fluttery hand. "It wouldn't take great power. Making a demon vulnerable to physical attack is magick anyone can learn. All it requires is the right words, the right hex."

Willow flexed her hands. The cinnamon cat could practically feel the magick that ignited in her girlfriend.

"But you know those words, right? Any idea who else does?"

Catherine stiffened, raising her chin imperiously. She shook her head in disapproval. "You little bitch," she whispered.

Willow flinched, hurt.

"I gave you the ultimate gift. Magick that the blackest hearts won't dare to use, and I handed it to you, and protected you from the consequences. I safeguarded you so that you could have your heart's desire. And this is how you repay me? This is your loyalty?"

Her voice rose higher and higher as she spoke. Though Tara could only see her profile, the change in her expression was equally unsettling. Her beauty turned ugly with rage and disgust.

Whatever Catherine had done to the other witches, Tara could not allow her to do the same to Willow.

The cinnamon cat closed her eyes and willed herself to change. It felt for a moment as though she were floating, and when she opened her eyes, she was Tara Maclay again, her blond hair tied back in a ponytail and her shirt untucked over jeans that never seemed to fit right.

"I didn't come here to accuse you," Willow said coldly. "But, gotta say, kinda thinking your reaction is a little fishy."

Catherine sniffed angrily. She glared at Willow, and then she shot out her right arm, fingers pointed, magick pulsing from her open palm—aimed not at Willow, but at Tara. The spell struck Tara in the chest. Her heart thumped the way it did when she stood too close to the amplifiers at a concert, low bass notes thundering in her rib cage.

Then came the pain, like swords driven through her chest. She fell to her knees, gasping, no breath left in her to scream. Catherine might have twitched her fingers, but a second hex hit her in that moment and it blew her up off the floor, off her feet, and hurled her the length of the corridor. Her outstretched arm struck the frame around the entrance to the kitchen and she felt the bone give way as she dropped to the kitchen floor and rolled.

Drawing quick sips of air, the pain abating in her chest, she tried to rise but could only stare back the way she'd come at the scene unfolding all the way at the end of the hall, in the foyer . . . so far away.

"Bitch!" Willow had screamed, but Tara only heard the echo now.

Willow hooked her hands into claws and the hex leaped from the fingers of both hands, a wave of light with the tainted yellow and purple hues of a bruise. Tara heard the words in Latin. She knew the spell. It would age Catherine so swiftly and so badly that she would be crippled by her ancientness.

With a wave of her hand, Catherine stopped the spell. That magickal light—a bit of magick not quite wicked, but darker than Willow ought ever to cast—seemed to freeze in the air. It shattered, fell like rain to the floor, and then became a thousand spiders of those same ugly hues.

Willow tried again, but Catherine struck her with a hex that hurled her against the door. The spiders crawled onto Willow's legs and began to spin webs. In seconds they seemed to cover most of her body.

Then Willow began to scream.

Tara shook off her pain and stood, staggering from the kitchen with murder on her mind.

Giles stared at the map of Providence spread out on the floor of his hotel room. Micaela had spilled honey on the four corners of the map—careful not to get too much on the carpet—and then sprinkled dried rosemary onto the open map. Any herb would do, really, but some worked better than others. If he could have found fresh rosemary, that would have been preferable. But still, this should have been enough.

Should have been.

"What's happening?" he said, staring at the map, brows knitted in consternation.

Micaela sat on the edge of the bed. He had been wishing she would stop doing that, but at the moment his mind had other distractions.

"Nothing, obviously," she said.

Giles took off his glasses and leaned against the bureau, tapping them against his leg. "We did the spell correctly. All right, the honey was a variation, but it did say 'pure' on the label. And the incantation was correct."

"It's pretty rudimentary magic, Rupert. It should've worked."

"Let's try it again."

Micaela gave a small shrug to indicate that she didn't think it would do any good, but was willing. Giles doubted it would make a difference either, but the result was so odd that he had to at least consider the possibility that they'd made a mistake.

They couldn't start over from scratch. The honey was already on the map. But they swept all the rosemary off the map and Giles picked up the bottle again.

"Incantation first this time," he said.

Micaela began. The words were German, a language Giles was only passably familiar with, but enough to know that they were performing the spell correctly. When they reached the end of the incantation, he began to tap out a small shower of dried rosemary above the map.

None of the herbs hit the paper.

They hung, suspended, above the detailed image of Providence.

Giles kept tapping the bottle until all the rosemary had sifted out, watching hopefully. The first time it had just scattered across the paper. This time it hung in the air, inches above the map.

Not moving.

"It's working perfectly this time," Micaela said.

But there was no triumph in her voice. The opposite, in fact. Giles understood. If the spell was working perfectly, the rosemary ought to have been moving, collecting, gathering itself into concentrated points to represent the influence of the Powers That Be, and to that end, their Champions.

"Could it be Malik and the others have left?" Giles asked.

"Anything's possible," Micaela said. "But it's odd that the herbs are just hanging there like that. You would think that with all the magick, all the destiny in play in this city tonight, the influence of the Powers would be everywhere. The Champions would show up as more significant, but the Powers are always at work when something this major is at stake."

Even as she spoke, Giles saw that Micaela was wrong. The rosemary did have a much higher concentration in one particular area of the city. But the location meant nothing to him. That didn't help much, however. They were looking for individuals, and the locator spell had not found anyone directly influenced by the Powers.

"What the hell's going on, Rupert?" Micaela asked.

"I'm not sure. But one thing is clear. There are no Champions in Providence tonight."

One of the vampires had a sword.

Faith laughed at him.

"What the hell's wrong with you? Might as well have made it rain holy water, dumbass."

The vampires swarmed all over one another trying to get to her. The smell of mint candy filled her nostrils. It seemed to coat the walls inside the old Charlotte's Candies factory. Huge rows of industrial windows lined the walls, high up, and many of them had been broken. Moonlight washed across the floor, the dusty, useless, broken-down machines, and the bloodsuckers that came at her like sewer rats.

But these things were lower life forms than sewer rats, and not half as smart: witness the sword.

Faith punched a stake through the chest of the nearest vamp even as she shot a side kick out, high and hard, crushing the throat of another leech. One of them—a long-haired female who screamed like a banshee—leaped off of the top of a piece of machinery. Faith grabbed her arm, twisted, and hurled her into the rushing swarm of vamps.

She ran at them as they fell and stumbled over her. With a quick shot of her left fist, she broke a nose. With the stake clutched in her right, she dusted another vamp. She planted her foot on the back of the long-haired vamp chick she'd just tossed at the others, stepped on the neck of a second, who was struggling to rise, and then launched herself into the air. The somersault took her in an arc over the heads of fourteen or fifteen snarling, fanged vamps, their faces all ridged and ugly.

When she touched down, she knocked aside a leather-boy vamp who looked like an extra from *Braveheart*, then found herself facing the moron stupid enough to bring a sword to this fight. He feinted with the sword, trying to protect his heart.

Faith jammed the stake through his right eye. The vampire went down, writhing and twitching but alive. As he fell, she snatched the broadsword from his grip, then swung it in an arc that took his head off.

"That's my one act of mercy for the day," she said. "You're welcome."

Already a vampire reached for her, long, pale fingers grasping for her arm. Faith pulled away, the claws raking her arm, drawing blood.

She took the offending hand off first, then the head.

Some of the vampires were at least smart enough to pause at the sight of a Slayer with a broadsword. Some of them, she felt sure, knew exactly who she was. Faith Lehane had a reputation among the vampires. The way she'd heard it, the whispers around the bloodsucker campfires gave Buffy Summers the edge when it came to efficiency and the whole resurrection thing. The smart vampires, the ancient ones, they were more afraid of Buffy than anyone because she was likely to bring down their entire operation. But the rank and file, the grunts and savages, they were more afraid of Faith because all the whispers said she liked it more. Buffy did the job. For Faith, killing them was a party.

The ones who didn't hesitate learned too late. The sword flashed in her hands. Some she decapitated, others she cut in half and returned to with a killing stroke afterward. The only time she paused was when she had to wipe the ashes from her eyes, because the smell of mint in Charlotte's Candies had been finally erased by the dry, scorched-earth stink of dead vampires, a cloud of dust that swirled around in the warm breeze of a humid summer night.

Sweat beaded her skin. Faith became coated with a grime from the ashes of dead vampires, but she kept killing. Grinning.

From outside the factory there came howls and roars that painted hideous pictures in her mind. Oz was busy as well, or so she assumed. The truth was driven home when the massive wolf leaped through the open factory door, clamped his jaws over the head of a vampire, and shook her like a rag doll, tossing her at a machine. Bones shattered and blood burst from her nose and mouth.

Oz bounded to the fallen vampire, put one huge paw on her chest and the other on her ruined skull, then separated the two. The vampire seemed almost to pop like a New Year's Eve confetti popper, dust swirling away.

Vampires launched themselves at the werewolf. One straddled his back, plunging fangs into his flesh. Maybe into his spine. Oz ran at the wall, leaped, twisted in the air, and left the vampire as a smear along the corrugated metal.

Faith had seen him as a wolf before, but she'd never seen him let the beast out like this before. Oz's savagery was a revelation. She was glad he was on her side.

A vampire lunged for her. She kicked him in the chest, knocking him back, even as she brought the sword around in a long arc that decapitated another. How many had been hiding in the darkness of this factory? Dozens, at least. They had been nesting, but seemed to have expected an attack—which meant that Christabel could not be too far away.

Three of the vampires, all pretty girls who looked like runaways, rushed at her. Faith raised the sword—

Only to feel cold steel punch through her back.

The point of the blade emerged just below her collarbone, above her left breast. She blinked, staring at it, saw beads of her blood glide down the blade and drip to the floor. Whoever held the sword gave it a twist and removed it.

Faith screamed and fell to her knees. Remembering herself, and her peril, she raised her own sword. But too late. The three runaway girls fell upon her, driving her to the floor. Her head struck concrete and she blacked out for a second. One of the girls yanked her head back. Another darted down toward her throat, fangs bared.

With a grunt, Faith kicked her in the mouth, breaking her teeth. The girl wheeled away from her, one hand over her bloody lips. The other pulled her farther back. Faith used the momentum to pull herself into a backward roll, swung her legs up, and wrapped them around the girl's neck, twisting and breaking it. That wouldn't kill the vampire, but it would slow her down.

Not enough.

The third girl snatched the sword from Faith's hand as several others fell on her. She heard the werewolf howl and then a whimper. Oz didn't seem the type to whimper.

Hatred burned in Faith. She was not afraid of death, but she despised these creatures so much that it disgusted her to think that her death might be at their hands.

"Well done," a silky, feminine voice said. "Stand her up."

The vampires dragged her to her feet. Faith was spun around. A wooden match scratched against the ground flared to life and she saw the beast himself, the child-eater, Haarmann, crouching six feet away from her with a cigarette dangling from his lips. He drew in smoke and shook out the match, then tossed it down.

Haarmann held the sword in his right hand. The blade was still wet with Faith's blood.

"Can't even begin to tell you how dead you are," she said.

Haarmann grinned, but he didn't speak.

Just behind him, one hand on his head as though he were some kind of pet, stood Christabel de Tournefort. Faith had seen portraits of her in books so old that the pages were crumbling away. Once she had been pale and fragile-looking, a girl made of bone-white lace. She had been rather plain-looking, but her eyes in those centuries-old pictures sparkled with raw intelligence.

Faith recognized the eyes. The rest had long ago been transformed by the demon inside. Christabel's nose was like a pig's snout, the mouth permanently stained red, lips perpetually drawn back to reveal teeth like long spikes, a bear trap of teeth that prevented the vampire from closing her jaws. All that remained of once black hair were oily straggles of gray and white.

But sheer power emanated from her and she looked down upon Faith like an empress upon a serving girl.

"You fight well, Slayer," she said.

Several vampires dragged Oz along the concrete in a thick net that had little bundles of something—wolfsbane, perhaps—tied all over it. The wolf whined, eyes on Faith. There was nothing she could do, of course. She wished he would quit it.

"I can't say the same for your front lines," Faith told her. "Seriously, I'd be embarrassed."

Christabel inhaled sharply, moist phlegm rattling in her throat. Or perhaps it was coagulating blood. Vampires didn't have to breathe, but they could when it suited them. When expressing anger, for instance.

"Haarmann," she said.

The butcher reached out with his cigarette—Turkish, from the stink—and pressed the tip into Faith's abdomen. Faith bared her teeth with the pain, but turned it into a smile.

"Gonna have to do better than that, de Sade. That kinda thing comes with the pillow talk where I'm from."

Oz let out a low growl. One of the vampires kicked him but he didn't even struggle with the net. Faith glanced at him and saw that the werewolf's gaze was still locked on her, as though he was waiting for something.

Faith arched an eyebrow, then looked at Christabel with renewed interest.

"You gonna kill me, or you just gonna stand there and whistle 'Dixie'?"

"I've never met a more insolent wench," the ancient vampiress said. "But I should not be surprised. Slayers are contrary by nature. We have spies in the city. Allies. We knew you would come, and our outriders watched you for miles. I have a message for the arbiter, and for the Dark Congress. We came to this gathering to protest the exclusion of our kind, but we have nothing to do with Kandida's death. Nothing."

Faith cocked her head. "We're supposed to believe you?"

Christabel's hand fluttered dismissively; her fingernails had grown so long that they had startled to curl, like the nails of a corpse long in the ground.

"I care nothing for what you believe. I give you this message, that is all. We came to argue for inclusion in the Congress in the future. What would be the point of assassination?"

"Never quite understood politics, myself," Faith said.

Christabel sniffed in disdain.

The tip of Haarmann's cigarette glowed orange in the moonlit shadows of Charlotte's Candies.

Faith glanced down at the werewolf, trussed up in the net on the ground. She winked.

The wolf surged upward, all four legs in motion, claws shredding the net. As he moved, Faith dropped to the ground, using her body weight to pull the vampires who'd been holding her down as well. She twisted her right hand, grabbed the one holding that arm by the throat, and shattered his head against the concrete. Then she snapped her head back, using her skull to break the nose of the one behind her. Cold blood dripped onto her neck.

Her right hand free, she pulled a stake from inside her jacket and plunged it into the heart of the vampire who'd been holding her left arm.

Others rushed her, but she was free.

The growl that came from Oz's throat sounded more like a roar. He bounded at Haarmann. The centuries-old butcher lifted his sword just in time and caught the werewolf in the chest, but the vampire was a fool. The sword wasn't silver, just steel.

Oz clawed the concrete and forced his own body down on the sword, and its tip came out his back. He dragged himself closer to Haarmann—close enough to reach out a paw. His claws flashed out and he tore the vampire's face off.

Haarmann screamed and let go of the sword, and Oz had him then. He took Haarmann's head in his jaws and bit it off, then spat it out as both head and body exploded into dust. The werewolf stood up on his hind legs and dragged the sword from his chest, tossing it to the concrete with a clang.

Faith and Oz both looked around.

"Where did the bitch go?" Faith asked.

Oz growled.

The vampires, mystified and wide-eyed, glanced around as well. Christabel de Tournefort had withdrawn from the battle. Her message delivered, she had left her minions to fend for themselves.

Slayer and werewolf were both wounded. There were a couple dozen vampires left in the mint-and-scorched-flesh-smelling factory. But the bloodsuckers didn't like the odds.

They ran, trampling one another to get out of there. Oz started to follow, but Faith called to him. The wolf stopped, hearing the man's name. After a minute or so, when it was certain they were alone, he transformed back into the odd little redheaded guitar player she'd always found such an enigma. Never more so than now.

Faith stared at him. "You believe her?"

Oz shrugged. "Kinda."

She chewed on that a moment, then pulled out her cell phone and dialed Giles at the hotel. There was no answer in the hotel room so she rang Micaela's, but still no joy. Faith had to leave a message.

"Hey. It's me. It isn't the vamps. Me and Oz, we're okay, but we're gonna have to catch our second wind."

When she hung up and put the phone away, she found him watching her curiously.

"What?" she said. "I've got a friggin' hole through me. So do you, in case you didn't notice. The bleeding's stopped, but I need a little time on the bench, coach. Giles'll call if he needs us."

Oz looked down at his chest, where blood wept from a thin gash. Like Faith, he was already healing, but it hurt like hell. He looked around the factory.

"Wonder if they kept a stash of those mints in here when they closed down. I'm a little peckish."

Spiders crawled in Willow's hair. Her heart thundered in panic and revulsion. She tried to shake them off, but they weren't just in her hair, they were all over her, and these things that Catherine's magick had spawned were unnatural—things of black magick. The spiders had nearly covered her body with webs. Her arms were held where they had been, frozen by webbing. She had struggled as much as she could, but the spiders had her. One of them crawled across her right eye.

Willow screamed, felt one on her lower lip, and clamped her mouth shut, breathing frantically through her nose and staring in venomous hatred—a righteous fury unlike anything she'd ever known—at this woman she had thought might be her friend and mentor. Catherine Cadiere had presented herself as elegant and sophisticated and full of wisdom, but her veins ran with evil.

"Try any spell you like, and I shall counter it," Catherine said. "Better yet, simply listen to me a moment."

Catherine had given Willow the magick to resurrect Tara, but now Tara came staggering out of the kitchen, bruised and bleeding from a cut on her hand, cradling a broken arm against her chest.

But Catherine had underestimated Tara. Tara's innate magick might not be as powerful as Willow's, but she had a bigger heart than anyone Willow had ever met. That made her a formidable woman, someone not to be trifled with.

"Leave her alone," Tara said, her voice measured, words clipped. "Get those things off of her."

Catherine Cadiere turned pitying eyes upon Tara. Willow wanted to rip them from her head.

"You misunderstand me, sister," Catherine said.

"I'm not your damn sister."

"No," Catherine said with a condescending smile. "You are my cat."

With a wave of her hand, she transformed Tara back into the cinnamon-furred cat that Willow had first seen sitting on the old witch's lap back in Athens.

"No!" she screamed, grief clenching her heart. "Please!"

Catherine seemed to deflate, a sadness coming over her. With a wave of her hand, the cat transformed again. Tara appeared, lying on her side on the floor. She scrambled to her feet, eyes full of regret and sorrow.

"Will," she said.

"Hush," Willow told her.

"No. You should see the other room. All those women we met the other night, the witches, they're all unconscious. She's done something to them."

Catherine ran her hands through her silver hair and smoothed her clothes, as though all of this was beneath her dignity.

A spider crawled across Willow's mouth and she blew it off her, twisting in disgust, trying to shake them away.

"Get them off!"

"Tara speaks the truth," Catherine said. "My sister witches are unconscious at the moment and the magick is my doing. I am borrowing a bit of their magick for myself—siphoning it from them. There is a reason I am as ancient and as powerful as I am, a reason I am able to perform dark magicks without ever giving in to them."

"Not giving in? You're stealing magick from other witches!" Tara shouted.

"They will never know the difference," Catherine said. "Save for lethargy and diminished power for a few weeks. And they will all have benefited from the magick I'm able to perform because of it. I have tasted wickedness, Willow, just as you have, but I've managed to escape its grasp. I could have taught you the same."

Willow's upper lip curled. "Yeah, I don't think so. If you think you can mess around with the darkness and not get tainted, you're wrong. I'm thinking you need a new mirror, Catherine—one that shows the real you."

Catherine lowered her head and sighed, then looked up at them again. She shifted her gaze from Willow to Tara and back again.

"My heart is heavy. I thought you, of all of them, would see the wisdom in my path. I was wrong. Whatever happened to Kandida, it was not my magick. I have already told you that such witchery is not especially difficult with the right spell. I could have done it. But I did not. And as for the two of you . . ."

Anger flickered across her features.

"I hope you will be very happy together in your hypocrisy. You have both been given your heart's desire, but you hide the truth from yourselves. The magick you spurn—my ventures into the darkness—gave you this gift. You will not be able to hide from that truth forever."

Catherine whispered a spell and gestured at Willow, and the spiders all fell away, now nothing but bits of gray dust. The webbing turned brittle. She went to the door, opened it, and walked out, closing it firmly behind her.

Tara ran to Willow and began to break the webbing. It came away easily now, like dry papier-mâché.

Willow stared at her eyes, but Tara would not meet her gaze, and she knew that they were both suffering the same weight upon their hearts.

"We've . . . ," Willow began, but could not continue.

Tara sat back, kneeling beside her while Willow tore the rest of the webbing away.

"Been in denial?" Tara asked, without looking up.

Willow felt tears burning at the edges of her eyes, blurring her vision. They spilled over, running down her face. How could she have been so foolish? Buffy had tried to make her see it, and so had Giles. Real, human death could never be undone so simply.

"There's this d-debt," Tara said, taking short, hitching breaths, her own tears beginning as well.

Willow sat up and took her hands. They were on their knees, facing each other, but still Tara would not meet her gaze.

"Debt?" Willow asked.

Tara nodded. "Wherever it comes from, the b-black magick,

whatever d-deity or whatever those spells tap into, there's a debt. Magick costs something. Always. I knew that. I j-just didn't want to think about it. The debt is too much, Willow. I c-can't owe my joy to that. And I can't let you do it either."

Panic stricken, Willow shook her head. "That isn't up to you! You don't get to decide!"

Tara paled, staring at her. "Once, you used magick to make me think everything was okay, and it almost destroyed us. Are you going to do that again?"

Ashamed, Willow looked down, shaking her head.

"Then it *is* up to me."

Willow's throat felt like it was closing up. "Baby, no."

At last Tara looked up. Her eyes were fierce with love and determination. She nodded. "Yes. I don't belong here. We b-both know it. You're needed too much for me to go now, but when this is all over . . ."

Her face twisted up and she reached for Willow, pushing her fingers through Willow's hair. Tara held Willow's face in her hands. They wept silent tears. Willow could taste salt on her tongue.

"When it's o-over . . . ," Tara began again, but she could not continue.

Willow knew she had to say it aloud, to say it for both of them.

"When it's over," she said, "we have to return Catherine's gift."

She choked on the last word, on the irony, on her anguish. Willow found she could not hate Catherine. The ancient witch might be corrupted by darkness, but Willow was grateful to her for even the little time she had spent with Tara. It wasn't enough. It could never be enough. But in life, the bullet had taken Tara away without their ever having a chance to say good-bye.

They had their chance now. Time for a proper farewell.

Willow took Tara in her arms and kissed her deeply. Slowly she stood, brushed herself off, and reached for Tara's hand. The town-house was quiet, and with the spell the witches were under, it would remain quiet for hours. She led Tara up the stairs of the Victorian townhouse.

She wished she could take Tara in her arms and hold her forever. But as always, the darkness encroached upon the world, and Willow had to stand against it. Tara knew. She understood, and always had. Soon, they would have to go back out into the city and join the fight again. The world needed saving.

But for just a little while the world would have to wait.

CHAPTER FOURTEEN

Giles stood at the top of the State House steps with Micaela, waiting to die. Not that he wanted to die—far from it. But he had never imagined being surrounded by so many demons and flesh-eating monsters without at least having some kind of weapon in his hands—no sword, no crossbow, not even a sharpened stick. If anything went wrong, they were both going to be very dead, very quickly.

"You bring me to the nicest places," Micaela said, a mischievous glint in her eyes. In the moonlight she had an ethereal glow.

"You inspire the romantic in me," Giles replied.

They exchanged a nervous grin and then both of them flinched at the sound of the State House doors being unlocked. Coming here had been the only logical next step. Either Buffy had had to surrender her cell phone or it wasn't working in the meeting chamber. Walking up the steps, they had received hundreds of suspicious looks and many hungry glances, but no one had challenged them.

Not until they'd knocked on the door.

Micaela had made a joke about coming to the Emerald City to see the great and powerful Oz. Giles hadn't been in the mood for humor. Their knocks at the door had been answered by a nine-foot demon with a bulbous head and a face that twisted with octopus-like tentacles. Xander had seen a number of them at Lovecraft's grave, but prior to this Giles had been certain that the Yurgoths were extinct. Apparently not. They had told the demon that they needed to speak to the arbiter, and that if he did not fetch her, the arbiter herself would deal with him.

It had locked the door, leaving them waiting.

So when they heard the click of the locks being drawn back, and the door swung inward, Giles fully expected to see the Yurgoth again. Instead, Buffy poked her head out the door, a wary curiosity on her face.

"Giles? You get that this is a bad time, right?"

Before he could reply, the door swung wider and he saw the Yurgoth behind her, along with a demon with blue-tinted, stringy hair, and eyes as wide as a character from Japanese animation.

"Who's this? What's it about, eh?" the demon with the blue hair asked.

Giles stared at him a moment, then looked at Buffy. "It's absolutely vital that Micaela and I speak with you a moment, alone."

"Impossible," said the stringy-haired demon. "She can't leave while the Dark Congress is in session. She's the bloody arbiter, you fool."

Buffy turned to look at him. "Back off, Dyer. I've got this." She shifted her gaze back to Giles. "Cutty Dyer. Kid-snatcher or something. Water demon. He's the speaker for the Congress. And he's impatient. What's going on?"

A breeze blew the door open farther. Grit flew up from the floor and stung Giles's eyes. He blinked to clear them, wiped something away, and saw that Micaela was doing the same thing. When he could look at Buffy again, a new figure had joined them. Behind her and the speaker, Trajabo had appeared. His body was sculpted from sand like a statue. Giles thought of the street performers he had seen in tourist cities from New Orleans to Barcelona, men and women who kept perfectly still until it was time for the illusion that they were carved from stone to be undone. Trajabo had his head wrapped like a desert tribesman, only his eyes visible, but even that cloth seemed to be made of sand.

"This isn't the ideal situation to—"

"Rupert," Micaela interrupted. "We don't have time. Cards on the table."

Buffy gave him an urgent look and nodded in agreement.

"Right. So be it." He studied Buffy's face, glanced at the speaker and then Trajabo, then looked back at the Slayer again. "the Council has records of Malik and each of his allies as Champions. But Micaela and I performed a locating spell, searching the city for the influence of the Powers in individuals. The short version is that there aren't any."

With a sound like sandpaper on wood, Trajabo stepped nearer. The speaker, Cutty Dyer, shifted to let the desert demon closer to Buffy. Giles stared at them, wondering what help he could be if they meant her harm.

"What are you saying?" Buffy asked. "Malik and the others have left? Not what I expected, but not exactly Earth-shattering news."

Micaela took a step toward Buffy, her gaze urgent. "We don't think they've left."

Buffy frowned. "But that would mean . . . they're not Champions?"

Giles pushed his glasses farther up the bridge of his nose. "We can't be certain of anything. This warrior you met might not even be Malik. But they do meet the descriptions of the individuals in the Council's journals."

"There's something else," Micaela said.

Buffy sighed. "Isn't there always?"

Micaela took the map from her back pocket and unfolded it. She held it outstretched in her hands so that Buffy could see the area that she had marked.

"This road here, along the Seekonk River, is called Riverside Drive. The location spell found an anomaly all along the road on both sides, a place where the influence of the Powers is slightly greater than elsewhere, without any obvious explanation."

Another gust of wind, more powerful than before, buffeted them. Giles swore aloud and shielded his face. Buffy wiped away grit that had stuck to her lips and tongue. Micaela brushed at her hair. As one, they all noticed that Trajabo was gone.

"Damn it," Cutty Dyer said, shaking his head.

"You were the one who wouldn't let them talk to me alone," Buffy reminded him.

The speaker of the Dark Congress looked old and weary. "Trajabo vowed to give you until dawn. We'll simply have to trust him to keep to his word."

Giles stared at him. "That's it? He overheard our suspicions regarding Malik and vanished. You'd have to be a damned fool not to see cause and effect. He's going to try to hunt Malik himself!"

"Rupert," Micaela warned.

But Giles ignored her, glaring at Dyer.

"Boys, kinda not the time for a school yard brawl, okay?" Buffy said. She stepped out the door.

As she did, Dyer grasped the back of her shirt and hauled her back in. Buffy responded on instinct, spinning and knocking his hand away, then striking his chest with a flat palm. Dyer staggered back and sprawled on the marble floor of the rotunda. The Yurgoth hissed and reached for Buffy, who dropped into a battle stance.

"Try it."

"Buffy, stop. You don't have time for this," Giles said.

"You've got to get out there and find Malik," Micaela said. "Champion or not, we've got to find out the truth. Our best guess is that the concentration of influence from the Powers has some connection to Malik and his crew."

"Fine. I'm going," she said, glancing at Cutty Dyer. "Hold the fort. Don't let them kill each other while I'm gone."

Dyer's wide eyes had narrowed at last. Sour and grim, he stood up, one hand massaging the place where Buffy had struck him.

"You can't leave, lass."

"Should be pretty clear that you can't stop me," Buffy replied.

"You don't understand. If the arbiter leaves while Congress is in session, then the Dark Congress is over. Kandida will have died for nothing."

Buffy threw up her hands. "What do you want from me? Trajabo's gone. I've got a decent lead on Kandida's killer. I'm going to go and take a look. You're telling me there's no way for me to get out of here?"

Micaela crossed her arms, staring at the speaker. "There is a way."

A flicker of alarm crossed Dyer's features. "Don't be—"

"Substitution," Micaela added. "I've read up on the Dark Congress since we discovered what was really going on here. The arbiter can leave whenever she wishes, as long as she chooses her own substitution."

Buffy stared at Dyer. "That true?"

The water demon nodded, stringy hair falling across his eyes.

Giles flinched when Buffy reached out to tap his shoulder. "Tag. You're it."

"What? No, Buffy. You cannot seriously—," he began.

"Just did." Buffy reached out and pulled him into the State House. The speaker stared at him with open loathing. After all, he was no Slayer, nor a demon or anything supernatural at all. He was an ordinary man.

"Rupert Giles, Cutty Dyer. Cutty Dyer, Rupert Giles, the new arbiter. I'm out of here."

She stepped out the door. Giles called for her to come back, but Buffy ignored him, turning instead to Micaela.

"You with me?"

Micaela shot Giles a regretful glance. "Sorry, Rupert. You know it's the only thing to do."

"Good," Buffy said. She reached into a pocket and pulled out her cell phone. Flipping it open, she glanced at the phone, apparently to make certain she had a signal, and then she handed it to Micaela. "Call everyone in. Tell 'em where to meet me. The numbers are programmed in."

"But I should—"

"No," Buffy said. "You shouldn't." She took the map from Micaela, wondering how long it would take her to find a taxi.

Giles could only watch as Buffy descended the stairs, nearly at a run.

"Gather the others," he told Micaela.

She nodded, a forlorn expression on her face. Reluctantly, he stood by while Cutty Dyer swung the door closed and locked it, shutting Micaela and the rest of the world out, and them inside.

"This is quite troubling," the speaker said.

Giles turned to the Yurgoth, who hissed at him again, tentacles writhing on his face, reaching out toward Giles but not quite attacking—not yet.

"Buffy's going to be the death of me," he said to himself. "Possibly tonight."

Dyer laughed softly. "Now you know how my kind feel."

Improvisation had become the theme of the night. Not that Buffy's cab driver had appreciated that fact very much. The white-haired, solidly built man had been sitting behind the wheel reading a book by the dome light in his cab when she tapped on his window. He had seemed disappointed to have a fare but had nodded and invited her into the cab. They were driving by the time Buffy told him where she wanted to be taken.

"Nah, come on. You don't wanna go down there."

"I don't?"

The driver shook his head. "Nah. Nothing but trouble down there. Not a spot for a tourist stroll."

"How do you know I'm a tourist?" Buffy had asked.

The driver had glanced into the mirror and smiled. "You're not from Providence, honey. That much I know. I'd say Florida or California. Maybe the Pacific Northwest, but you don't look all that earthy to me."

"California," she had admitted.

"You don't want me dropping you off on Riverside Drive."

Buffy had pulled a bunch of cash out of her back pocket, all the money she had on her.

"Actually, I do. I've got a little over a hundred and twenty dollars here. I'll give you every penny if you drop me off and let me have your tire iron."

That had silenced him. He had kept driving, staring at her in the rearview mirror. A few minutes later, she saw the river out the passenger side window, moonlight glinting on the water. When he stopped, it was slowly, car rolling to a halt.

"You sure about this?" he had asked, eyes kind and concerned.

"Very," she said, handing the money up to him.

The driver took it. Buffy had gotten out of the cab while he counted it, and then he'd popped the trunk and climbed out as well. He went to the trunk, retrieved the tire iron, and handed it to her.

"You watch yourself, all right?"

Buffy had smiled, stood on tiptoes, and kissed the man on his stubbly cheek. He blushed a bit and looked away, then closed his trunk.

"I don't wanna read about you in the morning papers," he said.

"I can take care of myself," Buffy told him.

The driver slid back behind the wheel and closed his door. "Yeah," he said, taking her measure through the open window. "I figure you can."

It had all worked out quite propitiously. Buffy had been in such a hurry leaving the State House that it had never occurred to her to ask Dyer for weapons. She had nothing on her at all. Getting the tire iron from the cabbie had been a moment of pure inspiration, and she was glad of it. As she walked along the Seekonk River, ignoring the parked cars and the sounds that came from the open windows— sounds of a sticky summer night—the only thing she had seen that would have made a decent weapon was a length of chain wrapped around a fence on the other side of the road. Breaking the lock would have been easy, but carrying the chain around would have been cumbersome when she already had the tire iron.

So she walked, and she wondered what she was going to find. Buffy had almost expected the air down by the river to have some kind of magickal electricity, that frisson of weirdness that some- times crackled around supernatural locations and events, like the way the air felt right before a storm. But the road seemed utterly ordinary.

Even at night, in the moonlight, it was easy to see that the city of Providence had dropped the ball when it came to Riverside Drive. The riverbank was strewn with garbage. Nobody came down here at night except people who wanted to do things without being seen. She passed a group of teenagers drinking and tossing their beer bottles into the river, seeing who could throw them the farthest. Buffy went by without slowing. A couple of the guys called obscene things after her, but they did not try to pursue her.

The road must have run for two miles. On one end, where the cabbie had dropped her off, was some kind of yacht club. By the time she approached the other end of the street, Buffy had almost given up on finding anything, and anxiety had set in. If Micaela and

Giles had misread the results of their spell, there was no telling where Malik was, or if he was even involved in Kandida's assassination.

And she only had until dawn before Trajabo started tearing the Congress—and the city of Providence—apart looking for his girlfriend's killer. Demons in love. Always trouble.

A Salvation Army thrift store stood at the far end of Riverside Drive, a blocky building with two tractor trailers sitting as though abandoned on one side of the parking lot. Other than those trailers, only one vehicle sat in the lot: a black SUV of the type supposedly favored by drug traffickers.

The headlights came on, momentarily blinding her. Buffy shielded her eyes, blinked, and then tried to peer through the bright glare to make out any more details of the SUV.

Buffy kept walking. When she got to the end of the road, she stopped at the entrance to the parking lot.

The SUV's doors opened. Behind the glare of the headlights, she could only see black shapes climbing out of the massive black vehicle. The one at the driver's door ducked back inside and then the headlights winked out. Silence and darkness descended upon the parking lot. Buffy could hear the river flowing by, and then she heard the crunch of heavy boots on gravel.

Her eyes adjusted. The moonlight gave greater shape to the four figures that approached her—one tall and thin, one even taller and massive, one dwarfish, and one woman who seemed to slink with predatory, feline grace.

"We've been waiting for you," Malik said as they drew closer and the moonlight picked out the details of his face, the darkness of his beard. "I'd begun to wonder if you were not quite as intelligent as I thought."

Buffy read their body language, and it confused her. From the moment she saw the SUV parked in the lot, she had known it had to be Malik and his cronies, and had expected them to try to kill her.

But now, as she tested her grip on the tire iron, she studied them and realized that none of the four seemed ready to make any move.

"All hell is going to break loose, Slayer," said the woman, Simone, in her French accent. Her red hair shone in the moonglow. "This is precisely what we predicted. You have come to join us?"

Buffy couldn't help it. She laughed. "Yeah, that's not really on the agenda."

Bors, the dwarf, clucked his tongue. "I told you, Malik. She's blind."

The hulking Tai said nothing, as always.

But Malik took several steps toward Buffy, leaving the others behind, stopping only a few feet away from her. His eyes had a hypnotic quality, a strange kaleidoscopic effect that she hadn't noticed before. Buffy gripped the tire iron harder, just in case he had some kind of mesmerism power.

"It isn't too late," Malik said.

"For a bunch of demon hunters sitting out here in the middle of nowhere, you guys are pretty well informed."

Malik cocked his head. "Don't you think we have our sources, Slayer? Do not insult us."

"Sources? Like from the Powers? The only problem with that is you aren't really Champions," Buffy said. "Any of you."

The other three went very still, glancing at Malik, wondering what he would do.

"Oh, but we are," was all the dark-haired warrior said. Buffy could see the hilt of his sword sticking up from the scabbard that he wore across his back, but Malik made no move to reach for it.

"You should have listened from the beginning," Simone said, taking a step closer, watching Buffy closely. "But if you will not stand with us, you would be wise not to attempt to stand against us."

"Depends on what your next move is, I guess," Buffy replied. She wished she knew for sure if they had been involved with Kandida's death. They were all zealots, all bloodthirsty, and they had predicted that things would fall apart. But that didn't mean they had murdered Kandida. So she asked them.

"Did you kill her?"

Malik smiled. "There will be war now over her death. The only way to stop it is to eradicate them all—all of the monsters who have gathered for the Congress—before this city spins further into chaos."

"And if I disagree?" she asked.

The warrior's smile vanished. "Then you're just another monster."

Xander sipped a pint of Ipswich Ale that he'd been nursing for forty-five minutes. He figured one beer wouldn't hurt, given that all he was doing was sitting around waiting for Faith and Oz to come back, or for Giles to give him new marching orders. He had left messages by now at the hotel for Giles, Micaela, Buffy, and Willow, not to mention on Buffy's cell phone.

He was bored out of his mind. So bored, in fact, that the demons and childhood bogeymen and folktale monsters in Dunphy's Irish pub were starting to seem like pretty good company. The Red Sox game was still going on above the bar—or maybe it was a double-header or something. Or ESPN was on and they kept showing bits of the game over and over again.

To kill the time, he'd gotten to talking to some of the demons and listening in on their conversations. One of the nicest of them, a Russian Kurlow demon whose name was something like Tralfaz—only it couldn't actually be that, because Xander knew Tralfaz came from an old *Jetsons* cartoon—had bought him the Ipswich.

The creatures in Dunphy's were not members of the Dark Congress. They had come to Providence just for the spectacle, for the rare camaraderie of a peaceful gathering, and for the party. Word had reached them of Kandida's murder, and opinions were loud and varied on the subject of who might have perpetrated such a crime, knowing the possible consequences. Xander paid close attention to these musings, trying to keep track so he could pass them on if his friends didn't come up with the killer.

One opinion that nearly all the demons and monsters in the pub shared was surprise that Trajabo had agreed to give the arbiter until dawn to find his beloved's killer. Apparently, the demon of the desert was well known for his temper. Many of Dunphy's patrons admired him for his self-control, but others thought it showed weakness.

Xander kept his mouth shut except when he needed to ask a question to prod further discussion, and when he did, he chose his words carefully.

What astonished him most was how comfortable he felt in that environment. Given that at any other time, most of the creatures in the pub would gladly have eaten his brains, he felt remarkably calm—calm enough to be bored.

Until the winged serpent slid across the floor and rose up like a cobra beside him. Once upon a time Buffy had fought and destroyed a demon called Machida who'd had a similar appearance—like a man-size snake with arms. But Machida had not had wings. This thing had moist, leathery things that twitched and rustled as it swayed back and forth, staring at him with hideous orange eyes.

"I know you," the winged serpent said.

Xander cocked his head. "I . . . don't think so. I'm not from around here."

That brought a ripple of good-natured laughter from the other creatures in Dunphy's. Xander smiled, but then the snake-demon darted its head toward him and he let out a cry that was almost girlish. The winged serpent hissed, showing its fangs and forked tongue, but it did not bite him. Instead, it seemed to be smelling him.

Xander didn't try any other wisecracks. He had a feeling his girly squeal might have detracted from his audience support.

"I know you," the snake said again. "You were there at the revelry at Lovecraft's grave. You were there at the massacre."

Silence in the pub. All eyes turned toward Xander. His mind raced. This was not good, and he wondered how the winged serpent could know such a thing, since all the demons at Lovecraft's grave had been slaughtered by Malik and his friends.

"That wasn't me," he ventured.

The snake actually laughed, a sibilant chuckle that rocked its head and made its wings twitch partially open. "Oh, I know. I saw you, though. I had taken to the air from my perch in the trees only seconds before the killers arrived. I saw them, and I saw you."

Xander let out a breath. The rest of the monsters in Dunphy's were still listening, but didn't seem quite so ready to tear him into tiny pieces.

"It was Malik," the serpent hissed. "Malik and those other Champions. They are more bloodthirsty than any demon. If Trajabo wishes to take vengeance for Kandida's death, he does not need to look any further than Malik."

Xander glanced warily around and when he replied, he did so quietly. "That was . . . really ugly. Slaughter. The guy's a barbarian. But he's a Champion for the Powers. Killing Kandida could lead to chaos worse than anything anyone's ever seen. No Champion would do that."

The winged serpent sniffed in disgust and started to turn away. "You think not? Perhaps you're right. But I have seen Malik and some of the others at work before. They are not like other Champions. They hunt monsters, but Malik and his ilk enjoy it far too much. They will kill anything that isn't human. Your friends should beware."

"My friends—"

"They will kill *anything* that isn't human," the serpent said as it slithered away. "Demons. Witches. Werewolves. Even Slayers are not human. To Malik, we are all the same."

Xander stared at the demon as it slithered toward the back of the pub and into a booth. He looked around at Tralfaz, or whatever, who only nodded sagely. None of the other demons were looking at him anymore.

"Oh, crap," he said.

He took off, leaving the rest of his pint on the bar. By the time he hit the street, he had his phone out and he was running.

"I'm a monster?" Buffy said. "You and your brotherhood of evil mutants slaughter a bunch of uglies in cold blood without stopping to figure out who's actually evil, and the monster is me?"

Bors actually laughed. The dwarf had one of those unsettling, salacious laughs that she'd heard at frat parties and bars: suggestive and putrid—a pornographer's laugh.

Malik shot him a dark look and then faced Buffy once more. A gust of wind swept across the parking lot of the Salvation Army thrift store and rustled the leaves in the trees along the river. Sand skittered in the breeze and for a moment Buffy wondered if Trajabo had arrived, and what she would do if he showed up.

"Evil is not easily defined," Malik said. His voice was a low rumble, almost a purr. Sexy as hell. But the warrior was deceitful and murderous, and there was nothing at all sexy about those traits. Buffy had seen enough of deceit and murder to last a thousand lifetimes.

"Yeah," Buffy said. "It's like art. I can't define evil, but I know it when I see it."

Simone narrowed her eyes, stiffening. "What are you implying?"

"Implication is for diplomats. If I have something to say, I say it."

Her tone made things pretty clear. Tai, the hulking Asian man, took a step nearer to her, off to Malik's left. Buffy supposed it was meant to be surreptitious, but she noticed. Without moving, she took his position into account.

"As I said," Malik continued, "evil is not easily defined, so we are more comfortable referring simply to what is natural and what is unnatural. Humanity is part of this world's nature. What is inhuman is unnatural."

Buffy tested the weight of the tire iron in her hand and wished she had brought something more efficient—like an Uzi.

"Y'know, I spent a lot of time in high school and college taking crap for not being the most . . . studious girl. But when it comes to Slayer business, I do my homework. The Powers have never interfered with a Dark Congress before. From the research my friends and I dug up, it pretty much looks like the Powers support the idea of the Congress because it's just so damned orderly. Order from chaos, that's what they love. Order tips the balance toward peace; peace maybe leads to more and more demons saying sayonara and lighting out for the dark dimensions."

The amusement that had been in Malik's eyes vanished. "Now *you* sound like a diplomat."

Somewhere far off, a truck engine roared. The river flowed. When Buffy had been walking along Riverside, she'd heard night birds calling, but there was no birdsong now.

"Right. Sorry. Bad me. How's this for direct, then? Whatever you four are, or were, you weren't called here by the Powers. You're not here doing their work. Whatever twisted psycho game you fruity nut-bars are playing here, it's *your* game, not theirs. And you're more dangerous to this world than any of the demons and bogeymen up at the State House.

"You're the monsters."

Malik seemed crestfallen. He shook his head.

Tai and Simone each took a step nearer to her.

Bors laughed that obscene laugh again. "Finally. Can we kill her now?"

CHAPTER FIFTEEN

Oz had kept a change of clothes in the car, so his T-shirt and baggy pants didn't have any holes in them, but the ratty old bowling shirt he wore over his T-shirt was tacky with blood over the spot where his worst wound had been. It had stopped bleeding, but the cloth had stuck to the skin and when he shifted it pulled painfully away, crackling with drying blood.

Faith looked rough around the edges, but that wasn't new.

They'd rested in the old factory for twenty or thirty minutes. It would have been best to wait until their wounds were completely healed, or at least completely closed up. But they had to settle for mostly. They had both gotten stir-crazy out there in the middle of nowhere, knowing that the real fight might already be going on elsewhere.

Faith drove and Oz searched the radio for something acceptable to both of them. His taste in music was pretty diverse, but she liked headbanger stuff, so the car thrummed with thrashing instruments as they drove back to the hotel.

"You're a scrapper," she said to him at one point, while they waited at a red light.

Oz arched an eyebrow. "If that's a compliment, I'll go with thanks."

Faith kept her eyes on the road and her hands on the wheel. "It is. Gotta be brutal in a throwdown if you want to come out the other side. Good to have you with me tonight. Could've used you in the prison yard."

"Chicks in prison," he mused. "I've seen that movie. Could be fun."

"It wasn't," she said, with no trace of humor or irony.

Oz let it drop. Faith rarely seemed serious about anything. If he'd touched a nerve, he knew better than to touch it again.

As they came in sight of the Hotel Kensington, Faith's cell phone began to play its ring tone. "(Don't Fear) the Reaper" by Blue Oyster Cult. She flipped it open and looked at the display.

"It's Buffy."

Faith pressed the button to connect the call and held the phone to her ear. "Hey, B. We're pulling up to the hotel now. What's your twenty?"

Oz watched her face, saw the lines appear on her forehead.

"Yeah," Faith went on. "We'll park in front of the lobby doors. We'll be waiting."

She shut the phone and started to turn into the circular driveway in front of the hotel.

"What's going on?" Oz asked.

"That wasn't Buffy. It was Micaela. Looks like that Malik freak you ran across might be our guy. Buffy's out hunting. She should've waited for us."

"She's never liked to wait," Oz said.

Faith scowled. "Me either, but some of us learn our lesson. Micaela knows her general vicinity. Looks like we get to hunt the hunter. We've gotta find her before they kill her."

"Kill her? But she's Buffy."

"Against four Champions?" Faith said. "What'd they call her? The Deathless Slayer? Damn, wolf-boy, nobody's deathless. Nobody."

Willow and Tara left Maggie Hood's townhouse when the witches in the back parlor began to stir from the enchantment that had been placed upon them. They slipped out quietly, walking down the hill in the wealthy neighborhood with weary smiles on their faces, hand in hand. The disapproving looks of the old woman walking her dog and the business suit parking his BMW—home quite late from work or from a dinner with clients—did not faze them at all.

The memory of their conversation earlier hung like the sword of Damocles above them, but Willow refused to acknowledge it. They would have whatever time they had, and she would cherish every moment that remained.

As they walked down the hill, Willow felt the cell phone in her pocket begin to vibrate and the ring tone played "Black Magic Woman." A shudder went through her as she retrieved the phone, and she promised herself she would change the ring tone at the first spare moment.

The display said it was Buffy calling.

It wasn't.

Xander sat in the back of the cab, but right on the edge of the seat, as though his urgency could somehow lend velocity to the vehicle. The driver glanced at him several times, apparently unnerved by the manic energy of the stubbly-faced one-eyed guy in the backseat. Xander didn't care. He had to get to Buffy.

He had tried her cell phone nine times in about four minutes. Now, as he rode toward the Rhode Island State House—the dome was visible from almost anywhere in the city, lit up with small floodlights—he opened the phone and moved his thumb to the button, ready to hit redial.

Instead, it rang. He'd never gotten up the proper motivation to choose a song for his ring tone, so it remained the jangling, old-fashioned bell that came programmed with it.

The incoming call was from Buffy.

"About time," he said when he answered. "I've got to talk to you."

"It's Micaela. And I've got to talk to you, as well."

"What's wrong?" Xander asked, panicked. "Tell me Malik doesn't have her already?"

Micaela paused. In that moment he imagined the most horrible things. But then she spoke, and he realized he'd misinterpreted her hesitation.

"What do you know about Malik?"

"No. Uh-uh. Tell me what's going on. Why do you have Buffy's phone? Did he already get to her?"

"Malik's not a Champion. But we think we know where he and his allies are hiding. Buffy went after them."

Xander swore. His empty eye socket ached, and his temples began to throb. "That's not what I hear. About him being a Champion. The way the demons in town tell it, they're all Champions, but they don't follow the rules anymore. If it's supernatural, they'll kill it. Slayers included."

"But that doesn't—"

"Look, just tell me where she went."

"We're all meeting there. Let me give you directions."

He listened, then barked orders to the cab driver. The guy looked at him like he was out of his mind, but did not argue. Xander closed the phone and slid back against the seat, trying not to think about what would happen when he got to the Seekonk River—what they all would find waiting for them.

Micaela snapped a branch from a fallen oak tree on the riverbank. The car was parked on the shoulder of the road, with the rental

Faith had been driving right behind it. She and Oz sat on the hood, talking quietly to Willow and Tara, who had arrived in a taxi moments after Micaela and Faith had parked there.

She wasn't one of them; Micaela knew that. They were a generation younger than she was, and though they'd all had their difficulties, their resentments, and their broken hearts, they had grown up together. They knew her, but she was an outsider. In some ways it would have been much simpler if Buffy had chosen Micaela to replace her as arbiter. Giles would have been here instead, and then their circle would have been complete. Despite their differences, they were all a sort of congress of their own.

But the clock could not be reversed. Giles was back at the State House, and Micaela knew that was probably for the best. Rupert would be able to deal with the diplomatic pressure of the Congress better than she would have. In his own life he had lost patience with diplomacy, but when the world hung in the balance, she knew that he would always know precisely what to say.

So Micaela simply had to do her best.

She snapped the twigs and small branches off the larger one, stripping it down so she was left with a Y-shaped branch, perfect for her purpose. Dropping to her knees, Micaela picked up an apple she'd bought at a market on the way over. She'd also purchased a paring knife, and she used it to peel some of the skin off the fruit. Quickly and vigorously, she rubbed the apple's white flesh all over the single jutting end of the branch, juice and bits of the fruit left behind on the bark.

Micaela began a low chant. The incantation was a variation on a locator spell, but one she had never performed before. Micaela had some facility with magick—she had been raised from childhood by a sorcerer of great power—but she had no inherent magickal ability, only what could be learned from books and persistence.

An engine rumbled. She turned anxiously, worried that all of this activity so close to the entrance to the yacht club would have brought a police officer. Instead, it was another taxi. The cab pulled to a halt and Xander jumped out, then reached back in to pay the driver. A moment later the cab was pulling away and he was trotting over to join the others. Once he had been a laughing boy, a big-hearted clown, but the dark patch over his empty eye socket had altered him in spirit as well as appearance. He was grim tonight.

Of course, they all had reason to be grim.

Micaela walked back to where the two cars were parked. She heard them talking, exchanging stories about what they had learned. Catherine Cadiere and the vampires had all been cleared as suspects in Kandida's murder. That came as no surprise now, of course. Xander had confirmed that Malik and his friends were Champions, though Micaela and Giles had been unable to find them with the locator spell that would identify the influence of the Powers in the city. There could be only one conclusion, and Micaela felt furious with herself that she had not made it sooner. Somehow the Champions had blinded the Powers to their presence here. Their connection to the Powers was diffused over a large area, explaining the concentration she and Giles had discovered with their spell.

"If Buffy found them, she could be in major trouble," Willow said.

"Ya think?" Faith snapped. "Two Champions, maybe, but four? She's screwed."

"Way to boost morale, Lehane," Xander snapped.

Faith flipped him off, but there was nothing hostile about their exchange.

Micaela stepped up to them, the Y-shaped branch—her supernatural dowsing rod—in her hands.

"Tara?" she said.

They all turned to look at her. Willow wore a strange expression, almost protective. Faith gave Micaela a glance that said she had only just remembered that the Watcher was with them.

"Me?" Tara said.

Micaela smiled, considered asking if any of the others were named Tara, but then thought better of it. The witch was shy and self-effacing, and making light of that would not win her any friends.

"I'll need your help to find Buffy. The locator spell I'm using is channeled through this branch and it becomes a sort of pointer. I'd like you to hold it while I finish the incantation."

Tara's blond hair fell across her face and she seemed to hide behind it. She opened her mouth as though to reply, but Willow moved up beside her and took her hand.

"Why Tara? If you've got a locator spell that can track Slayers, why does it have to be her?"

Micaela understood Willow's protectiveness. She had lost Tara once and feared losing her again. So she did not take offense at the powerful witch's tone or the wary light in her eyes.

"The spell doesn't track Slayers. But if it did, I'd need Faith to hold the pointer, otherwise it would simply point to her because she's closer to us than Buffy is. This spell is attuned to those whose spirits have touched the afterlife and returned. It's—well, honestly, it's usually used to find the walking dead, but it should work to track the resurrected. If I hold the branch, it'll point to Tara. If she holds it, it should lead us to Buffy."

They all stared at Micaela until she began to fidget.

"What?" she asked.

Xander grinned. "Nothing. It's just cool. If Giles were younger, female, kinda hot, and not so in love with giving lectures, he could be you."

He flinched, his smile vanishing, and glanced over at Oz. "Did I say that 'kinda hot' part out loud?"

The werewolf nodded solemnly. "You can't help yourself. You're Xander."

Tara reached out and took the pointer, holding the arms of the Y in her hands.

Faith slid off the hood of Micaela's rental. "Can I just ask, before we play cavalry, if there's a plan? I mean, okay, I know I'm not the having-a-plan type. Pretty much I go with what for most people would be the fallback option—y'know, 'beat the crap out of something.' But we're trying to do things differently these days, right?"

She glanced around at them. Micaela knew what Faith was talking about. As they had gone around the world gathering all the young, new Slayers, they had attempted to become more methodical in their operations.

"Tara and I were talking," Willow said. "If the Champions are blowing off the Powers That Be, the Powers are gonna be kinda pissed when they find out. We're trying to work out a way to get the message to them."

Faith nodded. "Cool. Other than that?"

Micaela glanced around at them. After a few seconds Xander threw up his hands. "What was that you were saying about your fallback option?"

Willow glanced at Micaela. "Are you sure you don't want me to do this spell? No offense."

Micaela shrugged. "None taken. You're a very powerful witch, Willow. More innately powerful than any I've ever met, I think. I'm just a magician, really. Petty sorceries, that sort of thing. But I've done this spell before, and done it well, and I don't think we have time for me to teach it to you."

Willow turned a hesitant glance toward Tara.

"She'll be fine," Micaela assured her.

After a moment, Willow smiled. "So, pretty much up to you. Do your thing." She kissed Tara's cheek. "Be careful, sweetie."

"Will you drive?" the Watcher asked.

Willow nodded and Micaela handed her the keys. Tara got into the backseat. When Willow started the engine, Tara rolled her window down and held the pointer out. Micaela got into the passenger seat as Faith started up the second car, with Xander and Oz riding along with her.

They pulled off the soft shoulder, moving slowly. Micaela started chanting the spell again. When she had finished, she glanced into the backseat at the shy, blond witch who watched her anxiously.

"Tara?" Micaela asked.

She watched the witch holding the pointer out the window. Tara moved it back in the direction from which they'd come and the Y-shaped branch jumped in her hands, its point bending in the other direction. Tara shifted, let the pointer lead the way.

"Keep going straight ahead."

Malik sighed. "Such a shame, but we've wasted enough time. Yes. Kill her."

The dwarf, Bors, whipped his arm out, unfolding a metal flail—a kind of whip made up of segments of black iron. Tai unsheathed a pair of silver daggers, intricately etched, ancient blades. Simone brandished no weapon save her hands.

The three of them came at her, and Malik only watched.

Buffy let them come, staring into the warrior's eyes. She might be fighting the other three Champions, but Malik was her true opponent.

The dwarf's metal flail whipped toward her. Buffy dodged to the right, practically into the hands of Tai and Simone. The silent, mountainous warrior slid into a smooth, swift attack—he held the dagger in his right hand back to parry any counterpunch even as he stabbed at her with the left. The attack had been coordinated so well with Simone that Buffy felt sure they had fought side by side many times. Simone dropped down and shot a kick at Buffy's right knee that would have easily shattered her kneecap if she had not moved.

Buffy leaped into the air, grasping Tai by the stabbing arm and diverting the blade in his hand. Simone's kick swept harmlessly beneath her. The Slayer twisted, using the hulking mute as a foundation for her motion. She grabbed Tai's right hand and drove it back, forcing him to stab himself in the shoulder with his own blade. Tai grunted, and as his blood began to trickle, Buffy shot her right leg down and caught Simone in the back of the head before she had managed to jump back from her own attack.

The redheaded woman fell forward, tumbled into a roll, and then leaped up, turning toward Buffy, enraged.

Tai glared at her, trying to twist her off, to free his left hand so he could stab her again. Buffy head-butted him, but it seemed to trouble him not at all and her skull rang hollowly.

She heard the metal flail whistle through the air and tried to move. Tai held her, turned her, and the flail struck her across the back. Buffy cried out as she heard bone crack in her back. Pain shot through her and she pulled her legs up, braced them on Tai's chest, and pushed away, tearing herself free of him.

When she landed, it took a moment for her to rise. The pain in her back felt like Tai was stabbing her with his silver blades, over and over again.

"I'm gonna guess you guys don't care about playing fair," Buffy said.

Simone danced toward her in an odd, elegant fighting style that reminded Buffy of capoeira. She did a kind of pirouette, which seemed like an opening. The Slayer ignored the pain in her back and shot a kick at Simone's chest.

The redhead leaped from her pirouette like a ballerina, using the end of her spin to knock aside Buffy's kick, and then she twisted, reversing direction, and slapped Buffy open hand across the face. Though it could not have the impact of a punch, the sting was sharp and startling and it staggered her for a single heartbeat—long enough for Simone to follow up. The redhead dropped into a crouch, shot a punch at Buffy's side that connected solidly, then leaned back to shoot a low kick, once more at her knees, trying to disable her.

Buffy snagged her ankle and spun her hard, twisting her off her feet. Simone went down hard on the ground. The Slayer tried to follow up, but Tai was already there. They traded several blows, then Buffy broke his nose. Blood sprayed down his shirt. Buffy knocked the dagger from his left hand, leaving him only with the one in his right, the one that already had his own blood on it. Tai snorted like a bull and started to pursue her. Simone was getting up.

This time Buffy heard the whistling of the flail as it whipped toward her. She turned, dodged, and then grabbed hold of the segmented metal weapon before Bors could retract it.

"Yeah, I don't think so," she said. "I didn't ask for seconds."

She ripped the flail from his hands. Bors ran at her, reaching for it. Buffy dodged the little man and then kicked him into the dirt. With a low grunt from deep inside him, the mute Tai thundered toward her.

Buffy hit him in his bleeding, broken nose with a quick snap of the flail.

The massive Asian opened his mouth in a moan of agony and she saw that he had no tongue. But that didn't stop her from taking advantage of his pain. Buffy whipped the flail at him again. It wrapped around his neck and she maneuvered around behind him, choking him, dragging him down. He tried to bring his other dagger up, but she kicked at his wrist, disarming him completely, and dragged him away from the weapon.

Bors and Simone came at her slowly, watching warily, not wanting her to kill Tai, looking for an opening to attack her. Beyond them Malik stood as still as ever. In his black clothes he seemed to be half invisible in the moonlight. His eyes even seemed black, set in his pale features, above that dark beard. The ominous warrior had not even drawn his sword.

"I didn't expect him to be real skilled in the banter," Buffy said, giving a tug on the flail to indicate that she meant Tai, "but none of you talks very much, do you? Where's the bragging? The threats?

No promises about eating my eyes or gnawing my bones or delivering me to everlasting torment? You guys really have to brush up on the bad-guy schtick."

Malik actually smiled. He strode toward her, but stopped when he was still a few feet behind Bors and Simone.

"Killing you really is regrettable, Slayer. You'd be quite an ally. And we could make you vanish the way we have vanished. We've blinded the Powers to us, made them believe we're dead. When we learned of the Dark Congress, there was no other choice. We simply cannot accept that peace might be made between the monstrous races. That could lead to peace between the forces of Light and Darkness, and we can't have that. Demons and horrors, hostile or passive, must be destroyed. Anything else goes against our purpose, our mission."

"Yeah, y'know, I was kidding about the speechifying."

Buffy dragged Tai backward by the neck. He choked pitifully, reached up, and tried to claw at her, to grab her, but she dodged and twisted the flail hard. He tried to struggle and she forced him down again. He might be much larger than she was, but Buffy wasn't an ordinary woman. She was the Deathless Slayer. The Chosen One among Chosen Ones. She overpowered him, kept him down.

"Didn't the Powers give you this mission in the first place?" Buffy asked.

Simone laughed softly.

Bors had lost his pornographer's grin. He glared at her now, full of hate. "The Powers don't understand the needs of the human race. We are human. We're flesh and blood. We understand what must be done."

"Good for you. What do you want, a cookie?"

Even as she spoke, Bors moved. His right hand came around from behind his back and he barked words in an ancient, guttural tongue as he whipped a handful of gravel into the air.

For a second Buffy was confused. The dwarf wasn't even throwing the gravel at her. Then the scattering of dust and tiny stones exploded in a burst of light, a fireworks display of tiny sun-bursts that blinded her for a moment.

Then they were on her. A boot struck her cheek. Hands grabbed fistfuls of her hair and dragged her down and then they were kicking her, circled around her. Spatters of Tai's blood fell on her as he crouched to hammer his fists down upon her. She twisted so that the blows fell on her back, but the pain pounded through her. The bones that the flail had cracked ground together.

Buffy tried to crawl away.

Her right hand landed on a leather boot.

The beating ceased and she raised her head to find Malik standing over her.

He had drawn his sword at last.

The demon of the desert slid along the roadside, nothing more than wind and sand. He followed the friends of the Slayer in their two cars as they tried to use their witchcraft to track her down. The cars moved slowly, just rolling along the road, slower than the rush of the nearby river.

The presence of the river hurt Trajabo's heart. All he could think about, so close to the gentle sound of the deep, rushing water, was Kandida. His grief and fury had merged and become one.

As he slipped along the road, watching the two cars, his very presence sucked the moisture out of the humid August night. The demon missed the desert. When he passed above grass, it dried to a crisp yellow, the soil becoming arid. Trajabo did not exert this influence on his environment purposely. It was simply his essence. The desert lived within him. And now his heart was as arid and unforgiving as the hard land of his origin.

The cars began to slow and then stopped. The engines were shut off, first one and then the other. The Slayer's friends climbed from the car. Trunks were opened and weapons removed—swords and an aluminum baseball bat and a crossbow.

The Slayer must be near, which meant that Kandida's killers were also near. Trajabo trembled. Vengeance would not restore her to life, or assuage his grief, but it had to be done.

Blood would flow.

CHAPTER SIXTEEN

Buffy stared up at Malik and at the glint of moonlight on his sword. Her body throbbed with the blows the other renegade Champions had delivered and she felt disoriented. She tensed, hoping she could dodge the arc of his sword, but he was so close, right above her.

"You were quite pretty," the brooding warrior said.

Apropos of nothing, Buffy thought. But she'd been drawn to him from the moment she had first seen him, and knew that in another life, things might have been different between them.

Malik raised the sword.

A low, growling noise came to them like distant thunder, but Malik did not hesitate. He brought the sword down in a killing stroke.

Oz struck him from the side, the werewolf plowing into him. Snarling, jaws gnashing, the wolf drove Malik to the ground and began to beat him about the head with his forepaws, claws slashing the warrior's face and arms, drawing blood. Malik managed to get his sword up, only to have it batted away. It landed on the pavement only a few feet from Buffy.

As the Slayer staggered to her feet, she watched Malik reach his left hand up to try to force the werewolf's jaws away from his throat. Oz bit the hand off, finger bones crunching in his teeth.

Malik cried out in pain.

Buffy found no pity in her heart for Malik. She picked up his sword.

As she did, Tai ran past her and leaped onto the werewolf's back, dragging Oz away from Malik. The wolf and the silent warrior began to roll over and over. Buffy saw a glint of silver and knew Tai had recovered at least one of his daggers—blades that could be fatal to Oz.

Malik started to climb to his feet.

Buffy held the sword in her left hand, hauled back with her right, and punched him with all the strength she could muster. She felt bone crack in his cheek and he went down.

"Oz! The big guy's got silver!" Buffy shouted.

But then Faith was there, rushing past her in the dark.

"Got it, B!" she said. Faith set one foot, then started launching kick after kick at Tai. She knocked his arms away from Oz, and when the silent warrior began to rise in fury, Faith leaped into the air, twisted into a spinning kick that landed solidly at the center of his chest, and knocked him backward. Tai rolled off the edge of the pavement and down an incline covered with prickly brush. He caught himself only a few feet from the river's edge and stood.

Faith went down toward the water in pursuit.

Malik cursed under his breath and started to stagger to his feet again. Buffy glanced down at him and raised the sword, pointing it downward. She wouldn't kill him, but if a blade through the shoulder would keep him down, that kind of pain was fine by her.

She heard the metal flail whistling as it swung toward her.

Buffy turned and held up the sword. The flail wrapped around it and Bors tugged the blade from her grasp. It flew out of her hands, spun away from the flail, and landed in the river.

"Good job, Lollipop Guild," Buffy said.

Bors grinned at her. Beyond him, Buffy saw that Oz and Faith had not come alone. Xander and Micaela were there, facing off against Simone. The redhead had her hands up, ready to fight. She lunged at Xander and Micaela shot Simone with a crossbow. The bolt sank into her chest just above her left breast and she cried out. She spun into the air using that same, dancelike martial arts move she had used on Buffy. Simone kicked the crossbow from Micaela's hands as Xander swung a baseball bat. He stepped into it, like he was swinging for the fences, and the bat struck Simone in the back. She went down, but rolled and sprang up almost instantly.

"They won't be able to help you," Bors sneered, starting toward Buffy, hands up, still wearing that salacious smile.

Stiff and hurting, Buffy lifted one corner of her mouth in half a smirk. "I don't need any help."

Bors held the flail in both hands now, preparing to attack. Buffy was unarmed.

"You think I can't hurt you because I'm small?"

"No. I think you can't hurt me because you're wolf bait."

The dwarf spun at the sudden growl and the sound of the werewolf's approach. He swung the flail. It struck Oz in the head, wrapped around the wolf's skull, and then Bors pulled the werewolf to the ground. Oz remained there for perhaps an eyeblink, and then he surged upward at Bors. The flail could be a devastating weapon from arm's length. Up close, it was useless.

Bors began to scream.

Buffy caught a glimpse of Willow and Tara standing together in the moonlight maybe fifty yards from the Salvation Army parking lot. The witches had their hands linked and raised between them. Their faces were turned to the sky, illuminated by the moon, and on the wind Buffy could just hear their voices rising in a low chant.

"Another master plan bites the dust," she said, turning back toward Malik.

But the renegade Champion was gone.

Once upon a time Xander would have had a hard time hitting a breathtakingly gorgeous redhead with a baseball bat. Since that time he'd nearly been eaten by a woman who was a praying mantis, seen hundreds of hotties turn out to be hideous demons or vampires, and had his ass kicked by many of them.

Simone grabbed Micaela around the throat and lifted her off the ground, sneering.

Xander climbed to his feet. Maybe the Champion though she'd hit him hard enough to take him out of the fight. But she had a rude awakening coming. He slipped behind her, slid the aluminum bat across her throat, and held on tight, tearing her away from Micaela as he choked her. Simone reached around, trying to claw at him, but Xander kept dodging his head.

Simone dropped Micaela, who gasped as she sucked in air.

The female Champion tried to kick backward. With the strength she had, she could easily break his leg with one kick. Xander raised the bat like a weightlifter, pulling her off her feet so that she thrashed against him, trying to get some kind of leverage.

"There's a joke in here about you liking it rough," Xander whispered in her ear. "But I ran out of funny a long time ago."

The redhead tagged him with a swift swipe of her hand, her fingers tearing off his eye patch. Xander winced, but then laughed without humor.

"Already lost that one, lady."

Micaela was up. She had one hand on her throat as she staggered toward them. In her other hand she held a small amount of sand and gravel she'd picked up from the parking lot. Micaela threw the sand into Simone's face, then darted in to clamp her hand over Simone's eyes.

"Rabiosa veternosa," the Watcher said.

The redhead went limp in Xander's arms. At first he thought she was sleeping, but as he put her down he saw that her eyes were open. She looked tranquil, drugged.

"What'd you do?" Xander asked.

Micaela sat down hard, exhausted. "Soothed the savage beast—for the moment."

Oz had his jaws clamped on the diminutive warrior's skull. He'd already had a taste of one of them, though he'd spit Malik's mangled hand into the tangled brush by the river's edge. Now he fought the urge to simply bite off the dwarf's head.

Pinning Bors to the ground with one heavy paw, he pulled his jaws back, growling low. Long ropes of thick drool slid from the werewolf's open maw to spatter the dwarf's clothes and face. Bors recoiled in disgust, but he could not escape. Oz had him. The metal flail was still wrapped around the werewolf's neck, but Bors could do nothing.

Which made Oz wonder why he was smiling.

With a grunt, the dwarf began to talk. He muttered something in a guttural language Oz did not recognize. The werewolf felt his skin prickling strangely, and realized that the former Champion knew some magick. One of them had to know magick to have managed Kandida's assassination, but Oz hadn't thought it would be Bors.

Wary, he started to back away.

The moonlight seemed suddenly very bright. Oz snarled and blinked, lowering his huge, shaggy head. When he looked up, Bors had climbed to his feet.

Oz felt a breeze off the river and it seemed almost cool to him.

That was when he realized he no longer wore the body of a wolf. Somehow Bors had used magick to revert him to human form. Oz was naked and weaponless.

The smile vanished from the cruel little man's features. He

reached around to his back and pulled out a small knife, then started toward Oz.

"Not so frightening now, are you?" Bors said.

Oz glanced down at his skinny, naked torso. "Some would disagree."

The massive Asian warrior moved far more quickly than Faith would have expected. She shot a kick at his groin and he snatched her ankle, dragged her toward him, and hammered her with a punch to the face. Faith went down hard, rolled away from him, and sprang up again.

But Tai had taken off running.

Faith frowned, wondering what she'd done to scare him off. Then she saw Bors and Oz—Oz had changed back to human for some reason and was standing there naked and pale and defenseless, the moron—and she realized Tai was the werewolf hunter among them. He still had a silver dagger in one hand, and he was after Oz.

"Not gonna happen," she sneered as she gave chase.

Bors struck Oz once. Then Tai was there. The silent warrior grabbed the dwarf and yanked him away. He said nothing, but Bors seemed to understand immediately.

"All right, my friend," Bors said, holding up both hands. "Take him."

Then Faith was there. She sprinted toward them and leaped into a flying drop kick. Her right boot struck Tai in the back. Something snapped in his spine and he collapsed to the ground as though an earthquake had shaken the mountain down.

Bors started to raise his hands to defend himself.

Faith only smiled at him.

Xander hit Bors in the head with the baseball bat and the renegade Champion flopped to the pavement beside Tai.

Oz stood just beyond them, hands covering his most vulnerable parts.

"Jacket? Sweatshirt? Anyone?" Oz asked.

Micaela averted her eyes.

Faith arched a suggestive eyebrow at him. "What for?"

With a shudder, Oz transformed again. Whatever Bors had done to him, it seemed to have faded. The wolf lumbered toward Faith, growling low.

"Get over yourself," Faith told the beast. "There wasn't much to see."

Wincing with pain, Buffy scanned the parking lot and the road and the trees and twisted bushes near the river's edge. It took a second glance for her to realize that the dark shape emerging from the water was not some fallen pine but the immortal warrior himself.

Malik rose from the rushing river, hair and beard shedding water and clothes soaked through, so that they hugged his thickly muscled form. He had retrieved his sword from the water and held it in his right hand. At the end of his left arm there was only a stump where Oz had bitten off the hand.

The renegade moved up the bank and pushed through a lattice of thick bushes. When he reached the road, he was bent and limping. From where she stood Buffy could hear him grunt with pain as he started to cross the road. She staggered after him, moving as quickly as her pain would allow.

When she glanced past him and saw Willow and Tara, still facing each other and clasping hands, still with their eyes closed and their faces turned toward the night sky and bathed in almost divine light, Buffy realized that Malik had made them his target.

All of her pain vanished.

"Willow!" Buffy shouted. "He's coming for you!"

But neither of the witches looked up or broke off their contact—their spell. Nor did Malik respond with so much as a glance over his shoulder. He shuffled toward them, sword gripped in his right fist. Buffy saw that what dripped from his left arm was not water from the river but a darker liquid. She reached the first splash of his blood and inhaled, breathing the coppery aroma.

"Malik! Leave them alone!"

The renegade did not listen. But he did not have to. Malik had kept on limping and Buffy had shed her pain, put it in a compartment in her mind so that it could not hinder her now. Tomorrow she would suffer for it. Tonight all that mattered were her friends. Willow and Tara had been given a second chance at the sort of contentment Buffy felt sure would forever elude her. She would not let some bloodthirsty zealot take that away.

She ran, stumbling just a little.

Malik heard her coming. Just before she reached him, he turned, brandishing his sword. Buffy dodged his first thrust with the blade. In that moment he was vulnerable. She stepped in and hit him in the temple, and Malik staggered away from her. Buffy moved in, swift and efficient, to finish the fight.

But Malik wasn't finished. The renegade shot back his left elbow and hit her in the throat.

Choking, gasping for air, Buffy staggered backward. Panic surged in her as she tried to breathe, and for a moment she thought he had crushed her throat and she would suffocate. Then she drew a ragged breath and relief flooded her. Her eyes were still wide, her hands still clutching at her neck, and Malik moved in to deliver the coup de grace. He brought the sword down in a sideways arc meant to decapitate her.

Buffy threw herself into a forward somersault, rolling beneath the blade. As it sliced the air above her, she sprang up from the roll and grabbed him by the wrist, twisted, and tore the handle of the sword from his grip. Furious, almost lost in some blind fury, she raised the weapon above her head and swung it with all her strength at the pavement. It struck the road and the blade shattered into half a dozen pieces.

The Slayer dropped the hilt of the sword and it clanged to the ground.

"Damn you, girl, for interfering! The future of humanity depends upon what we do here today!" Malik roared.

"At last we agree on something," Buffy replied.

Malik came for her. The Slayer caught his fist and pulled it toward her, using his momentum. She drove her knee up into his gut. He doubled over and stumbled back and Buffy clasped her hands together in a single, enormous fist and swung them around in one blow to the head that knocked him backward and to the ground.

Still Malik was not defeated. Hatred and disgust burned in his eyes. Wearily, he began to rise.

Tara had repeated the incantation more than a dozen times, perhaps two dozen. She held Willow's hands in hers, felt the warmth there, the familiar contours of her palms. Her eyes were closed in order to focus on the spell they were performing, but though she could not see the world around her, that only freed her to look inward instead. In her mind's eye, images and moments from their time together played over and over. Tara had lived eighteen years before she had met Willow, but they seemed a long and uneasy slumber to her. Meeting Willow had been the first time she had woken from that sleep, woken to a life like the sweetest dream.

Dying had simply been going to sleep again, but it had been a sleep without the dream she cherished.

They stood there together now in the damp heat of the August night, holding hands as they had done so often in Willow's bedroom when they had first begun to experiment with magick and spell-craft. Tara felt her eyes burning with unshed tears, welling with sorrow. Good-bye would come soon, but this would be the last time they would perform magick together. She sensed that, felt it with utter certainty.

When, as they began the incantation yet again, she felt the abrupt collapse of the magick that the Champions had used to hide themselves from the Powers That Be, a piece of her heart broke along with it. The sudden attention of the Powers was tangible. The summer night crackled with the electrical static that always filled the air before a storm. They were all being observed now. The Powers were aware. Tara felt it.

She cared nothing for their attention.

Eyes still closed, she wrapped her fingers more tightly in Willow's and pulled her into an embrace. They held each other so tightly that Tara could not breathe. Willow whispered a word that might have been "no," holding her fiercely, as though at any moment she feared someone might try to pull Tara away.

There had been shouting and cries of pain and the clang of metal weapons and the howl and bellow of the wolf while they had performed the incantation, but they had ignored it all. Even now they seemed to be on an island to themselves in the midst of the sea of conflict around them. Surrounded by violence and bloodshed, they had found sanctuary in each other.

For the last time.

"Willow," Tara whispered.

"Shh. Let's just . . . shhh."

Malik seemed almost to shrink. Buffy felt as though she *saw* the spark of immortality flee from his body. Whatever other gifts the Powers That Be had given him as their Champion must have fled as well. Cradling the stump of his missing hand, the warrior knelt on the ground and glared up at her with hate-filled eyes.

"What have you done?"

"Projecting much?" Buffy said. "I'm pretty sure this is about what you've done. I'm guessing the Powers don't approve."

Malik forced himself to his feet. Surprised he even had the strength, Buffy tensed, ready to defend herself. But the renegade had no interest in her now. He staggered past her.

"My friends . . . ," Malik began, but he could not get another word out. His voice was filled with grief, and the way he gripped his severed wrist with his remaining hand, he seemed almost to be pleading forgiveness.

Tai, the silent warrior, had fallen. He too seemed diminished. He bled from half a dozen wounds and his body twitched as though recovering from some kind of seizure. The seductress, Simone, knelt beside him. The Powers may not have given her immortality, but their gifts had slowed her aging and now those gifts had been withdrawn. She was an old, withered crone, face all drooping leather and hair nothing but white wisps. Simone wept and shuddered, leaning against Bors. The dwarf seemed the least affected of all of them. Hatred still burned in his eyes. But he, too, bled from many wounds, including puncture marks on his face where Oz had held the dwarf's skull in his jaws.

Faith, Xander, Oz, and Micaela had gathered in a half circle around the Champions, exhausted, bruised, and bleeding themselves, but also wary of their enemies.

"What's happening to them?" Xander asked.

"Payback," Faith said.

Buffy glanced over at Willow and Tara. The witches held each other close, the rest of the world closed off from their intimacy.

"They used some kind of glamour to hide themselves from the Powers That Be so they could do whatever they wanted and not face any of the consequences," Micaela said.

"Willow and Tara took away the glamour," Buffy said, unable to look up at Xander, her gaze locked now on the pitiful wretches before them.

Malik stumbled and fell to his knees beside the fallen Tai. Neither Simone nor Bors so much as glanced at him, though his features were contorted in a mask of regret that was hideous to behold.

"And the consequences begin," Faith said.

The wind gusted. At first Buffy thought nothing of it. Then it gusted again, more powerfully than before. Sand and grit flew into her face and she shielded her eyes. Her throat went dry, as though all of the moisture around her had been sucked away.

"No," she said.

Turning, she saw the dust devil swirling across the road, saw it take form and sculpt itself in the shape of a man.

"No!" she shouted. "We had an agreement. You gave me until dawn!"

Trajabo stood a dozen feet away. His golden eyes were narrowed with anguish and hatred. He started to walk toward her. All of Buffy's friends moved to stand by her, to bar the demon's approach. A bitter taste came into Buffy's mouth as she realized that they were protecting Malik and his allies, these monsters who had been responsible for so much horror, who had risked the fate of the world for their own arrogance and bigotry.

"My agreement was with the arbiter," Trajabo said. His features, carved in sand, had seemed almost human before. Now they were as monstrous as any demon, resculpted, cruel and twisted. "You are no longer the arbiter."

"You can't kill them," Micaela said. "the Congress is tenuous already. If you murder them, the entire thing could collapse."

"You'd be just as selfish as Malik, risking the world to serve your hate," Buffy told him.

"The arbiter will persuade the Congress to forgive me. What choice do they have? They have taken Kandida from me, from all of us. And these creatures are not members of the Dark Congress. They are our enemies. the Congress will not condemn me. They'll make me a hero."

"You don't know that," Buffy said.

The four renegade champions were wounded and weak. Yet Bors and Malik had a quiet dignity. On their knees, they would sink no farther. Buffy glanced back and saw them glaring at Trajabo like condemned prisoners awaiting the hangman's noose.

Trajabo hesitated, softening. "You cannot understand. My life has spanned thousands of years. In all of that time I found love only once, and I know I never shall again. Not real love. Once, she was taken from me by callous murderers. Then she was returned to me. A gift. A miracle. Only to be taken away again. The only bit of divinity that I shall ever have in my life, torn from me. It is a cruel joke. You cannot possibly understand."

"You're wrong."

The reply came from Willow. Trajabo turned to watch as she and Tara approached. He had a sneer on his face, disdainful of the witch's claim. But Willow was not intimidated. She and Tara walked toward the demon of the desert, hands linked.

"We understand completely," Willow said. Her voice was tight and there were tears in her eyes, but she held the demon's gaze and spoke firmly. "I wish we didn't. We understand better than you'll ever know. But you're missing the point. You just don't get it. A cruel joke? How can you say that? You got the best gift in the world, and then it was given to you a second time. I know it hurts, but that's what it costs. That's the price of love. Once, I thought the price was too high, that love wasn't worth it. But it is."

Willow glanced at Tara. "It is."

Trajabo seemed taken aback. Buffy stared at him, wondering if Willow had gotten through to him. But then the bitterness and fury flashed in his eyes again, and she knew that his thirst for vengeance was beyond any logic or sentiment.

"Don't do it," Buffy said.

She rushed at Trajabo, but before she could grab hold of him, the demon of the desert burst into a cloud of sand and grit. The dust devil spun to cyclone force, twisted her around and hauled her off the ground as though she were weightless. The sand scoured Buffy's face and arms, and she closed her eyes and tried to reach her hands up to cover them.

The wind dropped her. She plummeted to the pavement, collapsed to the ground, and knocked her head on the road. For a second oblivion nearly claimed her. But she fought off the pain and shook the disorientation of the blow away and staggered to her feet. Trickles of blood ran down her face and arms, everywhere her skin was bare and the sand had abraded her flesh.

Micaela screamed her name. Xander, Oz, and Faith tried to shield Malik and the other Champions. The whirling sandstorm plucked them off the ground and hurled them away. Xander landed in the parking lot. Faith struck several trees by the river, and Oz plunged into the rushing waters of the Seekonk.

"Willow!" Buffy shouted.

With a glance, she saw that Willow and Tara both had their hands up, trying to cast a spell that would slow the sandstorm or shield the renegade Champions.

They could not stop him.

The sandstorm swept Malik up in gusts of wind, then one by one it plucked Bors, Simone, and the unconscious Tai from the road. The swirling sands made it difficult to see more than silhouettes in the moonlight, but their shapes were all so distinct it was simple enough to tell them apart.

When the sand started to erode their flesh, the mute Tai must have woken, for Buffy heard him scream, a long, unintelligible, and mournful wail of pain. It ended abruptly. The sandstorm raged, pulsing as though with a life of its own. Wet, tearing sounds could be heard from within the storm.

One by one, the bones showered down to clatter to the road.

Then, with another enormous gust of wind, the sandstorm blew out over the river and disappeared into the night sky.

EPILOGUE

On Sunday night, the lounge at the Hotel Kensington was near capacity. Some kind of medical convention had come to Providence, so the bar was full of doctors and various other business travelers who'd come to the city for Monday morning meetings.

Buffy had managed to get a large table in the rear corner of the lounge by arriving in the late afternoon, before the pre- and post-dinner rush. She and Faith had spent most of the day sleeping and then loitering ineffectually and anxiously in their room. She suspected that Oz and Xander had passed the time in similar fashion. Of Willow and Tara, there had been no sign until late in the afternoon, when everyone had arranged to meet in the lounge.

There had been tears and grief and profound regret, and then the witches had departed.

Hours had passed since then. Buffy sat across from Faith, silently condemning her for not being more lively. Oz had the chair beside her, but Buffy had no expectations of him. In fact, she was surprised that the werewolf had not already left the city, trying to put all of this behind him, as was his nature. Instead, Oz just sat there sipping a glass of ginger ale—what must have been his ninth—more reticent than ever. Buffy would not have imagined it possible, but he was living proof.

Faith, though . . . Buffy had expected more of her. Unable to find any way to lighten her own mood, she had hoped that Faith would oblige. But Faith seemed to have been drained of her usual rebellion and sarcasm. She had begun the afternoon with a double shot of whiskey, and now, after they had ordered dinner that they had only picked at, she nursed a beer and leaned her chair back, propped against the wall. Buffy always thought of Faith as beautiful, but tonight hers was a tragic, porcelain beauty that seemed delicate and fragile. It troubled and surprised her to think of Faith in such terms, and she hoped it never happened again.

"Come on, guys," Xander said, returning to the table with a beer for himself and a Pellegrino for Buffy. "You've gotta keep it down over here. The bartender's about to throw us out."

Buffy raised her eyebrows. How Xander could maintain his humor under the circumstances, she'd never know. But she did know *why*. If he let his guard down, let himself sink into the sorrow that had touched all of their hearts, he might never recover.

"Thanks, Xand." She took a sip of the Pellegrino.

"Anyone else hungry?" he asked, looking around as he slid into his chair.

Faith stared at him. "You just ate."

Xander nodded. "I just ate dinner. Now I'm thinking about something of the snack variety. Curly fries? Anyone?"

Oz shifted in his chair as though waking up from a trance. "I could go for curly fries."

"See?" Xander said, pointing at Faith. "You just don't understand the magick of curly fries."

"Which is?" Buffy asked.

Xander rolled his single eye, an unsettling reminder of the

emptiness behind his patch. "Which is? Hello? They're curly!"

"Ah," Buffy replied, "now I understand. I have seen the light."

"Then you'll partake?"

"Will there be cheese on these hypothetical fries?"

"Hypothetically," Xander sort of confirmed.

Buffy smiled. "I'm in."

Triumphant, Xander took a long gulp of beer and got up again to go back to the bartender to put in the order. Buffy thought that was good for him, keeping himself busy, keeping his mind on anything else but where Willow and Tara had gone. They had done the job, here in Providence, had tracked down Kandida's killers and made certain the Dark Congress could go ahead as planned. But it didn't feel like victory. Maybe that was because there was no way to know what the Congress would decide now, if their debates would end with the world safer, or with apocalypse.

But tonight apocalypse didn't seem the worst thing that could happen.

"Hey. Cyclops," Faith called.

Xander paused halfway to the bar and turned to look at her.

"Better make it two orders."

"There you go," Xander said, pointing at Faith. "Curly fries for everyone. Now you're getting it."

While he was at the bar waiting for the bartender to make his way over, Buffy glanced at the entrance to the lounge. Every time she caught movement there out of the corner of her eye she had to take a closer look, wondering if it would be Willow.

To her surprise, Giles and Micaela walked into the lounge.

"Guys," Buffy said.

Faith rocked forward on her chair. Oz frowned deeply. Micaela smiled weakly and waved to them and Buffy waved back, but her focus was on Giles. In all the years she had known him, he had never looked so tired, or so old.

"What happened?" Buffy asked as they came to the table. "It's only been like sixteen hours since Trajabo turned himself in to the Congress."

Giles quietly asked a trio of businessmen if he could have the fourth chair at their table, and when they agreed, he dragged it over to join Buffy and the others. Micaela sat down at Xander's seat.

"It appears that the world will not be ending just yet," Giles said.

"Not tonight, at least," Micaela added.

Faith and Oz stared at them.

"You mean it's over?" Buffy asked, shaking her head. "How can that be?"

"Okay, B, are you missing that we averted a potential apocalypse?" Faith asked.

Buffy ignored her, staring at Giles. "Spill. How is it over?"

Giles locked eyes with her for a moment, then glanced away. Buffy turned to Micaela.

"Rupert acquitted himself admirably as arbiter. Several quarrels were settled with his help. And the Congress itself went ahead as planned, with old truces renegotiated and territorial disputes put to rest. But it ended the way every previous Dark Congress ended—with the various factions unable to come to any consensus about the future of humanity."

"Considering most of them are demons, that's probably for the best," Faith said.

Buffy shushed her with a look and turned back to Micaela and Giles.

"But they were in session for one day. It's like they didn't even try. After all these years, they just walk away? That doesn't make sense."

"They pardoned Trajabo's actions," Micaela said, "which we expected. But this afternoon he was given a chance to address the Congress."

Giles picked up the salt shaker from the table and studied it as though it were the most fascinating artifact he had ever encountered, as though all of the secrets of the universe could be found inside.

"From what I could discern, Kandida had always been the more dynamic of the two," he said. "She could hold the entire Congress in thrall. Many feared Trajabo, and respected him, but it was her they *loved* and respected. This afternoon it was as though he had inherited that love in the aftermath of her murder."

"What did he say?" Buffy asked.

Micaela gave a tiny shrug. She, too, looked exhausted. "He convinced them to adjourn."

Oz narrowed his gaze. "Adjourn? They just went home?"

"Essentially," Giles said. "In his address Trajabo asked all the parties involved in the Congress to pledge a century of détente so they might all recover from the drama and horror of this weekend— so they could catch their breath and rein in their anger. They vowed to gather again in one hundred years to decide the future of the supernatural in our world."

Faith laughed softly. "Bunch of candy-asses."

Xander had returned in the midst of this exchange and now stood behind Micaela. "They were probably looking for any excuse to avoid having to try to work out their differences."

"Looks like there's not a whole lot of difference between human politics and demon politics," Oz said.

Buffy sighed. "I wish I could be surprised."

Giles stared at her. Soon they were all looking at her.

"What?" she asked, self-conscious.

"You're smiling," Giles said.

"I am?"

She was.

"Care to share with the rest of us?" Xander said.

"Guess I'm just glad I won't be around for the next Dark Congress. All the tension and suspicion and the bitterness . . . I won't have to deal with any of that. But part of me is disappointed, too. I mean, things could have gotten so ugly here so fast. The end could have been a nightmare. But it didn't have to be. They had a chance to make things better, and they just turned their backs and walked away. They're just leaving the hard work for the next bunch of suckers that comes along."

No one had a reply to that. Xander picked up his beer and took a long sip. He glanced at Giles and Micaela.

"We've got curly fries coming," he said. "Cheesy, curly fries."

Micaela smiled wanly. "I'm starving."

But Giles glanced around the lounge, brows knitted. He turned to Buffy. "Where are Willow and Tara?"

Xander took another sip of his beer and looked away. No one seemed to want to answer the question.

"Willow will be back," Buffy said. Her throat felt tight with emotion and her eyes burned with unshed tears. "Tara . . . Tara asked me to tell you good-bye."

In the end it was Tara who burned the scroll.

Willow had held on to it ever since Athens. Magick that powerful— no matter the consequences, it had seemed wrong to her just to tear it up or throw it away. She had been aware all along that she should not be carrying it, but she had told herself that she was keeping it for the benefit of others, in case she ever needed to pass the magick on to someone else.

As if she would have entrusted magick of that magnitude to anyone.

Catherine had made clear when they had last met that the scroll had not contained the only magick that had gone into the spell. The ancient witch herself had cast spells to protect Willow while she performed the incantation that had brought Tara's spirit back to the world and merged it with the cinnamon cat who had been Catherine's familiar. But at the time, Willow had not known that. She had hung on to the scroll in the same way that some addicts might hold on to drugs they had come into possession of—to keep them out of the hands of someone else.

All lies.

But in the end, her compulsion had saved them. Willow had always been far more innately powerful, but Tara had been more perceptive. She could see to the heart of a puzzle, understanding the inner workings of a ritual or a spell, how it originated and what it was truly meant to do. And it had been Tara who understood how tenuous life was, who felt herself tethered to the cinnamon cat and to Willow, rather than anchored there.

"If we're both willing to just let go, the spell will be broken," Tara had said.

"What if I'm not?" Willow had asked, shaking with her tears.

Tara had kissed the tears away, but could not prevent new ones from falling. "You know what has to be done. This isn't . . . it isn't right. It's tainted."

"Maybe we can live with that."

Biting her lip, Tara had shaken her head. "I can't. And I won't let you. Everything we've ever been to each other . . . you want to taint that?"

Willow had been unable to respond. They sat together on the grass in a small park. The ground still felt warm from the heat of the day, and the scent of the earth was redolent in the air, but after the humidity of the night before the weather had changed. The night was dry and a cool breeze caressed them.

For what might have been forever, they held each other. In time Tara whispered in her ear, urging her on. Willow had taken the small yellowed scroll in her fingers and held it up. In her other hand she had a cheap plastic lighter that they had borrowed from the bartender at the hotel and promised to return.

Willow had spun the thumb wheel on the lighter several times, but only managed a spark. Her hands were shaking too much. Tara had taken her hand and held it, helped her get the lighter working, and then moved the flame beneath the scroll.

When it started to burn, Willow had dropped it with a sob that shook her whole body.

Tara had embraced her then. She had whispered her love—forever love—and asked to be released.

Now Willow sat on the grass in the park with the cinnamon cat in her arms. The last ember of the burning scroll flickered on the ground and then went dark, leaving only moonlight and the distant glow of the lampposts along the park's pathways to reflect from the eyes of the cat.

No other light—internal or otherwise—shone in those eyes. The cat felt warm against her, the cinnamon fur soft and sleek. Soon the feline began to fidget and strained against her arms until Willow let her go.

Her heart swelled as she watched the cat stretch and begin to walk away. She wanted to call after the animal, to plead for her to stay, to shout her love and her loneliness. But she said nothing. And as the cat made its way to the path with a light, almost bouncing step, and then into the bushes on the other side, Willow found that her tears had ceased.

"Thank you," she whispered to the night, to Catherine Cadiere—wherever she was—and to that sleek cinnamon cat.

After Tara's death she had often said that the only thing worse than saying good-bye was never having the opportunity to do so. Now, somehow, she felt a lightness of spirit within her that she had not felt since the earliest days of her time with Tara, when they were just falling in love. Whatever the future held in store for her now, she felt that she was ready for it, that she could open her heart to destiny.

She spared a final, yearning glance toward the bushes where the cinnamon cat had disappeared, and then she rose and made her way out of the park, and back to her world.

Back to life.

ABOUT THE AUTHOR

CHRISTOPHER GOLDEN is the award-winning, bestselling author of such novels as *The Myth Hunters, Wildwood Road, The Boys Are Back in Town, The Ferryman, Strangewood,* and *Of Saints and Shadows*. Golden cowrote the lavishly illustrated novel *Baltimore, or, The Steadfast Tin Soldier and the Vampire* with Mike Mignola. He has also written books for teens and young adults, including the Body of Evidence thriller series, which was honored by the New York Public Library and was chosen as one of YALSA's Best Books for Young Readers.

With Thomas E. Sniegoski, Golden is the coauthor of the dark fantasy series The Menagerie, as well as the young readers fantasy series OutCast and the comic book miniseries Talent, both of which were recently acquired by Universal Pictures. Golden and Sniegoski also wrote the upcoming comic book miniseries The Sisterhood, currently in development as a feature film, and BPRD: Hollow Earth, a spinoff from the fan favorite comic book series Hellboy. Golden has authored several original Hellboy novels, including *The Lost Army* and *The Bones of Giants*, and edited two Hellboy short-story anthologies. Golden has also written many novels, nonfiction books, and comic books—and created two video games—based in the world of Buffy the Vampire Slayer. Working with actress/writer/director Amber Benson, he cocreated and cowrote "Ghosts of Albion," an original animated supernatural drama for BBC Online, from which they created the book series of the same name.

Golden was born and raised in Massachusetts, where he still lives with his family. He graduated from Tufts University. Presently he is collaborating with Tim Lebbon on *Mind the Gap*, the first novel in their series The Hidden Cities. There are more than eight million copies of his books in print. Please visit his website at www.christophergolden.com.